CATCH YOURSELF ON

Katherine Cowan

best wishes,
Katherine Cowan

©Copyright 2005 by Katherine Cowan

First published in Great Britain in 2005 by Katra Publishing

The right of Katherine Cowan to be identified as the author of the work has been asserted by her in accordance with the Copyright, Designs and Patents Act 1988.

All rights reserved. No part of this publication may be reproduced, stored in a retrieval system, or transmitted in any form or by any means, without the prior written permission of the publisher, nor be otherwise circulated in any form of binding or cover other than that in which it is published and without a similar condition being imposed on the subsequent purchaser.

All characters in this publication are fictitious and any resemblance to real persons, living or dead, is purely coincidental.

British Library Cataloguing in Publication Data.
A catalogue record for this book is available from the British Library.

ISBN 0 9550937 0 8

Design by Hawkins Communications, London.

Printed and bound in Great Britain by
Antony Rowe Ltd., Chippenham, Wiltshire.

Katra Publishing, Nadder Park,
Nadderwater, Exeter, Devon.

Acknowledgements

With many thanks to those who helped so much,
in particular :
Brigid, Bryan, Andy, Ros, Sue, Paul, Jennifer, Trevor, G.,
Betty, John Fox, Dinah.

For Ralph, Lucy, Laura and James

CHAPTER 1

West London, 2003

Graeme Ward had one thing on his mind as he eyed his wife Eleanor across their bedroom floor …. sex. He'd been thinking about it for days and still couldn't find the right words. Middle aged and middle class – and in a real mess.

They'd flown back that morning from their seaside holiday home in Northern Ireland to London Heathrow – with Eleanor in discomfort throughout. Neither had had a good time away – though each for different reasons. He stood in the bay window, watching the traffic on West Hill, and waited for her to come out of their bathroom.

"You've got a dose of the clap," he blurted out. "I'm so sorry – I don't know what to say – it's all my fault," he finished lamely.

Eleanor thought she'd misheard him at first. Frozen in the doorway, she tried to see his expression. With his back to the window, the remainder of his hair was lit by the thin sunlight, a fuzzy halo topping off the fleshy face with the wet lips she so hated. Sloppy wet kisses with a little pointed tongue to follow. The tongue was currently licking the lips, getting ready to speak again. She wasn't listening, she felt sick and cold – going back into the bathroom, she quietly closed the door and vomited.

Graeme sat down on the chair in the window and listened. Eleanor, fastidious Eleanor, retched and sobbed, then needed yet another pee, for once uncaring about being heard. In Graeme's eyes this was one of their problems – her hang-up about anything to do with the body. He was the opposite; once it had bothered him, now with power and money it seemed to matter much less. He'd never had any trouble getting a woman once he started making it.

1

WEST LONDON, 2003

He presented well, his lack of height compensated for by an air of authority and wealth – along with the expectation of getting what he wanted. Having heeded Eleanor's advice, his impeccably cut suits hid the excesses of too many rich dinners. He had charm – bags of it – talking his way out of most difficult situations. This one, however, would call for more patience and skill than he was accustomed to having. He loved her of course – hadn't they been married for over twenty years ..? and most importantly – she was the mother of his children. Did he fancy her though? Well… no.

"Eleanor, come on now, we have to talk – let me explain. Come out and listen for Christ's sake – let me talk to you … please…" With his hand trying the handle, Graeme leaned his head on the door. The continuing silence was more than he could take.

"Look it's a question of you seeing a specialist and taking some antibiotics – that's all; it can be cleared up quickly and I swear – on my life – that it stops now, it's over – I'll catch myself on – honestly."

Eleanor stood with her back to the door, staring at herself in the mirror: with red blotchy face, swollen eyes and running nose, she watched as more tears came. This was Graeme all over, even down to delivery – always crass, always insensitive. She felt defiled, dirty and livid. Livid for having put up with his behaviour for so long and believing in the love and loyalty crap. Now, so many years on, they were a rich couple with four grown up children, two homes, and nothing in common – except a disease.

Sex – she watched her head shake in the mirror – what sex? She and Graeme had sex, a quickie, maybe once a month these days. He didn't seem to mind and she was so unmoved by the whole thing that it didn't really interest her any longer. What sexual frisson that had existed between

CHAPTER 1

them had been when their naivete was their sexual thrill. Two inexperienced people freed up from their religious and cultural hang-ups, finding out that you didn't go to hell, necessarily, and good girls do do it. She'd always known that Graeme screwed around – she'd known from the very beginning. Her first pregnancy had been the end of her innocence.

His pattern was always the same, durex in the golf bag, an increase of oral debris left to bake on the bathroom mirror, topped off with a shifty restlessness. But this – she couldn't believe how sick she felt – how completely betrayed. She heard his words alright – was she meant to feel lucky or something? She'd been a virgin when she'd married him, there had never been anyone else, and now all she needed was antibiotics to treat her very own venereal disease – unbelievable!

His mobile rang and she listened as he moved across the room and out on to the landing.

"Yes, I know. Look, I've a couple of things to sort out and then I'll be right over. No, I'll ..."

Eleanor knew that he'd already be half way down the stairs in a hurry to get to his study on the ground floor. Naturally secretive, Graeme always worked on a need to know basis – and a wife didn't need to know that much. She came out and quickly changed, choosing what to wear carefully. She would have it out with Graeme, he'd compromised her health and she'd had enough.

Graeme heard her coming down and finished his call, following her into the sitting room. She sat and listened as he paced and talked up a storm. The wonder of it was she didn't finish the phrases for him, she'd heard them so many times before. She was quite cold, making him write the

3

details of the consultation down, hearing him assure her that his chap would sort it all out. He was waiting for her to say something – anything; she let him wait and stared at the fireplace. Her appointment was for that afternoon; she would go by taxi, alone. The silence hung between them, Graeme fidgeting with the change in his pocket.

"Right now I've nothing to say; I'll talk to you sometime when I feel able, or actually want to." Trying to control her voice, she stood up to leave the room.

She knew that Graeme, as ever, would expect her to forgive him; the child in him unable to handle rejection – this time she didn't even feel like trying, She knew exactly where she stood in his eyes: wife, mother, and homemaker, nothing else. Smooth running homes, well groomed and well mannered – all part of being Mrs.Graeme Ward. She had cultivated a polite little shield while she watched.

She had watched it all; Graeme's games, the deals, the chat-ups, he would be shocked at how much she knew. She knew even now that the V.D. was only part of his anxiety, he was also thinking of his important 'do' that she was to organise for him. Without her it could not happen and both of them knew it. What Eleanor didn't know was just how important it was to Graeme.

CHAPTER 2

Belfast, 2003

Sam looked respectable these days, gone were the clothes and the stance that had made him look a wee hard man. Nowadays he wore a safe tweed jacket, flannels, shirt and tie – always a tie. He'd softened the harshness of his accent, spoke quietly, and was clean in the eyes of the security forces.

In his forties, he had been a member of the organisation since his teens, rising up through the ranks. These days he had nothing more to prove; those who mattered knew, that was enough. His current task was to go to London for a couple of days to collect an answer in person to the proposed deal, which could run into millions. Nothing was to be written, recorded or discussed on any telephone or computer – it was all far too sensitive. He carried nothing apart from clothing, washbag and a thriller. At Belfast airport he blended in well with the crowd waiting for the next flight to London Heathrow. Just a wee bloke going over for a break – his second since Christmas. It was time for Graeme Ward to give his answer, and Sam's job to cut the best deal.

Security, more than ever, was tight and Sam had checked in extra early. Settled in at the bar with a large one, he watched the crowd. Unused to flying – this was only his second flight – he preferred to drink and wait rather than cut it fine and run the risk of making a mistake.

A few weeks earlier it had been a different story; he had been nervous and paranoid, avoiding eye contact, tense all the time. Recalling it now made him half smile. He'd been so knocked out by the sheer size of the city. For him Belfast had been a huge place once, but London – that'd been something else.

5

BELFAST, 2003

The flight had been short and dull, nothing to see when you're in the seat by the aisle except the other passengers, and Sam had had nothing to say to anyone. Warned, that on landing he could be questioned by the Special Branch officers at Heathrow as to the purpose of his visit, he had his answer ready. Rugby – plain and simple.

In fact he needn't have worried, there had been a politician on board that day. Not one of the major players, but important enough to warrant priority and attention. Sam had just melted into the crowd waiting at the baggage carousel – being so short had its good points.

Within an hour he'd been away, the slow crawl down the M4 into London giving him his first feel of the size. His driver was from Ireland, the Republic of, but Sam couldn't quite place the accent, he reckoned County Meath. On asking, he got told bluntly that it was County Kilburn. He'd left it there, annoyed by the rebuff, and they'd travelled on in a tight silence. Christ – he'd only been trying to pass the time of day, stranger in town, etc., but the bloke wasn't having it, or had been told to say nothing. Arriving at the hotel had been a relief.

Sam had done as he'd been told, checked in and waited in the bar. He'd been so impressed by the chain hotel – it was way out of his league – a mini bar and a bathroom! He'd looked exactly what he was, a little greaser in a cheap suit and out of his depth.

Graeme Ward had been late and Sam had spotted him bustling into the bar, looking for him; burly guy with broad shoulders in a classy dark suit – sleek and prosperous. Fleshy face with small eyes and a smile as real as a politician's, he had his hand outstretched yards before he reached Sam.

"Och hello, how are you, sorry to have kept you waiting

CHAPTER 2

– you know what the South Circular's like – here – let me get you a drink, I know I could use one."

Sam, bemused by the gush, had ordered his drink. He'd recognised Ward from the photos he'd been shown, but Sam also knew his face from somewhere else, way back. Ulster is a small place and for over fifteen years Sam had moved around Belfast and the rest of the country as a collector for the organisation. Every multinational, every family business, pub, club, hotel, whatever – if they wanted to keep their businesses going – paid protection.

It was like a verb; you have to pay, you do pay, you'll always pay – such easy money. Graeme Ward fitted in there somewhere, but Sam had said nothing, sticking to idle chat whilst they had their drinks. He had let Ward run it – yer man was a great talker, but sharp enough with it. He'd been briefed on Ward's background – the guy was a big fish in the Ulster business pond. The family's failing building business had been turned around with a mixture of some money, good timing, but most importantly, excellent contacts. There was little that Ward hadn't managed to make money out of over the years of these 'Troubles' thanks mainly to his contacts – high and low. Sam's lot needed to set up a new system and knew that Ward, if persuaded, could deliver.

They'd soon left the bar and gone to Sam's room, keen to get down to business.

In a few hours Sam would meet Graeme Ward again, back at the hotel near Ealing Common. He had been given a lot of leeway with regard to the size of Ward's commission. His organisation was prepared for Ward's greed, they wanted his acumen – they needed it – urgently. So many routes had been closed since September llth that few shipments made

7

BELFAST, 2003

it through to Northern Ireland. Graeme Ward hadn't been put off by that – as he'd told Sam – 'like women ... there's always a way in!'

The final call for the flight to Heathrow came as Sam finished his drink. He joined the queue, insignificant and unnoticed.

CHAPTER 3

February 2003

Graeme left the house in a hurry, keen to get away from the glacial atmosphere. He hated his wife's cold withdrawal, especially knowing that it was justified. He was genuinely sorry, he'd taken a huge risk and it had all gone wrong. She hadn't really listened to anything he'd said by way of explanation, which on reflection was no bad thing. He could hardly come from a 'never before, never again' stance, could he?

He never meant to hurt her – but Eleanor was so boring in bed, he needed a thrill rather than a duty. He'd just got carried away, and this time had been caught.

It'd been the night that he'd met Sam, business and pleasure all rolled into one, something that he was good at – and Sam had been more than ready to enjoy. On first sight Graeme had been far from impressed by him. A short, wiry man, dark hair cropped so short that his white scalp had shone through, flat pale blue eyes in a tensed face. He'd expected someone with a bit more of an air to him, not so awkward looking.

What Sam had lacked in social skills, he'd made up for over the business deal. He'd pitched it just right for Graeme, earning respect along the way. Both keyed up when they'd finished, they'd quickly eaten a bland steak and chips meal in the 'Bistro' of the hotel – Sam's safe choice of food.

"So what about this club like?" Sam had asked at the end of dinner. He'd been keen ever since Graeme had mentioned it earlier. That had been all that Graeme had needed, he'd been more than ready to make a night of it.

Christ, they'd had fun; Graeme had taken him to a discreet little club near King's Cross – any sort of girl, anything you wanted. His own taste that night had been for

9

FEBRUARY 2003

the 'nurse' from Prague: full, firm, and exhausting. He couldn't resist her second time round, paying extra for the feel of her inside. Expensive error, but Graeme had needed the risk. As for Sam – he'd had the boyish girl who would deliver 'golden rain'. Graeme had been amazed that Sam had been so turned on by someone pissing all over him.

Sitting in his big Merc waiting for a gap in the traffic, Graeme stopped his recall, and pulled today back into his head. It was busy, with Sam flying over later from Belfast to get his answer. He had decided to go with it, but would wait and hear the size of the commission; since 9 – 11 the risk factor was huge. As for Eleanor, he would have another go later at bringing her round. He pushed his way in to the traffic, earning himself an angry blast from the guy he'd cut in on. From upstairs Eleanor watched his leaving, it was always the same – all revs and pushing.

She went to telephone his mother.

CHAPTER 4

Reflections

Olivia Ward hadn't wanted her son to marry Eleanor Clarke in the first place – she didn't dislike her, it was just that she wasn't one of them – being half English. There'd been problems with both families but, as ever, Graeme had got his way. They'd had a stiff formal little wedding, where no one really relaxed or mixed. The grandchildren had been the only compensation.

However, after more than twenty years, she'd come to appreciate how well Eleanor coped with being Graeme's wife. He might be her son, but she wasn't blind to his behaviour – he'd always been the wilful one of her three children, the first-born. The other two, Tom and Christine, were easier – less angrily hungry.

'Were,' thought Olivia. She hadn't heard from Christine in months; and as for Tom – well, he'd be 47 this year, if he had lived.

He was only 19 when they shot him in the face in 1975. He'd been visiting friends on the other side of Belfast city and had died immediately. Shot for opening the front door. Dead because they thought he was someone else. He'd been her favourite child, she couldn't help it, his happy, easy going nature had made him so easy to love.

"Can you get that, it'll be Anna," had been the call when the bell had rung.

"Right," had been Tom's reply as he had got up to open the door – and that had been it. Two shots, a car driving off, and in less than a minute it was over.

She had disintegrated. The news, the wake, the funeral, she had gone through it all at a distance. Everything muffled by the Valium, tea and whiskey. She had buried her parents,

11

her husband even – their deaths could all be understood, but this one – never. Part of her had died at the graveside in the rain that day. Great creamy lumps of clay thumping on top of him, as Graeme and Christine held her upright. Nearly thirty years ago now, years of such anger, pain and impotence, with an ache that only her own death would ease.

Now at 72 she appeared a very composed, elegant woman. Medium height, slim going on thin; she tended to wear dark clothes and no jewellery at all. Her face was a controlled one, good bone structure underneath the lines, but lacking any spontaneity. She had learned the mask in the clinic. That was where she'd gone after the funeral, unable to face life in Belfast, in Northern Ireland even. Graeme and Christine had organised it all for her: discreet, private, and close to London. She had been totally compliant, malleable – the place had been a warm and safe cocoon and she had retreated into the soft cushion of drugs for months.

They were left to sort out her move, shocked at her decision that she would never return to Northern Ireland again, and convinced that she'd regret it. Graeme had argued that it was a knee jerk reaction, and that when she was 'more herself' she'd see things differently. Olivia knew that it would never happen. She couldn't bear to be known within her home town, she didn't want consoling, counselling, old contacts – just privacy and anonymity. When she finally came out, she was healed enough to perform the basics and pass muster. It was a veneer that worked – sort of.

The big house in Belfast had sold quickly, she hadn't cared, it was all too full of the past. The holiday house she had

CHAPTER 4

given to Graeme and Christine equally. She was content to have her belongings, her history, packed, shipped and stored, to be dealt with later. She had switched off entirely.

Up until Tom's death, Olivia had always believed in the system. The State, the government, the police, the judiciary. It was how society worked and was fundamentally just. You did your duty as a citizen; they did the job of running the country. Work hard and life could be very good – her husband had tried and had done well until his health had failed. She had lived very comfortably, bringing the children up in the large Edwardian house in the city, with the holiday home up the coast. They had both been bought just after the war when prices had been rock bottom.

The Belfast house had been a real find, a semi-derelict, five bedroomed villa up the Lisburn Road, with an overgrown garden of half an acre. Despite the original plumbing, 'hairy' electrics and a leaking roof, they had bought it for two thousand five hundred pounds, with a further one hundred for some furniture and fittings. So soon after the war had meant that there was little to buy, and they had been so glad of what had been left behind; the nearly worn out runners and the huge Edwardian wardrobes, the mangle in the yard and the disgusting meat 'safe' alongside.

It had taken them years to do it up, ending up as a light and welcoming home. Never smart, always a bit battered, but a place where the kids would happily bring their friends. The garden, despite their father's protests, had been used for every kind of childhood camp, den – even a tree house built with the other kids in the avenue. So many different pictures of the children's lives; their innocence. To Olivia it had been a great place to bring them up in, and to let them go from.

Graeme, Tom and Christine, all strong and healthy, well educated at their grammar schools. Their whole lives ahead of them as they say. It had all changed that night with Tom's death.

'So sorry to hear of your trouble,' she had heard repeated like a chant. Her 'trouble' – some euphemism for a murder. It had been impossible to comprehend that her child had gone, that someone described his murder as an unfortunate mistake. She had believed in justice until then.

When she had left the clinic she had stayed with Graeme and Eleanor for a couple of weeks. Little to do except wait to move into her new home, she had spent days in her room as much as possible. Staring out of the window, but seeing little. She had taken to counting everything, the repetition soothed her. So many paces, so many stairs, so many dead. Nothing made sense anymore. Just pop another little pill to take the edge of her already blurred day. What did it all matter anyway – as long as she could 'perform' at dinner when Graeme came home, smiling in the right places and looking interested, she would get through another evening, then take her sleeping pill and blot it all out.

Graeme dealt with his pain by working harder, coming home late and irritable, spoiling for a fight over nothing. Dinner, a few whiskeys and a slump in front of the telly. He was her son, and yet she felt that she hardly knew him. Tom had been the link, the one who had 'translated' between them. Now without him, neither of them made much of an effort – both wrapped up in their own little worlds. He'd do anything for her in a practical sense, but the depths of her depression alarmed him. A quick hug and a query as to how she was feeling, answered by himself before she could say a word: –

CHAPTER 4

"Bit better today eh? Good, good – Hi darling sorry I'm late," as he passed on to Eleanor.

He was oblivious to the moods of the two women in the house, he was home expecting to be looked after – that came first, as always. Olivia had been desperate to leave.

London, 1976

Olivia had finally moved into her new home in Southwark. Not ready to live on her own, but unable to live with her children either, she was afraid and trying not to show it. At forty-four she had aged in the last few months and looked laden, lethargic. She'd always imagined that at this time in her life she and her husband would've been living in their holiday home more and more, enjoying the golf and their circle of old friends. Gradually leaving Belfast – getting ready for the grandchildren coming to stay by the sea.

Instead she had lost her husband, her favourite child, her faith, and part of her mind. Now she had to start her new life, in a part of London she barely knew, alone. She knew she could create her haven, but dealing with life outside would be difficult.

Graeme had been unhappy about her choice of area; it wasn't safe; the SE1 postcode had little 'social cachet' (he was learning about these things), too far from him, etc. He hadn't dissuaded her, she'd found what she wanted, and had infuriated him by insisting that the house 'just felt right'. The small Victorian terrace house in a side street near the Walworth Road.

The street was a cul de sac; most of the houses had long term sitting tenants, with one young professional couple renovating their recent purchase. Olivia knew that the place would change, but had liked the contrast between the Elephant and Castle's endless traffic and the forgotten street within walking distance. Graeme's suggestion of an annexe on his house had been quietly dropped.

She had let him handle the purchase, knowing that he was convinced that anything more complicated than a

Chapter 5

shopping list was beyond her. It made him feel better, having control.

With his contacts, any building and decorating had been quickly done. Eleanor had helped her choose the bathroom and kitchen – Olivia's simple tastes made it an easy task. White bathroom, basic kitchen, and whatever size Aga would fit – Eleanor had taken her to the outlets, Graeme had organised the rest. His workmen worked very hard to ensure that Mr. Ward's mother got exactly what she wanted. Olivia had kept taking the pills, letting the days bleed into each other.

Today's task was painful and unavoidable; her container load of belongings was coming out of storage. All that she still owned packed by Graeme and Christine long before in Northern Ireland. Olivia had no recollection of deciding what she would keep. It was they who had done it all; the clearing, dumping and shedding of a family's shared life, the separation of all the strands.

She knew she'd still have too much furniture – Graeme had insisted that she could choose what to keep when it had been unpacked for her at the house. Needless to say he had a gang of 'lads' available any time to do the moving. He'd dropped her and Eleanor off at the house earlier, before bustling off to the storage depot to oversee the job.

Having told them that it'd be midday before the furniture van arrived, Eleanor was now making tea in anticipation of their imminent arrival. Olivia didn't know where to be, and retreated to the little yard at the back.

By late afternoon it was done; the lads had had their beers, been paid and Olivia was taking stock. It had been a grim time seeing the familiar pieces in the strange, small place. Too much stuff overcrowding the rooms, and Graeme

LONDON, 1976

hovering as always, wanting to help. She felt flustered and chivvied by his haste to settle her in. It was cool Eleanor who was helping most.

Seeing that it wouldn't be long before one or other of them snapped, she'd organised Graeme into doing the job that would keep him out of harm's way – the storage of the excess furniture into the second bedroom. Olivia could deal with it some time in the future. It'd been a compromise that he'd accepted, having had his ear bent quietly in the hall by Eleanor.

"Your mother is about to fall apart, can't you see what this is doing to her? For God's sake Graeme, let's finish off quickly and go home. She needs peace and rest."

Olivia had listened, and thanked Eleanor in her head – they'd never be close, and yet were close by their sharing of the same man. She wanted them to leave, to let her feel her way round her new home, to decide quietly and slowly where she would like to have things.

"Right Ma, that's it all done," Graeme had announced within the hour. Eleanor and Olivia had a drink ready for him, and they toasted the new home in the sitting room. It was chaotic, but already pieces were finding their places, except for the old button leather chair which was in the way. Both women knew instinctively what was about to happen, both were hoping that he wouldn't say it. Eleanor was trying to catch his eye; Olivia turned her back and looked out of the window.

"This room looks great now Ma, doesn't it? It's all turning out really well don't you think? You still have a stack of stuff to sort out in the back bedroom – but sure you can do that some time when you're ready. As for this old friend, I'd like to have it, it reminds me so much of Tom, and it

Chapter 5

won't fit in here." Graeme had paused, hand on the back of the leather chair, ignoring Eleanor – Olivia couldn't move.

"I mean, only if you like – you know, if you don't mind." He stopped, aware of the silence. Olivia was counting in her head, trying to hold it together.

"No, Graeme, that's all right, and there'll be plenty more to come as I sort out the rest," she finally managed to say, turning to face her son, seeing him so clearly and wanting him gone.

As if on cue, Eleanor stood up, and hugged Olivia.

"Goodnight from us, we'll talk tomorrow, sleep well… come on Graeme" and waited. She watched him kiss his mother goodbye, and thought she'd been quick enough to stop it going further. Olivia's face was so pale and drawn.

"Goodnight then Ma, and I'll call in tomorrow after work, see how you're settling in – okay? He had his arms round her, and Olivia could sense him getting ready to make his next move….

"Tell you what, why don't I take the chair now, it'd fit in the car, and be something less for you to worry about," he finished.

Olivia had never seen this side of her son before; it was so unutterably thoughtless and selfish that she agreed abruptly. She could feel Eleanor's anger and embarrassment as she left the room to open the front door for them to leave. Olivia stood at the sitting room window watching as Graeme became exasperated trying to angle her chair into his car. She could hear him urging Eleanor to 'do something to help, for God's sake, don't just stand there.' Finally it was in, and he quickly drove off. She remained at the window, weeping; they hadn't looked back. She took her medication early and went to her new bed – missing

London, 1976

Tom, actively disliking Graeme.

Despite the tablets it had been a fitful sleep, but she enjoyed the pleasure of getting up in her own place. No need to pretend, come round at your own pace. She was free until Graeme came round in the evening, and by then she'd have made an effort to achieve something. After her breakfast she'd spent time putting stuff away in the kitchen, acknowledging as she did so just how well Graeme had organised it all for her. She had to give him that, but how she'd feel when she next saw him she couldn't tell. His avarice over the chair had been the last in a series of signals, and the first that she'd chosen to see clearly. She'd mull it over during the day – she had the time.

On one side of her lived a retired couple. She'd watched them leave earlier, pulling their little shopper, as she opened the sitting room curtains. Tidy little people off to East Street market for the cheap deals. On the other side was an elderly woman, a sentinel in the bay window. Everything that they'd been doing to the house over the weeks had been watched, culminating in the embarrassing finale last night. When the builders had told Graeme that the woman never went out, had meals on wheels and district nurse calling, he had ruled her out immediately as a potential 'keep an eye on my mother' contact. He had his eye on the young professional couple instead. There was nothing Graeme wouldn't do for his mother, even if she didn't want it. She decided that she'd introduce herself to the woman.

Mid morning and Olivia went next door, her first solo effort for a long time. When old Florence finally made it to the front door on her Zimmer frame, she'd welcomed Olivia and invited her in. It was stiflingly hot and stuffy in the sitting room, with an overpowering reek of dog and the

Chapter 5

carpet sticky underfoot. Florence's shuffle to her chair in the window was slow, giving Olivia time to swallow the rush of saliva as she gagged. Breathing through her mouth she looked at the old dog in its basket, its eyes weeping and crusty, a recent fart lingering.

"He's nephritic," Florence had given out firmly, as if that could explain the smell.

It didn't, and Olivia was sure the dog had left a pile somewhere in the room, it was such a warm and ripe stench. She declined the offer of tea, not wanting to imagine what state the kitchen would be in. Florence hadn't minded, she had her flask of tea from the night before when the Social Services' carer had put her to bed. She made it last until the Meals on Wheels lunch arrived; they'd take the five minutes to make her a fresh one.

Olivia stayed for nearly an hour, perched on the edge of the sticky moquette covered sofa. She realised quite early on that she was there to listen to Florence's woes, and be added formally to the viewing schedule from the window. Consequently she'd felt less defensive, and on leaving had been pleased that she had managed to visit. That she'd taken some sort of a step without someone beside her

Back in her own house, several hours later it had started – in her hair. She'd worn it pinned up loosely, now she was pulling out the pins, scratching her scalp and panicking. She had picked up more than local information, she had picked up lice; she was crawling with them. She couldn't bear it – the thought of anything crawling on her was too much. From feeling quite buoyant, she sat and wept, then popped another pill.

She rang the Council, the Public Health Department, rather than the doctor's that Florence had advised her to sign up with. She didn't mind a surgery having her medical history, but lice – she would rather not. The snob in her remained, and the anonymity of the council department helped.

"Just go to the cleansing station, and they'll sort you out proper. Best to get it done there, those home treatments don't always work," she had been told promptly.

"It's just off the Old Kent Road – where'd you say you lived? Yeah, you could walk it from there."

She'd walked it, A to Z in hand, feeling unclean and itching all the way, finding it half way down a dingy little street. It was a single storey shabby building, with the opening hours displayed on a card covered in cellophane hanging in the window. The wrinkled plastic, coupled with the dirt on the window, meant that Olivia couldn't read it anyway, so she tried to open the door. It was locked, but beside the cheap bell push on the doorframe, was another note advising her to ring. She did, scratched, and waited. The woman who opened the door had been alarming; short, squat, and ugly, standing back to let Olivia pass inside. She was astounded at what she saw; it was like a time warp.

She was standing in a large, warm, room with a huge bath in the middle of the floor, old wooden duckboards on either side. To her left were two cubicles with curtains the size of elongated tea towels and more duckboards. There was another woman, sitting in one of the two chairs by the side of the bath. Fat, with a frizzy perm and bulging nylon overall, it was she who answered Olivia's embarrassed ramble about the reason for her being there. She had stubbed out her fag in the full ashtray beside her chair, and nodding in the direction of the two cubicles said "Strip!"

Olivia soon gave up trying to rig the curtain so that they

Chapter 5

couldn't watch her. She stripped off, leaving her clothes neatly folded on the narrow ledge, as there wasn't a hook either. She put her head round the curtain and asked what she should do next.

"Come and get in the bath and we'll delouse you – your hair is probably full of them," the bulging overall had replied. Olivia looked for a gown, a towel – there was nothing. She walked, naked and mortified towards them waiting by the bath.

"Your clothes'll need baking, the heat kills the lice you see; give them to Dun here and she'll put them on, they'll be done by the time we've finished," she added.

Olivia could now read the badge on the woman's huge bosom. 'Angela', and underneath, 'Supervisor'. She fetched her clothes under the gaze of the two women, turning round with her pile of clothing in time to see Angela smirk. The squat woman, Dun, had taken them off her and put them in the huge machine at the back of the room, slamming the door and setting the controls quickly.

"Just get in please" – and she had, climbing awkwardly into the deep, chipped, enamelled bath, the water hot and milky with an eye-watering smell. One woman on either side of the bath, and they had bathed her. Bathed, – it suggests a gentle soak and wash. Angela was a vigorous scrubber, with a preference for women. Olivia became aware of it as the woman lingered over her favourite bit, the pubic hair. Olivia felt invaded and humiliated. She had every part of her body rubbed and scrubbed in what could only be described as Jeyes fluid, by a woman whose fat fingers had managed to insinuate themselves into her. Twenty minutes later and it was over, she was pink, glowing, and stinking, with a small thin hand towel to dry herself on.

London, 1976

Inside the cubicle she had made no attempt to hide her nakedness when Dun had brought her clothes back.

"Here you are – mind out, they'll be hot," Dun had said as she passed them into the cubicle. They were – Olivia had to yank the zip of her trousers away from her abdomen, its metal teeth too hot to touch – she was close to tears.

"Do I have to pay?" she asked when dressed, wanting to run away.

It was Dun who answered, and for the first time Olivia looked at her properly, simultaneously clocking the accent.

"No, this is a free service, provided by the council, you know."

Olivia had muttered an 'okay', picked up her bag and followed Dun to the door, ignoring Angela who was back on her chair, fag lit and kettle on. Dun had opened the door for her, and stepping out, Olivia paused on the pavement.

"I know where you're from," she said.

"And I know where you're from," had come the answer, as Dun stepped out on to the pavement and looked up at Olivia, closely.

Olivia nodded and waited, looking down the street to break the stare between them. She was surprised when Dun had not continued, remaining silent. Usually the Northern Ireland game is played to a pattern, and Dun wasn't playing.

The first comment establishes the country, the second pinpoints the area. Generally, which county would be easy to establish, there are only six. City, town or village – give the name and wait for the reaction. It could vary from no knowledge whatsoever, to instant ability to discuss it in graphic detail – with the local genealogy as bonus. The next step is always the toughest.

"And which school did you go to?"

Chapter 5

On that it would all hang, deciding which way the conversation would go, and anything else that might follow. It told you which foot they dug with, so to speak.

Dun looked at Olivia and, as if deciding she was right about something asked instead:

"How come you turned up here?"

"Och it's a long story, I've only just moved in – the far side of the Walworth Road – it's all still a bit much you know." Olivia paused, unsure where to take it, if anywhere. Dun was a still person, silent, but she felt no threat in it, no heavy waiting. Looking away she went on:

"I couldn't take Belfast anymore, needed to get out, to start again. I've a son over here already, in Putney." She stopped, abruptly, facing her.

Dun's only response was a sympathetic nod, she knew better than to push for answers. She went on calmly rolling up her smoke, lighting up quickly. She didn't want this to end, this bizarre meeting, but felt uncertain about how to prolong it.

"I've got to get back soon, my son will be calling in later, and I can hardly meet him smelling like a drain – it's awful stuff, isn't it?" Olivia was aware that she was talking just a little too fast. She had difficulty in doing the chat bit anymore, generally it was an exhausting waste of time, but right now she too wanted to be able to talk.

They had spent ten minutes together, Olivia's hair drying in the breeze, Dun relighting her cigarette, talking quietly. Both had sensed the serious damage in the other, increasing their caution in the topics raised, but giving it a chance. It had been Dun who had brought it to an end – she had to go back in, the cleansing station closed at 4p.m. and there was clearing up to be done.

"Right, better get back then, or she'll be after me. Very

LONDON, 1976

nice to have met you Olivia, and safe home now," she had got out, too politely, but meaning it.

"Of course you must – sorry," Olivia began awkwardly, feeling anxious that there'd be trouble, that it was her fault. Dun gave a little smile, shaking her head. "No – it's no problem really – she's just a miserable cow at the best of times. Anyway, just before I go, I was wondering…would you like me to show you where to get the best stuff – like good breads and meat – down the market sometime?" She asked, hopefully. It was the only thing she could think of – they were both from the same country, but worlds apart.

"That'd be great, Dun. Thanks." Olivia answered quickly, pleased by the thought.

"Right, how's about Saturday – I'll wait for you at the library on the Walworth Road – say 10ish?" Dun had started to go in, pausing for her reply.

"I'll be there – and thanks again." Olivia's voice was husky.

With a quick nod Dun closed the door behind her, and Olivia moved off down the street, feeling dazed by the day. The degrading delousing had been abusive, yet out of it had come something; someone who hadn't known her before – and whom, ordinarily, she would never have met – with a lack of confidence to match her own.

By the time Graeme called in that evening Olivia was re-bathed, clothes in the washing machine, and lots of musky perfume on. Nonetheless he had noticed the smell – but had accepted Olivia's explanation that she had been cleaning the drain in the back yard – Jeyes fluid – just to be sure.

He had walked round downstairs – drink in hand – making suggestions that she didn't listen to. They needed to

CHAPTER 5

talk, but not about where he felt her things should go. She sat in the sitting room as he inspected the kitchen, willing him not to go upstairs. He'd only go on about how little had been done. Needless worry, Graeme had other things to do on his way home that evening. He reckoned that a brief visit to Olivia would still leave him enough time – without winding Eleanor up – to call in on his mistress as well. Her husband was due back from the States this week and it would be a pity to waste what was currently on offer.

Olivia didn't tell him much about her day, apart from having met a neighbour and unpacking. Graeme had half listened, swirling the last of his drink round the glass and finishing it with a gulp. He was good at the big things, wasn't interested in detail, and he wanted to be off. Minutes later he left, with Olivia agreeing that she would call, she would visit them, she wouldn't shut herself away. He and his restlessness took off, driving too fast as always. Olivia poured herself a large Jameson's and sat in the warm kitchen, sipping slowly, and thinking – what a day!

Back in her flat, Dun too was reflecting on her day, with Special Brew and a spliff by the two bar electric fire in her spartan living room. She was an ideal neighbour on the estate, never complaining about anything, and there could have been plenty.

The Cross Estate was a post war effort, four floors to a block, ten blocks of pure sink estate. It was a dumping ground near the Elephant and Castle. She'd been re-housed there after her re-habilitation; first floor, number 10, Brook House. In her time there the name had been changed twice, but the type of tenant – never.

They were the usual collection – the drug users and the small time dealers, the men who put their women to work on their backs across the river, the bad tenants from other areas, and the glorious 'care in the community' contingent. As a female, and alone, Dun could have been intimidated by the place and its people, but she had never had any trouble, ever. She knew how she seemed – pug ugly and hard, with a case file a foot thick at the local social services' Mental Health team's office. She knew also that it was this reputation that protected her.

She thought of Olivia by way of contrast – posh, soft, and a real pill head. Dun had immediately spotted the slow reactions and the dead eyes – daytime sleepwalker. She had been there herself, with far stronger stuff too – Sectioned and restrained more than a few times in the past – but Olivia, she looked like she'd been coshed. Living round the Walworth Road would be tough for her, Dun knew, but Olivia had strength in amongst the damage, and in a way her innocence could work in her favour.

Dun was pleased with her day – job satisfaction was rare and Angela was a mean boss ever since Dun had refused to shag her. Finishing her beer and spliff, she went to bed.

CHAPTER 6

Whitehall and Islington

"Quite frankly, I'd tow the bloody place towards Iceland, and sink it – who needs it?" the speaker asked Mark Bateson, as they took their drinks to the table in the corner. Two civil servants having a drink after work, talking shop. On a bad day Mark might agree – he wouldn't say it out loud, of course – Northern Ireland was an unsavoury mess, with talks about peace talks and politicians exaggerating the likelihood of the two sides reaching agreement. To him it was all talk and little to show for it – just more clever delaying tactics.

His job was minor, a junior civil servant in the Whitehall office that has covert links with MI5, Northern Ireland Section. He had nothing to do with the big political guns; he was no fast track man, just a very civil servant. In his twenties he had been earmarked for big things in the Service, but his background, or rather lack of it, went against him. Now, at 44, he had accepted that as a grammar school boy he'd climbed as high as he could. He didn't mind – his job was interesting and not too taxing. It paid well, and had a well protected pension scheme, along with some great perks.

Currently however Mark was flavour of the month, he had become useful. Following September 11th all the rules had changed. What had been accepted – a tolerance of certain levels of terrorist activity, in return for political concessions – was no longer the deal. All levels of activity were to be checked out, no exceptions.

That was his usefulness; he had a longstanding social contact with one of their 'clients', Graeme Ward. According to the FBI, Ward was keeping company with some interesting people. Mark was to do an initial assessment, very low key – his part a tiny fragment of a massive and delicate operation. He was good at this kind of job, moving easily in most circles, always appearing calm. That was the work front – his domestic life was a nightmare, and probably another reason for his lack of progress within the Service. Some days he thought it amazing that he had done as well as he had, with a wife like Fiona.

She was a forty-year-old loose cannon, sure to say the wrong thing, every time. How her behaviour affected their social life was evident by the lack of invitations, the gradual phasing out of any circle outside her own family – stifling, but better than nothing.

They had been a good-looking couple in the beginning, but these days Mark looked a lot younger than Fiona. She had been a petite blonde, fine boned with a fabulous smile. Now she was a hard faced 'blonde' with tight lines round her soured mouth, and a drink never far away. He, at just under 6 feet, looked fit and healthy, with no excess weight unless you counted his wife.

They lived in Islington of course. Fiona adored it, Mark hated it, and her family had helped pay for it. They had paid for her notions for years, bought her anything and everything she had demanded. They'd accepted Mark at her insistence, he hadn't been quite their sort socially, but she had had her way. Anything to keep her happy – happy enough to stay off the bottle. It had been a huge wedding, and had soon turned into a huge mess.

She was a devious, impossible drunk, out of control. She would describe herself as a 'bit tight' when to friend, hosts, and taxi-drivers she was an obnoxious drunk. Easier not to invite really – and so they weren't – except by one or two, like the Wards.

Chapter 6

That was his current problem, how to get her to go to, and behave at, Ward's forthcoming party. The last time she had attended a party there she had drunkenly called Graeme a 'thick Mick', resulting in a hurried departure and him having to call round the next day to apologise in person. When he had gone round after work only Eleanor had been at home. They had stood and chatted whilst she prepared dinner, she happy to leave the difficult topic for him to raise. They were old friends, not very close, but had spent many hours on touchlines watching their respective sons start their rugby playing, socialising afterwards, and then meeting occasionally for dinner.

Eleanor knew that Mark had his hands full with Fiona's behaviour, and hadn't been surprised that it was he who came to apologise. He would, it was typical of him – and just as well that Fiona hadn't come – Graeme had been beside himself with rage and Eleanor wouldn't have banked on his even being willing to see her. When Mark did ask her opinion of how best to handle Graeme she was honest:

"He won't forget it in a hurry, Mark. She has really done it this time – honestly, if she'd been a bloke, it would've ended up outside." She'd turned to look at him, and he had seen that she wasn't exaggerating. Soon afterwards they heard Graeme's car pulling up by the front door, and Mark had quickly gone to the door to meet him.

"Graeme, I apologise unreservedly for Fiona's appalling behaviour. She was totally out of order and completely pissed – I can't tell you how sorry I am, and…"

Before Mark could finish, Graeme had accepted the proferred hand and the apology – he wouldn't forgive the bitch, but Mark had introduced him to a lot of useful people, and it was so good to be able to say that you had a friend at Westminster. "Forget it, forget it, it's in the past," Graeme had responded, untruthfully, "come on in and have a quick drink." Mark had, relieved not to have lost yet another friend.

This was their first invitation to Ward's since that night – Mark was determined to go, not just for work, but also for the chance to see Eleanor again. He'd forgotten how easy they were together, comfortable.

He thought he had chosen a good time to discuss the invitation, and its implications, with Fiona. She had been calm when he had got in from work and he had showered in peace, joining her in the sitting room on the sofa opposite. He could never tell at this stage how much she'd had – she could pull it off so well, the pretence of sobriety. There were always glasses left round the house, with anything from neat Vodka to plain water in them – he could only gauge the amount by her behaviour and then play it by ear – tricky at the best of times. Her self-hatred was what drove her, thriving on old feuds, imagined slights, and the possibility that Mark would leave her. Already she was furious with him for having accepted the invitation without consulting her. He'd tried to explain, but it wasn't going in, she was topping up her drink and not listening.

"Look Fiona, I bumped into Graeme today, and he asked if we were coming. Frankly, in view of our past record I said we were, and that our reply was in the post – Christ, what else was I supposed to do? insult him again?! You know how touchy he is – we should have replied earlier," he had added, coming over to stand beside her. When she turned to reply he had seen her eyes, dull and trying to focus.

"I do not want to spend another evening with those Micks, they don't like me – and I can't stand them," was the

Chapter 6

reply, as the glass reached the mouth. He had misread the signs — she was more than well on the way. Lately Mark had let her get on with it, coming back to clean her up and put her to bed later, but this was different. He took the glass from her and made her sit down and listen, she owed him.

CHAPTER 7

Belfast 1975

It was raining when the two men got into the car. Stolen earlier in the day, the dark Ford was ideal for the job. Finding the house was easy as they had been told, and they knew he was in. Their informant lived at the end of the street with a clear view of the house – all they had to do was to prove that they were up for the job; they could do it.

Picking up the gun from the office above the bookies that morning, he'd been surprised that it was an old 9mm Browning. The only training he'd ever had had been on a Glock – but like the quartermaster said – 'never worry, same result.'

Both tense, they knew that this was their chance to make their mark, but neither realised how hard it was to get it right. Driving past earlier in the downpour, they had seen him moving in the bedroom, the cheap curtains affording only an illusion of privacy. He was alone, no family living with him. That was all they knew about the man they would kill in a few minutes; all that they needed to know. The order had come – it was up to them to deliver. As an initiation to the middle ranks of the organisation, their success would mean a level of status and respect both had been trying hard for. Sam was to ring the bell and kill him when he opened the door, Frank would keep the car running, door open. Sam had specifically volunteered for this one.

There was no longer a gate to what was euphemistically called a front garden – just the gap where it had once been. Sam was cool, he'd told himself he was, all the way there. In a matter of minutes he'd be away, back in the social club, his name on a pint or two.

CHAPTER 7

Standing on the front step, he rang the bell. He'd no worries about any interference from the neighbours – quite literally it would be more than their lives were worth to get involved. Seconds later the door opened and he saw him – and fired once.

He didn't know it but the bullet had gone into the head just above the right eye, as the man had tried to duck. The second shot had hit him as he had begun to slump, a falling body shot, catching him just below his left ear.

They'd screeched away in the car – the door swinging shut, narrowly missing the parked cars. It was a few minutes before either of them spoke. For Sam it was a chance to pull it together, to hide how he felt, whilst Frank got them into the sedate line of traffic heading into town.

"S'okay" was his only response to Frank's query. He couldn't say more, he felt almost let down by the job – there'd been no kick in it for him, it had all been too impersonal. Like it could be anybody. When Billy, their C.O. had seen them, Sam had stayed back to have a quick word in private. Sending Frank off to take the gun in for cleaning and storage, he'd decided to push for something else. He'd never minded what he'd been told to do – people, their pets, their homes- it didn't bother him, it was just a job. After tonight though he wanted something else, something to let him get close enough to smell the fear.

"That job Billy, it wasn't my cup of tea at all – any chance of a change in a while?" Sam asked the stocky wee man in the corner of the 'office'. He knew he was being cheeky, but didn't care.

"I wouldn't know about that now – that wouldn't be up to me, best leave it for a bit." Billy had replied, whilst wondering who the hell Sam thought he was. One hit and

35

he thought he was somebody – certainly the lad had come on, always stayed cool, but he was just too pushy. Billy didn't want to discuss it further, wanting instead to get home for his tea. They had kept him waiting for over an hour, and he was already late picking the kids up from their swimming lessons.

"Tell you what, why not come over tomorrow, and we'll talk about it then – alright?"

"Fine Billy, see you tomorrow," had been the last exchange between them.

Sam could feel the other man's rush to get away, and it needled him.

For his part, Billy had been surprised at the complete detachment of the young man – at his age Billy had been active, but reluctant to get into some of the areas that Sam seemed to enjoy. He left the building hurriedly, more worried about the likely nagging from his wife than the result of the 'action' taken. He would be told what to do later, when they had eavesdropped on the security forces' radio and heard the reaction to the latest killing. Right now though Billy was just a family man in a hurry to get home.

As for Sam, he went down to the club, had a couple of drinks in the grimy bar, made no friends, and went home to bed – picking up a wee fish supper on the way. He was looking forward, not back. One thing that he would never tell anyone was that just at the moment of firing he had frozen, not something to be proud of. Sam was scornful of lack of bottle – he definitely needed a change.

The change came rapidly, shattering his sleep- Billy's voice on the radio telling him to get over to his place, now. He had moved quickly, not just because of the tone of the voice, but also because it was the family's 'spare' room. What

Chapter 7

that meant was that it hadn't yet been added to the partial DIY central heating system and was permanently cold and damp. Linoleum on the floor and sash windows that didn't fit, made him hurry to get dressed.

Twenty minutes later he got to Billy's, entering by the alley along the backs of the houses; Billy was in the kitchen, the rest of his family peacefully asleep upstairs. He was a milkman in the real world, friendly and reliable, always kind to the pensioners. It was always a good cover when checked by the security forces – what could be more normal than a pinta, eh?

"Who the fuck did you sort out?" He had opened with as the door closed behind Sam.

"Yer man, just like you said," Sam had replied calmly, not sure what it was all about.

"Well not according to what we've been picking up," snapped Billy.

"He's dead, believe me – I got him twice, twice in the face at close range, for fuck's sake. C'mon, what's the problem here – he's dead and I'm knackered." Sam had answered angrily.

"You got the wrong fucking man, that's what the problem is. We don't even know this guy – he was just some wee lad visiting his mate. People are going apeshit over this, apparently his family are seriously respectable – no dealings with either side." Billy had spat the words at Sam, flecks of spittle on his lips. He had had such a bollocking from higher up over the cock-up – they were livid at the obvious increase in security checks that would follow, the potential 'lifting' of men for questioning. It was a pain, and Sam would have to leave the city for a while.

They'd already decided where, all Billy had to do was to

37

deliver Sam to the collection point, in the milk float, within the hour. Billy looked at Sam, wondering how best to tell him. Sam was numb; he had done what he had been asked to do – now what?

The answer was a shock to him, leave the city now, and go to the country 'for a while'.

That was it, clear and non-negotiable.

In the early damp dawn they had left the house together, walking round to the lock up where Billy kept his car. Sam didn't need to return to his digs – they would be cleaned by the woman of the house long before breakfast. All 'landladies' used by the organisation knew what to do and say after a sudden departure, should anyone ask.

Anything he needed would be bought for him, he had no personal effects – the few items he had kept had been stored in the loft at his grandmother's house, way up the coast. He couldn't go anywhere he was known, and wouldn't be welcome in other areas that now felt the heat of the security forces' investigation. Sam had a fair idea of what it would be like- he had listened to others talk about it, in the club late at night.

It would be on one of the numerous isolated farms up in the hills. Small farms with a collection of outbuildings, a clatter of unfriendly dogs, and a taciturn, reserved farmer. He would be passed off as a cousin if necessary, but more likely he would be left to wait and brood.

Three months he had spent there in the end – no one had forgotten him; he'd been kept informed, however briefly. Sam had reckoned that that was a good sign, that he hadn't completely blown it with the C.O., that if he kept his nose clean he would get back – no problem. The investigation into the murder had been intense at first, but

Chapter 7

had eventually eased off. Sam had wondered how some cases got dropped quietly – the word was that deals could be, and were, done between the various sides and the more secret parts of the security forces. Certainly after the initial expressions of horror and revulsion, and condolences to the family, most politicians would have difficulty remembering the case.

Only the relatives would remember it, live it. As for Sam, his view was simple – no regret that a complete innocent had copped it by his hand. To him it was a cock-up, a serious threat to his progress up the organisation's ladder, caused by some other git's ineptitude. He had sorted his head out on this one: he would run any future job from start to finish; no relying on half-baked surveillance from some sad bugger who needed money for drink.

The last time he had been in their social club in the city he had been contemptuous of some of the 'older' lads, the experienced ones, in the bar talking. They'd rabbit on for hours for the price of a few drinks, each drink enhancing their descriptive powers, their small parts in jobs growing into major ones. Their pathetic contribution to the cause – to Sam they were all a security risk. They were of the old school, bloody romantic notions about their country and their suffering at the hands of everybody, anybody. For Sam they'd lost the plot, their day was long gone. For every 'patriot' these days, you could count many more who were in it for the same reason as Sam was – money and status, but best of all, power.

He didn't share his politics, or lack of them, with many – naturally enough. He would wait, his chance would come, and when it did he'd found the reason bleakly funny... Billy had been blown up, blown to pieces getting into his car, his precious car that he kept in the lock up. It had provided the privacy to fit the device; no prying eyes, plenty of time, and one pathetic lock to pick. Billy had trusted the security of the lock rather than his own eyes. It had demolished the entire block of lockups, a new round in the murderous tit for tat game This had been the settling of an old score, and had been done away from the eyes of his family, almost a favour Sam had thought.

His return to Belfast had been swift, one quick call and he had been picked up within hours. Two lads he knew vaguely, with little chat in them beyond the cursory checks and greetings. Sam might be one of them, but he didn't relax, you never knew who your friends were when you'd been away. He was to be taken to meet the new man, pronto.

Billy's death meant his cock-up was buried, an irrelevance now. He had seen the T.V. coverage of the car bomb – it had had a ten second sound bite on the national news – described as the latest sectarian killing in 'Northern Island', before the newsreader moved swiftly on to something lighter. A sunny piece to wipe any thought of murders and bombs, it had worked in their favour for years.

Sam had thought long and hard during his 'wee jaunt', now he was keen to put it all to the new man. He knew there was no way he would be promoted now, all he could hope for was a chance – and he was far from disappointed.

Kevin, his new boss, was a surprise; there was barely ten years between them, and what struck Sam most was the man's style. He noted that the slogan T-shirt and grotty jeans with pre-requisite leather jacket had gone, replaced with an attempt at jacket and trousers and neat de-greased hair. The quality of the stuff was appalling, the trousers an

Chapter 7

indestructible nylon and the jacket a curious 'crease-free' blue number with fake gold buttons. His white nylon shirt was open at the neck, with ginger hairs showing.

"All right there Sam? I'm Kevin, good to meet you."

Sam had nodded his reply, looking at the face across the room. He had been brought to the office, which had actually been organised. Gone was the usual clutter of mugs and glasses, ashtrays and old papers. Instead it was clean and aired with Kevin very much the man running the show.

He was taller than Sam, with a broad freckled face and thinning ginger hair. Clean shaven, with the bright eyes of someone who drinks less than the rest and misses little. Unlike Billy, always in a rush, Kevin was calmer and willing to listen. They'd got on well, each understanding what was really being said under the surface pleasantries. Kevin was more than interested in what Sam had to offer – he could spot a like-minded lad dead quick these days. Things were moving in the city and different approaches needed to be made.

They all liked their gravy train, but lately young tearaways had been stepping out of line, attempting to act independently and keep the profits. Their activities raised the profile of the organisation, making serious action even tougher to arrange and execute. Kevin was going for a hard line policy regarding them. It had been agreed at a General Council meeting, and he couldn't wait to get it started. Punishment was to be swift, violent, and guaranteed – no exceptions, no second chances. Sam was knocked out when Kevin offered him the chance to run it. Yeah, Kevin would run the big stuff, but a tiny little piece would be for Sam to run – enforcement and punishment. He was well pleased; in fact, it was 'sticking out.'

He had been given new, nicer digs down near the river, and a 'taxi' had been laid on for him. Just a car that looked like a mini-cab, with its stickers and door logo, it was one of several that they used to move people discreetly around the city without comment. They owned them only for a few months and the drivers were all on the books of the Mini-cab Company next door to the office.

It'd taken time and contacts to establish their base, and it had stood up to many inspections by the authorities. The local community was their protective shield.

People were generous when it came to a good cause – imagine how generous they were when persuaded to see how good the cause would be. Not necessarily for them, the people, but for a few of them definitely. Sam was feeling the benefits – take his new flat for starters. The legal tenant had conveniently 'agreed' to move out, but the DHSS would continue paying the rent and heating bills.

He was home free as they say, and keen to go to work.

CHAPTER 8

Punishment

The pair worked well together, putting into place a much tighter network and a tough code of practice. There was a professionalism about Kevin that Sam admired and learned from. Kevin was good at weeding out the weak ones, the ones who would sell their granny for a drink, and particularly those who needed 'sorting.'

Sam would take over from there – he'd got it down to a fine art. Once he had the name he'd set aside a day to check it all through to his own satisfaction. Actually, he loved it, the preparation, the savouring of the detail of other people's boring little lives. It could take him anywhere in the Province, watching their routines, and choosing the best time. Not necessarily the best time for them, but the one that gave Sam the best time, his own, personal, 'match of the day' as it were.

In wry memory of Billy, Sam had rented a lock-up near the cemetery where his scraps of body had been buried. It was a no-go area for the security forces, the fire brigade, and latterly ambulances. You could forget buses – they had all been burned years before in the riots – which left taxis, if you could get one to come. An area where if you hadn't been born there, or had a local (with clout) to vouch for who you were, you'd be wise to stay out of. It was perfect for Sam's purpose, and the only security needed was a child's play Yale lock- the old fashioned kind that meant the door could be opened any time, and the place seen for what it was: a crappy workshop with nothing worth nicking- unless you were desperate enough to want an old table with one of its legs propped up by a brick, or a wobbly kitchen chair. There were two shelves high up, with the usual rusting tins of paint and a bag of rock hard putty next to the power supply.

Sam knew that once he got started the word would spread and he would have little trouble keeping people out of his way. His jobs ensured that he was on flexi-time. For the personal debts collection was always best in the evening. Likewise the pubs and clubs protection money – everybody knew when their payment was due, and soon any late payers from the old times got the notion to be punctual.

For the ordinary business protection payments – well Sam liked to do those in person, on a Thursday. Always on a Thursday; the other side collected their money on Fridays. All neat and organised – business during office hours. It was just like that, everybody knew the rules, and better still they were learning not to piss about with Kevin's lot.

That took care of most of the week save Saturdays, which was the part of the job that made it all worthwhile. Sam's sexual thrills were hard to come by, always had been. He had had it, of course, but not the way that others fancied. Take the wee 'girl' in his life – she was just something to shag: (those who had seen her, and there were not many, reckoned he had only done it for a bet) ugly, hard as a man, and with a loyalty that could be alarming. Sam liked being with her, (not going out much, but just enough to make her feel grateful that he would take her out) because she made absolutely no demands on him, and would do anything he asked for, anytime.

He had met her at the farm, at first thinking she was as dumb as the animals she tended, then being fascinated by watching her work. He had asked his host about her, who was as unforthcoming as Sam hoped he would be in relation to his presence on the farm.

CHAPTER 8

"She's the wife's cousin's girl. Gets a bit overwrought every so often, grand wee worker though, when she's here" was as far as he would go on the subject.

Tess was her name, much shorter than Sam, who could barely pass for 5'5". She was wide hipped, big arsed, with thick powerful legs and huge pendulous breasts. Sullen faced with coarse black hair cut badly, she avoided eye contact, preferring to look down, fiddling with the skirt she inevitably wore. That, a large pullover, and a pair of wellies on her bare feet, was it. Her age was hard to work out, she could have been as old as 30, but with a tough life it could be less, he thought.

Sam's only experiences had been with the city whores, thin and carping, money up front, job done. Tess – he just knew he could have her, for free – made him hesitate. He was the only one on the farm who used her name, he'd noticed, and she liked it. He noticed too that the response from her was brighter when he did.

He made a point of meeting up with her after the early milking, admiring her arse as she shooed the four cows back into the field, slapping rumps to get them through. In the steady rain the rutted lane to the field was already a bog, they were both wet but, for them, relaxed.

"Why on a day like this, don't you give in and stick on a pair of jeans, Tess?" he teased her as she shut the gate. Her reply wiped him, and established the first real link between them.

"Sure you never know when you might get lucky," she had countered.

He had laughed until he saw her face, not laughing like he was, but grimacing. He was curious but knowing, and as horny as hell. Afterwards, never having done it up against a tree before, he appreciated the simplicity and bluntness of it.

Christ – she was like one of the puppies on the farm, pathetically grateful for any hint of gentleness, and generous with the body too. She had none of the cloying baby talk crap that so pissed him off when with the city whores. Instead she answered his few questions like a bloke rather than a woman.

Yes – the farmer shagged her, yes – his mates shagged her too – but less often. No, she didn't like it, and yes she had wanted to shag Sam. The others were a bit of a local tax if you like. Sam hadn't liked, and had had a word with the farmer. It had been easy for him to sort it out with regard to her, there was little persuasion needed – his wants came first. He found out that she had been coming to the farm since childhood – once or twice a year – and had been repeatedly raped by her relation and his mates since 'an early enough age.' Even Sam couldn't work that one out – and the farmer had said no more.

It wasn't that he cared about her; he cared more about the risk of catching something.

A few years before, fresh to the city, he had laughed along with the men in the bar at their explicit jokes. Half the time he hadn't understood what they were describing, he was so wet behind the ears. These days he was specific about what he liked, and always paid well – he could afford to.

Sometimes, as his name got better known, he would get the nod at the club – the barman sending him a large one, pointing out the woman who had sent it. Often a young widow or an older one whose husband was still inside. He didn't mind those 'sometimes' – by the time he poured them into a taxi and took them home they could barely walk, never mind talk – which suited him just fine. A quick screw, tuck them up and he could be home in time for the

Chapter 8

late movie. They were just one of the many perks, the freebies.

As for Tess, she didn't know it, but she was his perfect whore – older, experienced and grateful, with a basic earthiness he found exciting. He decided that when he was back in the city he would send for her, give her a week or so in Belfast with him which should square it – then forget her. She'd be up for it – she was glad to be wanted, no matter the reason.

Chapter 9

Battery

On the first Saturday that Sam got going it had been a mild, dry day. It had meant that he'd had to change the timing a little as the children, with their father, stayed out longer on the swings, reluctant to go back indoors until the last of the day had gone, and what remained of the street lights had come on.

It had gone perfectly. His two men had waltzed up to the front door like he told them to, interrupting the family tea, telling the snotty nosed kid to run and fetch his da. The man had come down the hall and had listened to the message, wiping his mouth with the back of his hand.

"Tell your missus you'll be back in an hour or so, quick now."

Mrs. Short didn't believe her husband when he told her he'd be right back, touching the heads of the children as he left the room. She heard his hurry down the hall and the car driving off – seconds later the first question came immediately from their son –

"Where's Da gone?"

She couldn't answer – she was too afraid to put it into words. Instead she sat with her food untouched and waited, looking at the kids.

Sam was waiting at the lockup when they brought the man to him. A wee runt called Short to be punished for doing over the Post Office further down the road. A sad little start in a way, but the message was to be unequivocal so Sam gave it his best shot. Well not a shot really, that would come later in his plan. For now he had decided to keep it dead simple – just a Black and Decker drill and some gaffer tape.

Short had spent his brief time in the car sweating, trying

CHAPTER 9

to think of how to talk his way out of what was coming. He didn't know Sam, he knew of him, and had heard that he was a picky bloke who fancied himself. Short reckoned that he was in with a chance, first offence as it were. He came into the lockup twenty minutes after leaving his Ulster fry in his neat wee house with his family. Within another twelve minutes he was a cripple, slumped in a chair.

Sam drilled through his kneecaps, his right one first. Having watched Short play footie with his kids in the park, he knew which one he kicked with – quite neat really he thought. Any bluster that Short had considered trying had vanished when he had seen Sam standing at the back of the lockup, by the table. The welcome had been far too friendly, too smiley. He was right to sweat and be terrified – Sam was in top form, he'd been anticipating this all day, looking forward to enjoying himself.

When it happened he was delighted – Short wet himself!

Sam had quietly told Short that he was going to have both his kneecaps drilled, to teach him a wee lesson, and he'd only gone and pissed himself. Sam had been aroused by the sight of the urine stain spreading down the legs, puddling on the seat of the chair – it gave him such a buzz.

He couldn't listen to what Short was babbling – some quasi-religious shite, begging for help – like God's definitely checking out the lockups, and then the sentimental calling for his Ma, sad get. He'd plugged the drill in whilst they taped his mouth, then held him steady as they tied his arms and legs. The smell from the drill had been another kick – he had used the slower speed setting so that he could guide it, and make it last that bit longer. By the time he started on the left knee, Short's head was lolling – they'd had to take the tape off his mouth as he'd begun to choke on his vomit.

He'd been sick down his left side, the vomit staining downwards, to meet the urine soaked arse. As Sam lent over he could smell it all; the sick, the piss and the fear – and watched happily as the blood stains grew, like all the stains were trying to join up.

Afterwards, instead of abandoning Short on the wasteland, to lie for hours in screaming agony, they had – literally – dropped him off outside the Post Office, where he had originally 'sinned'. That had been Sam's final touch – he knew that even as they drove away the word would be out, ensuring that every little runt on the estate would get the message. He knew too that no one would have seen or heard anything.

As for himself, well it was barely eight-o clock on a Saturday night, and he was happy to get the drinks in for the lads back at the club. All of them felt that it had been a good one – a view echoed by Kevin coming in later to join them. That had been important for Sam; he and Kevin had agreed that it wouldn't be long before people wised up, caught themselves on. It wouldn't take many such lessons to get things running even more smoothly.

It had been a steady and productive period for them. The other side had proved less well organised, whereas they had gone from strength to strength. The money from the protection rackets was phenomenal – anyone with any sense just paid, too afraid not to. The clubs were raking it in – people drinking like it would be banned the next day and as for the drugs, well that side was expanding nicely. Some of his men weren't keen on the drugs side, despite the increased income. Sam listened to their chat and then reminded them that there were three taps in Belfast – two for water, one for valium – they were only giving the

Chapter 9

people what they wanted, recreational drugs. 'Where's the harm?' he'd ask, and paying them well for their evening's work, Sam would watch their doubts recede, helped by the wad.

Over the years Sam had consolidated his position. He'd stayed in various parts of the city for a few months at a time, each place better than the last, and for those with clout like him, always free. One of their most useful contacts worked for the Northern Ireland Housing executive – huge budget, jobs for the boys; and houses all the time. He was thinking bigger these days – he had few outgoings – with free food, (who would risk charging him for food, as he collected protection money from their restaurant?) free living, and more free drink than he would ever let himself have, he had serious money to spare.

The idea that he could become a home owner had never occurred to him – his family had never owned anything, relying on Church handouts just to survive – but Kevin's proposal had made sense and was a promotion in itself. Within thirty miles of the city, land had been bought by a company, on behalf of the organisation. There would be no problems with planning permission. The planning officer had been bought off long ago and the building plots would be decided soon – did Sam want in? Obviously those really high up, the ones being groomed for T.V. appearances as the world's press sought their opinions, would be looking further afield. For Sam it would be like your middle executive development, terrorist style. Of course he wanted in! What other sort of a job would reward a semi-literate thug so well? From nothing to the jackpot in just a few hard years!

He had seen the change in himself in the mirror. Not the

51

bathroom one, but the one in the bar which had caught him at an angle – he'd been taken aback when he'd twigged it was his own reflection. Christ – he had changed so much in a few years.

Gone was the thick near black hair, it was thin, dull, and slicked back, emphasising the thin, pale, face below. His face had always been thin and pointed, with sharp blue eyes that were never warm. They had multiple bags under them now, and his mean little mouth seemed smaller than ever, tight and lipless. He kept his mouth shut literally, as well as figuratively, his dental problems were severe but he wouldn't go to see a dentist. The thought of lying in a chair, giving total control to some stranger – no way. He'd put up with the pain, and those who got close enough could put up with the chronic halitosis.

His height, or rather lack of it, had meant that over the years spent in the city he had perfected the wee hard man's 'shuffle,' a way of walking with the shoulders hunched up, bomber jacket collar turned up and hands in jeans pockets. Leading with the shoulders, there was a tough rhythm to it, and the heels of the Doc. Martin boots were worn down at the back from the dragging. T-shirts, even in winter, and wrap around sunglasses for funerals, the hard man's uniform.

Tess had been happy enough with him though – he'd given her a good time in the city and she in turn had pushed all his buttons. She had a fair idea of what he got up to, but as it didn't affect him, unless there was a hitch, she wasn't curious. She'd seen the likes of him before when moving round the Province; men from active units being sent to the country for a break after a tough job. Some of them were sullen, morose drinkers, living out their

Chapter 9

nightmares in their heads. Others were manic, wanting to talk but unable to beyond a few hints, head shakings and large rounds of drink – twitchy and paranoid. Sam was one of them, but he never brought his nightmares home, he didn't have any. It was just a job, he did it well, and life was good. His worry was that it might stop and they'd all have to be frigging milkmen or the like – some drop in money, and fun, that.

Kevin had met Tess, by accident and to Sam's annoyance. He had an image to project, and though great to shag and get rough with, Tess was an embarrassment. Calling in on Sam on the off chance, Kevin had glimpsed her as she headed off to the kitchen, out of sight. He had raised an eyebrow, looking at Sam questioningly, but got no answer, and had let it be. Sam had been a very successful enforcer for them, an important part of the unit. He wasn't a leader, too much of a loner for many, but was powerful and had earned serious respect from the men. Intelligent and thorough – definitely, but Kevin felt that Sam had little else going for him outside of the job. Most of them were family men; divorced, remarried, living together, whatever – there was someone waiting for them, not just whores (and seemingly old ones at that) but your woman, loyal and silent. Less of a security risk.

"Just passing on my way over to meet some of the wife's relations, they're over staying for a while – fancy coming along?" he asked, looking out the window, down on to the river.

Sam didn't hurry to reply; he didn't believe Kevin's story about just passing, and was weighing up the possible reason for the visit.

"It's all right, just a few bevvies, bit of food, and some

craic – thought you might fancy a change – the wee lad is in the car, he'll drive us," Kevin had continued.

That swung it for Sam. Kevin wouldn't be trying anything on with his son present. The son was clean, very clean; he lived well, dressed well, had everything that his father had missed out on in his own childhood, and the rest. As soon as he had passed his driving test the new car had been sorted for him – driven over from Germany by two of the men sent specially. There'd been some comment in the club about it, but Kevin hadn't given a shit, his boy had passed his 'A' levels for Christ's sake. Sam found the lad pleasant enough, if a bit up his own arse, but no problem for an evening. He was ready to leave in minutes, having squared it with Tess, and was feeling less paranoid.

On the way to the seaside town they had chatted easily, keeping off any contentious topics. There would be a chance to walk and talk, drinks in hand, later. Sam knew that there was something on Kevin's mind that he would only hear about then. Three hours later, well oiled, that something had turned out to be innocuous.

Kevin's sister in law had taken a shine to Sam, and she and his wife had nagged and cajoled until Kevin had agreed to fix it so that they could meet away from the club, the lads, and their comments.

"Och sure you know what they're like – once they get a wee notion, they never let up," Kevin admitted to Sam.

Sam didn't know what they were like; he had never bothered to get that close to a woman to find out. He did take note though of Kevin's hint that despite being in the running for moving up, the other contender had the edge – better liked and more sociable.

"Fuck him Kevin, I'm a far better man than he is – I just

CHAPTER 9

don't do brown nose jobs, c'mon inside and let's make your wife happy," he replied tersely.

Stella he recognised from the club's social the previous year. A neat little hazel eyed brunette, quietly spoken and not one of the brightest; she was easy to be with. Kevin, apart from pouring huge Jameson's, helped ease Sam over the awkward gaps – when Sam had gone silent and Stella found the silence too hard to fill. It was obvious that Sam had few social skills, trying to cover his lack in this situation by being cool. He had no chat-up lines, he had never needed them, and any previous experiences with women would be of little use here.

Despite being brought by, and therefore vouched for, by Kevin, he could feel this tight knit family busily checking him out. He couldn't deal with the closeness of it all, the social side of life alarmed him; he felt that he wasn't able to deliver what they wanted. On the way home, in the wee small hours, he apologised to Kevin for how he'd been. Kevin couldn't understand why there had been a problem, but had certainly seen it, and had been triggered into helping – glad now that he had. Hearing Sam apologise gave him a good indicator of how hard the man had found it. Kevin had never heard him do so before and despite, or more probably because of, both of them being four sheets to the wind, he felt like pushing it a little.

"Was that your woman at your place tonight?" he asked.

"Not at all, she's just a wee millie who stayed over, why?" knowing full well that there was more to come. Christ, what a night.

"It's just that she was there like, seemed a bit at home you know," Kevin felt his way, carefully.

For Sam the choice was clear, talk or be questioned. At

55

least if he did the talking he could control how much, or what came out. With questions, you never knew where they might end up, he reckoned.

Up until then he'd been concentrating on the journey, with the hope that he could make it home without spewing up in the car. Now he was having to deal with this, along with the effects of at least half a bottle of Jameson's on top of the lagers. He'd drunk far more than usual, anxious not to cause offence by declining hospitality – at least he knew the rules on that one – but he was feeling the signs of a 'Hughey' increasing as he tried to think. All that saliva gathering in the mouth, and the stuff on the rise from his gut coming to meet it.

"Pull over – quick!" was all he got out, before trying to open the door.

The car had scarcely stopped moving when he was out, helped by Kevin, spewing violently onto the grass verge by the side of the empty road.

"Oh God – that's desperate," was all he could say.

"Och you're all right, it happens to the best of us, better out than in, eh?" Kevin replied, with his hand on Sam's shoulder. He'd been there many times before, knew the drill; no crap on his shoes at least. Sam was paler than ever but indeed better – he hated himself for being in this state, and was trying to get his mouth to work. He and Kevin leant on the boot of the car, the dawn coming up, in silence.

Sam, in the end, had been the first to speak.

"I've not had that much time, like, with women, you know, like, doing the old chat stuff – you know," he said, "never really found it easy. I dunno, maybe I'm just not or it's not – och, do you know what I mean?"

Sure Kevin could, just about, remember being that

Chapter 9

awkward about women. Mind you, it was more than twenty years ago now – at this rate Sam should have acne. When he did answer, it wasn't to his enforcer, the man who scared the piss out of people, but instead the wee bloke with boke on his shoes, who couldn't handle the closeness of a family at all.

"C'mon, it wasn't that bad – they can be a pretty intimidating bunch, I know. I'll fix something up for next week – say me and Renee take Stella out for a few jars, and you could join us later. That way you can sort out how long you want to make it – it'd be easier, eh?" he said gently.

"Now let's get back in the car and we'll get you home."

With that he opened the door for Sam, giving his son the wink. The car was warm and the smell from Sam was foul, so it was windows open for the rest of the journey, trying to keep the smell down. Kevin and his son sat up front, exchanging the odd word, while Sam slumped in the back, head back, mouth open. It seemed he'd just closed his eyes and now they were pulling up at his place already. He gathered himself together enough to decline any help getting in. No way was he being carried home.

The reception from Tess hadn't been good. She'd waited up for him, as she'd said she would, and was asleep on the sofa – telly on and bottle empty. The place stank of fags and her perfume, and god she looked rough. He sat on the chair opposite and watched her, trying not to compare her with Stella. Right now, he and Tess were two drunks together – and he disapproved of them both.

He didn't want to touch or speak to her so just left her there, unwilling to even put a rug over her in case she woke up. A long hot shower followed by a long, cold one helped him come round enough to decide – Tess had to go.

Whilst the coffee was on he made the call, then took her a cup, hating the smell of her foetid breath as she struggled to sit upright. Stiff, cold and badly hung over, she looked appalling and felt worse. He wanted her gone; he felt that he needed to avoid people for a day or so until he got himself back on track. Consequently his need came first and between them both. She was way behind on the caffeine stakes and wasn't up to speed when he gave her his take.

"It's been dead good and all that, but there's a problem about me giving you a lift home today – I've got a job on and it can't be done tomorrow, has to be today, so you'll be getting a lift back this morning, ok? " Sam said quickly.

His call earlier had been to get a driver for her – he used one of his men who would do, and did, the odd funny job for him. A hopeful, just as Sam had been years ago, hoping to get noticed, particularly by Sam.

Most of what Sam had said had gone straight over Tess's head, she was trying to come round faster than her body would allow. What she had heard was, she was out. Her leaving hadn't been mentioned before, but the message and the feeling was clear – leave now. She knew better than to ask questions, this had been the best time she had ever known, but this hurt, God it hurt.

She had just enough time to quickly wash and have another coffee before the guy came, waiting as she put her few bits in a bag. Sam said goodbye hardly looking at her, she repeated her farewell but still he avoided her eye. Both still pissed, they'd parted – him shutting the door before she'd even reached the half landing on the stairs. He didn't watch her go; he didn't want to look at her in the daylight really. What they'd had was best in the dark. He thoroughly cleaned and aired the flat, boiling the sheets – a feeling of

Chapter 9

order returning, calming him

Tess didn't cry at all on the journey, the driver would say later. She'd just sat in the corner of the nearside back seat, gazing out the window, inviting no conversation by totally ignoring the driver. He didn't mind – there were worse ways of earning a hundred quid. She felt like she was disintegrating, sliding; within a few hours she was back in the farmyard feeding the scrawny chickens, dead inside.

Sam sat in his clean space, waiting for the call to come to say that she had been delivered. As soon as it came he felt better, able now to get his head round the idea of Kevin's sister in law.

Politically it was a wise move, and she was a nice, quiet girl – the biddable sort. She came with a ready-made family, so to speak. He had found out from her that she had two small kids, and was on her own. Her man had been killed 'in action' six months previously – Sam had heard about it, of course, but hadn't realised there were kids. He hadn't taken in much detail apart from the fact that the guy had blown himself up trying to fit a device to a policeman's car. It had been a 200-pound bomb with faulty wiring – his own effort. There had been nothing but bits of him left to bury, but they had anyway, with sandbags as ballast in the coffin to give an illusion of presence.

Financially she'd never want, but she had no place anymore in the pecking order – her man hadn't died a hero, hadn't made his mark at all. Her man had screwed up, and only because he was related to Kevin by marriage was he given a military funeral, with death notices in the paper, extolling his efforts for their cause. Now the reality for her was that, apart from the odd outing with Kevin and sister Renee, she had no social life. She stayed indoors, looked after the kids, watched the telly, and went to bed. In the past she hadn't gone out much, and only with her husband, not with a bunch of the 'girls' – she was too quiet for their parties and clubbing, not able to hold her own in their shrieking banter. But it was so lonely when the kids went to sleep – silence until the morning. When he'd died so many people had called in, so many things had needed doing. The cold, hard, time was about a month after the funeral, when they'd all gone, and the shock had worn off. Then it had really hit her – this was how it would be, there wasn't anyone coming home, ever. Sometimes she and the kids stayed over at Kevin and Renee's, but it was a strain all round. Kevin found the demands of small kids wearing, and Renee didn't like anything that upset her Kevin.

Stella would have loved to feel the same, to still have her man to look after. She was lost without her purpose – from a young age all she'd wanted was to get married, have kids and be a wife. How could it all be over when you're only twenty-five? She needed a man, but not for sex. Sex for her was a treat for her man, she didn't much like it, but he had. For her it was the comfort of having someone to care for, to be able to talk to at the end of the day. Not a lot to want, and just about what Sam could deliver.

Kevin and Renee had actively promoted the awkward courtship. Kevin found his sister in law a bit dull, and when depressed she was like some misery trailing round his house, reminding him of what a dick she'd married in the first place. He rated Sam, found him a bit of a misfit, but maybe with a good wee woman behind him he might come out of himself a bit more. As for Renee, she'd done her bit and wanted Stella to move on – there was only so much a sister could do after all.

Chapter 9

The wedding was small; Sam didn't appear to have any family, or anyone he wanted to let on about, and Stella felt that it wasn't right to put on anything bigger, coming so soon after the funeral. Just her, the kids, Renee and Kevin – quiet, just how she and Sam liked it. She'd make him a good wife, and he'd soon see how little it took to keep her happy. She had got what she wanted, and what he wanted he could get elsewhere – she didn't need to know his true sexual proclivities. As long as he gave her one, once in a while, she'd be fine, he knew that. Anything fancier he would buy, away from home.

CHAPTER 10

Party Planning

Eleanor needed someone to talk to, someone outside the normal circle of family and friends. She didn't confide easily in people, preferring to mull things over privately, but these days there was so much that she was unsure about, unclear as to what exactly was going on. Prior to this she had felt that she and Graeme had struck a balance, a way of staying together, now that the children weren't there to cement it. She'd accepted her role, it was the price for the so called 'good life' they shared.

Now it was different, she felt different – Graeme's 'deal' was unacceptable. That was how he operated, everything a deal, to be haggled over and usually ending with him coming off best. She was fed up with being taken for a mug – she couldn't even bear to imagine how many times he had taken her for one, lying was his first language, emotional blackmail, his second. There was no thaw in their relationship; she remained cold and polite, whilst he tried to think of some way to bring her round.

In the past he'd always succeeded, but only because she still wanted to believe in him. Opera or concert tickets, a good dinner, champagne – they'd generally do the trick – papering over the cracks, pretending afresh. Once they'd even joked about it, his 'penance' – hours of music, which as usual, he'd sleep through.

She would do the party for him, it would be her valediction – but he didn't need to know that. The remaining three weeks would give her time to plan, not just the party but also her departure. Right now a grotty one bed roomed flat seemed more attractive than this diseased sham.

She had been nervous about even sending out the

Chapter 10

invitations. If she'd had her way they'd have been simple, black on white, 'At Home' – easy. Not for Graeme – nothing better than the faux Irish script, complete with Celtic borders and green print. She knew better than to argue over it, she'd tried when he had given her the guest list – a political and social nightmare. Forget the etiquette book, there was no solution to this one. It was an Irish rugby night with business on the side; and what business.

She'd baulked when she had seen his list – these were people the Wards met separately for obvious reasons – how did he think that the heavy-duty loyalists and nationalists would get on? How did he hope to bring together some of his 'rougher' contacts with the likes of the Honourable Richard Oliver and wife? It all seemed badly thought out, so unlike Graeme.

They'd spoken earlier that day, efficiently and briskly, checking replies and her catering plans. She'd finally given in over the row about domestic help – she didn't want it, but had agreed that for the party she'd put up with it.

Just as she started to clear her notes away the `phone rang, it was the call she had been waiting for, Mark Bateson. She'd tried to reach him earlier, his snooty secretary promising he'd call her back by the end of the day.

"Oh hello Mark, thanks for ringing me back," she began, and then hesitated, suddenly feeling a bit shy.

"I wonder, if you're not too busy, if we could have a chat about a couple of things? I'd appreciate a bit of clear thinking," she waited for his answer, playing with her keys on the work surface.

"I'd be delighted to Eleanor, but I'm about to go into another meeting – why don't you meet me for lunch tomorrow, I'll have more time then?" Mark answered smoothly, hoping she'd take up the offer.

"Oh, well, yes – I suppose I could – you'll have to give me clear directions though – you know what I'm like – but yes, I'd like that." Eleanor was sounding a mixture of hesitant and pleased, Mark could feel it. He was smiling as he gave her the venue, his friendly Italian restaurant. It was far enough from the office, but handy for discreet meetings.

"So, see you tomorrow, at noon at the Trattoria then, Eleanor, and I'm glad you called me." Mark spoke quietly, his secretary signalling to him that he was running late. He didn't mind; this call had solved one of his problems for him.

"All right then Mark, I'll be there, and if I'm…" Eleanor started,

"Yes, if you're late I will wait, don't worry – now I've got to go, my master waits – take care, and I'm looking forward to seeing you," he finished, remembering her late arrivals in the past.

With that he was gone and Eleanor had hung up, feeling brighter. As she finished off in the kitchen she realised she had a real smile on her face – these days a rare sight.

Closing the kitchen door quietly, she headed for her room, wanting to think about tomorrow, to savour her own secret – privately. She had done her lists, and planned her menu. Her 'big shop' tomorrow would take minutes, then she would be free – and that felt good. Upstairs in the bedroom she took a hard look at herself and decided to start with a long bath and a face pack, it might help.

CHAPTER 11

God bless America

Graeme Ward had done business with the Irish-Americans for years. Their generosity was famous and their patriotism to the cause was unquestionable. They might all sing the Star Spangled Banner, but nobody who had been to a Northern Ireland fundraiser in the States could doubt where their passion, their romantic idealism, lay. The tickets were never cheap, but at the end of the evening it would be the silent collection that really counted; thousands upon thousands of dollars, with more to come.

The organisation couldn't have survived without the support of the US and the other countries – their arms, money, training, and banking systems. It was all there if you knew the right people – and for this job Graeme reckoned he did – Jack Barnes.

Originally from Northern Ireland, Jack had left when he'd got his degree in psychology. He'd settled in the U.S., becoming a citizen as soon as he was able. Ulster had 'blown up' again and he had turned his back on it, wanting the success (and subsequent lifestyle) of an American professional instead. His career as a private therapist had been successful and lucrative; his early retirement letting him set up a couple of retail businesses. He didn't need the money; he needed the buzz of something new, rather than the predictable professional book that would use his case studies over the years.

He was a well-respected member of the community, wealthy and proud of his success, keen member of the golf club, and never attended any church of any kind. His clientele as a therapist had been monied and connected. Personal recommendations had given Jack some powerful clients – political ones particularly – he had a very smart network indeed.

One thing that had never changed in him however was his passion for the game – rugby. He could afford to, and often did, travel over for the matches, part of him still feeling the pull. He combined it with a bit of business, but nothing compared to the roar of the crowd at the matches. That was where he and Graeme had been introduced to one another, corporate entertainment at Twickenham, in a posh marquee – England versus Ireland. They'd got on well immediately, and Graeme had invited him out the following evening for dinner. Jack had been impressed by Graeme's ability to get a table at The Ivy; he had never yet achieved it.

After an excellent meal they had gone over to Ronnie Scott's, Jack having heard of it and wanting to taste some 'real' London. The music had driven them away, too busy and loud. They left, preferring instead the black cab tour round the city, with a final couple of brandies at Jack's riverside hotel suite. They'd established their link; they could, and would, do business and pleasure together. Jack had travelled back to the States in the middle of the week, with Graeme even taking the time to see him off at Heathrow airport. Graeme's next trip to the States would open up new links with the well-heeled and politically sympathetic connections Jack could come up with. It was a mutually satisfying relationship.

Graeme was certain that Jack would be interested in the deal, and would want a chance to do something before he got any older. That was how Graeme had read him on his last visit. Jack, sentimentally drunk, recalling his early days in Ulster, the memory bearing no resemblance to what existed now. His rose tinted vision of Belfast was one that Graeme

Chapter 11

could scarcely remember without an effort. Most of what Jack was talking about had been blown up, burned, long since, he just went along with the ramble; it was the tedious part of their drinking together. Now, however, the emotion would be used to drive the new business – potentially it was all there to be tapped.

Chapter 12

Islington

Mark woke early and breakfasted peacefully in the kitchen, looking forward to his day. Due to be picked up at 8.30, he'd be taken south of the river for the meeting. It'd be his first visit to the premises, the new secret anti-terrorist unit operating out of a warehouse in S.E. London. Any previous contact had been on a secure line, never in person. Even the driver wouldn't be anyone from their pool in Whitehall, the commander of the unit preferring to send one of his own men. Mark had been well briefed the previous day and wasn't anxious about his ability to deliver the Minister's viewpoint. Privately he doubted whether the unit would take much notice, but it had to be done – even if it was off the record.

He had taken care when getting ready and looked good in his dark suit and pale blue shirt. Hair still damp and especially well shaven, he looked healthy and positive – in sharp contrast to Fiona who was struggling to come round in the bedroom. He'd brought her tea in bed to delay her arrival in the kitchen. With any luck he'd be out the door before she came down. He hadn't allowed himself to think much about his lunch date, trying instead to keep focused on the task ahead.

In Putney however, Eleanor was trying on something else that she found she didn't like anymore. Behind her on the bed was the pile she'd already discarded – how come it was so hard to find something appropriate? Graeme was off on an early site visit in northwest London, a huge contract for the local council, which gave her the place to herself.

She was nervous about going to meet Mark – uncertain about what to say. Her taxi was due at 10, and she hadn't

Chapter 12

even started on her hair and makeup — cool Eleanor was more than a little ruffled. Four hours later she wondered why she'd worried.

Mark watched her getting out of the taxi, slim and attractive in a straight-skirted suit with crisp white shirt. As she came over to join him he got up to greet her.

"Eleanor…great to see you — you're looking well," he said with a big smile, kissing her cheek. Already half way through his Pastis, he'd been enjoying the anticipation of her arrival. His meeting had been productive, the Minister had been briefed and now he was free for the rest of the day.

"And you Mark — sorry I'm a bit late. Yes, I'd love one." The smile was real, taking some of the strain out of her face for a minute.

Her makeup was clever, Mark thought, but the eyes gave it away — they showed the worry and tension.

"How did the shopping go?" It was the easy way into the subject, after they'd done the weather and chosen their food. She played with her glass of water and took a deep breath. Determined not to cry, but finding the words sticking in her throat, she gave a little shrug and said:

"It didn't happen — I got held up at the house and in the end came straight here. I've no idea where to begin with this — it's as though everything I believed in is actually fake. Graeme is worse than ever — if that's possible — and as for his business, he's up to something that I can't put my finger on, but it's not good."

Mark watched her and then waited as their food and wine arrived. Once the waiters had left them alone he raised his wine glass to her, toasting her.

"Good health… now, we've all afternoon to eat and talk.

Everything seems better after a good meal and some wine – believe me," and began.

It was quite true – a couple of glasses of wine later and most of their meal eaten, they were leaning across the table talking non-stop. Mark knew all about Graeme's women – at one stage he had been invited to one of Graeme's 'jollies' but had happily got out of it, tarts were really not his thing. Listening to Eleanor, he marvelled at the crassness of the man, the lack of any insight into the pain he caused her.

Mark had always seen Eleanor in control, never letting go, remaining loyal despite the provocation. Today she was showing another side, some healthy anger that he felt was long overdue. Eleanor found the fact that Mark actually listened to what she was saying quite novel. With Graeme it was more a question of him telling her to listen to what he had to say – then ignoring her point when she tried to put one to him.

"I know what Graeme gets up to – the other women. He says they mean nothing, that he'll stop, but he never does – I don't believe he ever will Mark," said Eleanor, looking directly at him. She'd decided that she couldn't tell him about being infected by Graeme's latest mess – not yet anyway.

Mark ordered more coffee and Stregas, aware that he knew a lot more about Graeme's games than she. The likelihood of Graeme stopping was as plausible as Fiona becoming teetotal; the man loved the risk. Take the golf trip last year as an example – he had been the only one not to laugh at Graeme's story of his favourite little Greek restaurant. The other men in the bar had found it hilarious and daring – Mark had found it simply distasteful. Graeme's love of good food was well known; all had been out for vast

Chapter 12

dinners with him. They knew too his need to be recognised by the patron, to have his own table. It made him feel good, and he had made the little Greek taverna his haunt. So much so that he took everyone there – the wife and the mistress. He'd almost giggled his answer to the raised eyebrows over the pint glasses.

"No it works, really. When I take the wife we have my usual table, and they know who she is. When it's a bit of stuff, I have one in the corner, and they never let on. That way I get to eat what I like, and the women are none the wiser – mind you the tips can be astronomical!" Graeme smirked, enjoying the 'what a man' ripple from his audience. Mark had stopped going on the trips, he didn't fit in – he actually enjoyed women's company.

"I think you're right Eleanor – the man isn't going to change – why should he?"

Mark's reply surprised her – she felt it would be more like – 'why wouldn't he change?'

"Look at it this way," he continued, deciding to give her some more of the picture.

"Graeme, you say, has never been faithful to you throughout your married life. He likes variety and quantity, you've seen the evidence – and then afterwards I bet he asks you to forgive him, and you do, every time, don't you?"

"Yes," she replied miserably, it sounded so pathetic described like that.

"Well it obviously isn't making you happy – he's got you on a string. Your loyalty gives him free licence, and I think you know that." Mark added.

"I've learned a lot in the past few weeks Mark, and yes, that's one of the changes I've made, and I think he knows it now – I can't go on with this farce. What I'll do – I don't know yet; there are other angles to this that don't add up." Eleanor finished her Strega and looked to Mark for his reaction.

He was surprised to hear how far she had moved on – this was no little doormat talking. It'd be a very difficult road for her to go down – Graeme dumped people, not the other way round. She wouldn't be allowed to leave him, not without a major fight – at the table they both knew it without saying.

At least there wouldn't be any financial hardship for her, he reckoned. She knew that they were well off, rich even, but not the detail. Mark knew more, so did MI5 – part of his meeting that morning had filled in some more of the jigsaw that was Graeme Ward.

The man was worth millions – he didn't need to work another day in his life. His financial rise had been rapid, his decision to invest in a commercial glazing company at the start of the current 'Troubles' had been inspired – or a tip off.

Either way, after every bomb in Belfast, there were his vans, replacing the glass. His name cropped up everywhere; his father's small company was now huge, always in the front row when council contracts were being dealt out to the chosen few.

"Apart from everything else, there is the bloody party too," Eleanor was saying, the alcohol making her flushed.

"It doesn't make sense, the mix of people he's insisting we invite – God, I know I'm not one of them – but even I can see that this is a recipe for disaster. I'll be back in a minute," and left for the loo, aware that he was watching her make her way across the floor. She didn't mind. It was so good to be able to talk and be listened to. Mark signalled to the waiter for more coffee, Eleanor on his mind.

Chapter 12

"What are you going to do about the party, anyway?" Mark had asked her as soon as she'd sat down again.

"Well the food is the easy bit for me – I'm cooking for forty but it's not a difficult menu. Graeme's annoyed that his favourite smoked eel isn't appearing, but apart from that it's all going well." Back on safer ground, Eleanor was sounding efficient.

Mark knew the food would be excellent – and the drink would flow like water. He wished he could get a copy of the guest list though.

Neither had wanted to end the meeting, even though they were aware they were the last diners in the place. With the waiters hovering, ready with their bill and wanting to clear the table, they reluctantly left.

Outside on the pavement Mark hailed her a cab, gave her a big hug, and arranged to give her a call in a few days. Eleanor sat back in the cab and enjoyed the cabbie's chat and moans as he crawled through the heavy traffic. The journey was over too soon for her. Seeing Mark had been more than a help – she was already working out what he meant by a 'few' days – did he really mean it? Would it even be a good idea if he did?

She knew the answers to both, and hoped he thought the same.

The house was empty when she got in, with a message from Graeme to say he was taking a client out for dinner. She was more than happy; it gave her more time to think things over.

CHAPTER 13

Elephant and Castle, 2003

Olivia couldn't watch the news for long, the images of war too heavy, too explicit. The post September 11th retaliation by the United States had finally happened. Despite what anyone else called it, she recognised it for what it was – revenge. The size and strength of the American reaction had amazed her. In Ulster, her country of birth, they had had thirty years of bombings, killings, negotiations, terrorist's rule, with governments unable (or unwilling) to stop the warfare, or to control its funding. She was just another person who would never know who had murdered her child, no one ever having been brought to justice for it. No witnesses, no evidence, no help in finding the killer. So many like her, left to brood and fester, wondering 'why?' Over three thousand dead in Ulster over the thirty years.

She had spent the morning in the library, checking her comparison, wanting to be able to tell Dun confidently when she went round later to her flat. She was 'weak' at Maths, i.e. hopeless, so working out a percentage had taken a long time, but she had got there, roughly. The United States, during the Vietnam war, lost 40,000 servicemen. She could still see the news clips from back then – the grim sight of the body bags being unloaded. The American public had had enough of seeing their children coming home in bits – the war had to stop, and it did.

Starting to feel agitated, she had finished off and left, walking briskly down the Walworth Road, towards Dun's. As she crossed the estate, Dun watched her from the walkway, hurrying towards the block. Dun could tell that she was wound up about something, by the way she walked, and could guess too what it could be. Ulster, or the family:

Chapter 13

or on a really bad day – both. It never varied with Olivia – this time it was Ulster. They'd sat having a cup of tea in Dun's kitchen, and she had waited for Olivia to start. It was best to let her get it out, let her calm down.

Olivia's counting habits varied, sometimes factual, sometimes just counting the people on the bus when they went out. They were her mantra, her way of trying to keep a lid on it. Mind you, it didn't always work – Dun recalled her distress when the schools turned out, too many, too quickly, on and off the bus. They avoided those times now, and the underground was always a non-starter.

"Remember Vietnam – back in the Sixties – all the bodies going home to America, remember – on the news?" Olivia asked, watching as Dun rolled a cigarette on the plastic tablecloth.

Dun had agreed, of course she remembered – didn't know any of the figures, but yes she could picture it. Then Olivia had proudly given her her latest numbers.

"You know, if you worked out the number of people killed since these Troubles started up again, it would come to about three thousand dead. There are about one and a half million people in Ulster, and two hundred and fifty million people in the United States. Do you know now many dead there would be in the U.S. if they'd experienced what we've been through for the last thirty years?"

Of course Dun didn't know, it would never have occurred to her to even try to find out.

Olivia's answer had shocked her though.

"Half a million! Half a million dead Americans – that's how many – if you compare them. Twelve times as many as Vietnam." Before Dun could reply, Olivia had continued: "and those are only the dead. I have nothing on the maimed, limbless, traumatised, living!"

Dun could feel it in Olivia; since September 11th she had changed, there was a new anger in her that Dun could sense. It wasn't ready yet, but it was on its way – Dun was an expert on anger.

"What gets me is that nothing was really ever done before about terrorists – it took September 11th to make it start happening. Doing things that could have been done years ago – stopping the money, hunting them out, locking them up – for God's sake why couldn't we have had the same, years ago?" Olivia paused, drank some of the tea, her hand shaking slightly.

"I feel as though I've been had, conned for years. I believed that our government was doing everything possible to root them out, and give us peace. In fact, that wasn't so, was it? We just go on and on. More people like me being told the same old story: sorry, we can't tell you who killed your husband, wife, mother, father, child – there is no hard evidence, no help from those who do know, but we'll keep on trying. It's so wrong – and the lawyers, the bloody lawyers, lining their pockets as ever. There's an Ulster lawyer asking four hundred pounds an hour just to look at the case papers, not to do anything, just read – it's scandalous. Och Dun, I go on and on about it all – you know me – and I never get anywhere with it. It all comes back some days, like new, raw and open. I'd give anything to be able to touch or smell Tom again – just once more. It never, ever goes away – the need never leaves me." Olivia stopped, eyes brimming.

"Here, take some of this," Dun had said, passing her spliff to Olivia. "Suck it in and pull it down as far as you can, then let it out slowly, slowly," as Olivia choked on it. It was always

Chapter 13

the same instruction, same reaction – but Dun was proud that Olivia even tried. In her eyes weak spliffs worked better for her friend than the huge amounts of anti-depressants, sleeping pills, and other shit she had been taking. Getting her off them had been difficult – Dun's personal experiences of 'cold turkey' had helped enormously. She felt responsible for Olivia, looked out for her.

She had made sure that the local yobs knew that Olivia was her mate, and was not to be hassled. Even so, Dun never let Olivia come to the flat without prior arrangement – she liked to check out what was happening – sometimes meeting her half way if there was trouble on the estate.

Olivia was calmer and sat quietly, elbows on the table, looking at the compulsory net curtain on the kitchen window. Every few minutes another outline would pass by, only feet away from them. The block was a hive, humming day and night – people's footsteps ringing on the concrete, shouts and fights, stairwells turning into urinals for the incontinent young coming home from the pubs. Before meeting Dun, Olivia had never seen young women squatting to piss in a stairwell in her life – Dun was relieved that her friend had noticed so little.

The flat had none of the middle class cosiness of Olivia's home. All the furniture had come from the either the WRVS' fourth hand furniture store, or worse still, the Housing Department's store of abandoned items from previous tenants. Basic and tatty, with lino (cutely re-christened 'cushion floor') throughout, it was nonetheless one of the few places where Olivia felt secure. It was here that, over the years, she and Dun had exchanged many of their lives' secrets. Tom, Graeme, Eleanor, Christine – Dun knew so much about them, and had never met any of them.

Elephant and Castle, 2003

Dun had even shown Olivia her scar – only once, when she'd lost her temper at Olivia's complaining about withdrawal – how much her body craved the magic pills. Yanking her hair back, she'd shouted at her, making her flinch. "For fuck's sake – your pain – this is what pain looks like – they fucking lobotomised me – that's pain! You'll sweat and shake and cry and then you'll get over it – they zapped my fucking brain for Christ's sake!"

Dun had bluntly gone on to describe her mental disintegration, and the treatments given, to a shocked, silent Olivia.

"It wasn't long after I'd come over here, to London. I was in a bit of a state still, `cos things had really gone bad on me at home. I'd been on some of your 'happy pills' but then I got in with a hard set, and swapped them for better things – like acid. I slept rough, drank quite a bit and got into trouble – just smashed a few windows when I was off my face, nothing serious. Then it all really began to slide and I lost it completely. I couldn't tell you how many times I went on the ward – bottles of Largactil and some shit called social therapy – then out again a few weeks later. It didn't get any better, I couldn't hack the hostels and the staff were all against me – so I left and went back to the streets again." Dun stopped, but Olivia said nothing, reluctant to interrupt her.

"They sectioned me, gave me ECT – I had a bad time with that. It didn't work and I got a bit violent. I was in for ages, always up for review, but never getting anywhere. I agreed to it in the end – a pre-frontal lobotomy. They all felt it was the best chance I had – the shrink was hopeful – and I saw it as a way out of there. It was a fucking disaster – didn't stop anything much inside my head – I can tell you.

Chapter 13

Let's have a drink now, and put it away for today." Dun had stood up and was already getting the glasses out of the cupboard, tired with the talking and the recall.

Olivia's knowledge of mental health was confined to friendly doctors prescribing for her, and the luxury of a private clinic. She hadn't fully understood all that Dun had referred to, but had felt her friend's bitter pain and anger. Her naivete was her protection, yet again. Had Olivia Ward been allowed access to Dun's file at Social Services, she might have been alarmed.

Dun was described on file as 'a paranoid schizophrenic; violent, manipulative, and not to be visited alone. Believes that the television sends out signals to control her, even when switched off. All authority figures are against her, actively out to get her. Regularly arrested for drunk and disorderly conduct and charged with criminal damage, and affray.'

'Voluntary patient over a long period, subsequently Sectioned as paranoia increased. Regular ECT showed little improvement – patient resistant to treatment. Since being lobotomised has shown slight improvement. Takes medication sporadically – G.P. refuses to home visit without police escort. Contact with department infrequent since being re-housed – client advised to contact department on an "as and when need arises" basis. Ring psychiatric social worker first before engaging.'

Translated, it meant that Dun had put chairs through DSS office windows, terrorised staff, held the G.P. hostage in her flat, and half throttled the social worker driving her to an out patients' appointment. Every department wanted her off their books – Olivia had unwittingly done just that, and Dun had responded.

Her name on the estate though had been well established, long before the advent of Olivia. When she'd been really bad she'd pick a fight with anybody, fighting with a ferocity and strength that seemed inexhaustible to the onlooker. Sometimes barricading herself into her flat, convinced that she would be taken by 'them', she had paced all night to keep awake, to stave off the 'attack'. Other times it was the throwing out of the television and the radio off the walkway, nearly braining the people walking below, in attempt to stop the control of her mind by 'them'. However, since Olivia's arrival, there had been a calm and a stability she hadn't had for years.

As for Olivia, Dun was 'for' her, plain and simple. Olivia's mother had had a saying, 'You're either for me, or agin me,' which had been her life rule. Olivia had come to understand what it meant – and so had Dun. They were completely interdependent.

"Cheers," said Olivia, raising her glass to Dun, "here's to the future – and the end".

Dun, at that moment, felt happy – she would give Olivia what she wanted; it wasn't hard, considering her life. What on earth had they got to lose anyway – their benefit?!

CHAPTER 14

Home Improvements

Dun had been looking for one for ages, but they had become popular with the trendies and were harder to find. The price had made her cross, a tenner for the old clothesline – and the bloke had got it for nothing on a house clearance job. Its ropes had perished, but the pulley was sound and the slats were easily replaced. It would solve her laundry problem; mounted above her bath she could hoist all her washing out of the way. She paid the bloke on the next floor to fit it for her – heavy-duty rawl bolts meant that she could hang even her rag rugs to dry. It seemed like another, calmer, step for her, away from the fights on the estate over who'd nicked, or kicked over, her washing this week. Everyone had similar problems, though most would buy a tumble drier on the catalogue at 50p a week for years. She preferred it simple; it went with her old twin tub and the lino.

Even the Housing department had finally got round to dealing with everyone's drains – unable to cope with the endless blockages with fag ends and worse, flooded walkways had vanished when they fitted the individual drain covers outside each flat. Currently all was bearable in Dun's world – she had food and shelter outside a psychiatric ward. She also had a plan, which Olivia would be pleased about.

"You remember what we were saying the other night – about doing something about it – getting one of theirs?" Dun asked, lighting up.

"Oh – I remember all right, and I've thought about it a lot. Don't quite see how we could ever do anything though," replied Olivia, her elbows on the table, no longer noticing the sticky plastic cloth underneath.

"It's finding the opportunity and going for it — just like they do with people's lives and families," said Dun, watching Olivia, who was fidgety, avoiding much eye contact.

Dun had worked out how to give Olivia her plan, and now it seemed she wasn't even here.

"Sorry — I just wandered off for a minute. I was listening but then other stuff just came into my head — go on, I'm with you now." Olivia replied, sitting up at the table.

"No, let's have your shit out now, clear the decks and be able to concentrate." Dun always did this with her friend. She believed in dealing with the crap as it happened these days, storing it up always seemed to make it worse.

"Here, have a smoke and talk to me — what's happened?" Dun lit up and passed it over.

"It's Graeme and Eleanor — not the usual old stuff, but this party that he's setting up is a funny one all right. Eleanor talked to me last week, she can't understand what's going on, and you know what Graeme's like about giving any information. So, unusually for my daughter-in-law, she asked my advice — I mean how likely is that?" Olivia knew that Dun would get the significance.

"It's the mix of Ulster people that he's putting together — all sides, whereas he normally deals with people separately, for obvious reasons. He's told her just to get on with it and to stop fussing — but I agree with her, it doesn't add up and could turn out to be a disastrous evening all round. She's getting on with it for the sake of peace, but the atmosphere in the house is dreadful," Olivia said, and before Dun could comment, added: "I put it in my bag, you know," which made Dun look at her sharply. Occasionally Olivia pocketed things when they were out, but hadn't been taking anything lately. It was Dun who squared it in the

CHAPTER 14

shops, suggesting to the shopkeepers that Olivia was a bit confused, couldn't always remember about paying.

"No, it's all right, I didn't take anything from a shop, I just took the guest list. I wanted to be able to look at it by myself to see if I could make sense of it. It won't bother them, they can print copies on Graeme's computer." Olivia finished, reaching for her handbag.

Dun took the list from her and smoothed it out on the table. Typical of Olivia to have folded and refolded it — her conscience pricking her, but her fingers hanging on to it — it was limp on the tablecloth.

"Let's have a look then," said Dun, moving closer.

They studied the list, Olivia quickly pointing out the obvious ones, family and old friends. The business side was harder, it brought in the politics but Olivia could place them, even the former planning officer

"Oh yes Dun, this is a great night he's putting together. Even the damn poacher's been invited, look." Her finger had stopped at an Andrew McFall, half way down the page.

"I can't stand the fellow, he's a smug hypocrite who has had many a good holiday and 'treat' from Graeme over the years, by way of a thank you. We've known him for years. I've watched him slide from a principled planning officer, protecting his patch from the greedy developers, to — get this — a planning consultant for the same developers — talk about gamekeeper turned poacher! He's in Graeme's pocket of course — all those council contracts are down to McFall's contacts".

Dun didn't react much; she wasn't really listening. She had seen the name, near the bottom, which had shocked her — Sam Hudson.

"Here, what about this guy — do you know who he is?"

Dun's finger pressed down under the name.

"He's one of the ones that Eleanor is wound up about. He's part of some new business venture in Belfast she's never heard of, and he's important. Graeme wants him to have a good time, and all he'd say about him is that he's awkward in company and there'll be a few people who might not understand all he says." Olivia hadn't looked at Dun as she spoke, if she had she'd have seen the change in her friend's eyes.

Dun knew Sam Hudson, knew him from N. Ireland more than twenty-five years ago – nearly twenty-eight years now. She'd kept track of what he'd got up to – it was easy for her. Take a four pack of Special Brew up to the Green and the dossers are your friends. She'd been one of them years ago, and had often met up with new arrivals from Belfast. Banished and afraid, they all could talk of Batman – her Sam. That was how she had seen him – hers.

When he'd dumped her, thrown her away, she'd fragmented. It seemed to her that the only chance she'd ever had had gone, whereas to Sam it had just been a prolonged bit of fun. She obsessed about him, had moved from the farm to Belfast to feel nearer to him. She learned of his increasing importance, his marriage, his extremes – all of it wound her up in different ways. She'd tried to see him once, months after he'd thrown her out.

At the headquarters – she'd been told that there was a good chance he'd be there, and so she'd gone after her shift ended at the abattoir, and asked for him at the door. She didn't get further than the doorstep. The heavy on the door had buzzed her request upstairs, and his reply had been swift.

"Doesn't fuckin' know you – clear off".

Chapter 14

She had, she had gone on the biggest bender of her life, and had cut up badly. Found unconscious under the bridge, she was hospitalised for a few days. Arms stitched and bandaged, clean and sober was how she left them. She was back within days, in a state of collapse, stitches cut through with a blade, and fresh cuts – her arms resembled the cross hatching of a sieve. The spiral continued until she was sectioned – even the threat of gangrene and amputation of her arms couldn't stop her chronic self-mutilation. On the locked ward of the old psychiatric unit she had refused to answer their questions after her medical. Her notes would show their concern about her denial of the damage to her vagina and anus – the great ridges of scar tissue where ruptured, torn, flesh had healed itself, painfully and slowly. She'd been frank about the cigarette burns on her body though – she'd done those, so that was okay.

Cleaned up and doped up she had been swift to get away on her release. By the time the psychiatric social worker was doing her first home visit to assess Tess Dunlop in her halfway house, Tess had got the coach to Larne and had crossed to Scotland. When she finally made it to London she had nowhere to go, so she'd hung out at the Green in South London. No questions asked; everyone in the same grotty boat.

She drank and took everything and anything – stealing to survive. Her strength matched most men, but her violence was in a class of its own. Regularly up before the magistrates for drunk and disorderly, well known by the police for affray, she finally got herself sectioned again following her attack on a Social Security officer. That was it for her, she was in the system and couldn't get out without co-operating – her final capitulation being the lobotomy.

The years she'd known Olivia had been the most stable she'd ever known, but now with her eye on Sam Hudson's name she could recall how far down she'd gone and how much she'd gone through – he was the one who could pay now.

"I think that I know quite a bit about this fine fella," was her opening move. The list finished, Olivia was waiting for her friend's opinion

"Most of these people mean nothing, they're just the rich buggers who've made their pile during the Troubles. But this one, he's a different matter entirely," Dun went on.

She'd decided that she wouldn't tell Olivia about her relationship with Sam, only his 'professional' life – and its rewards. She had never discussed him with anyone – he belonged to her.

"I've heard a lot about him over the years. He's one mean piece of shit; he was the organisation's main punishment man for years. I've dossed with men on Camberwell Green who've never got over what he did to them; kneecapped and beaten, unable to return to their families, crippled twenty year olds. Believe me, he's a little runt who has come from a shack and has ended up bloody rich, with the big pad and the posh car – all thanks to half killing people and enjoying it." Dun was watching Olivia's face for a reaction.

"Why would Graeme get into business with someone like that? He can't know what sort of a man this Sam is, or maybe it's a different person?" Olivia was trying and Dun could understand why.

"No Olivia, you don't get to meet Sam Hudson easily. He's a really important man, one that most people have never heard of, especially the security forces. Only a few know what he really is. On the outside – well, he looks just

CHAPTER 14

like a wee jockey, but really hard. Graeme couldn't have just 'met' him somewhere – no way. There must have been a meeting organised by someone else. Your boy, for some reason, is really mixing with a serious, fucking terrorist – with very bloody hands. They know each other, they must do, otherwise he wouldn't be coming to the party. " She stopped herself as Olivia leaned back on her chair, a sad old woman whose eyes were full of tears.

"I'll get us a drink, alright?" Reaching for the Jameson's, Dun gave Olivia a breather before she went on. She loved her friend as much as she'd ever been able to love anyone – but now her mind was on revenge, and the most glorious opportunity for it.

"Take a good swig of that, and listen. I don't believe for a minute that Graeme knows all about Sam Hudson. I know a fair bit, but then I've been in places and know people that you and your family would never have heard of. Anyway – that's not the point is it? You want an eye for an eye, you want your justice – well there he is. Readying himself for an early retirement – plenty of money, no worries or conscience. He's never been caught or punished for anything – who says crime doesn't pay!" with that Dun went off to have a pee, leaving Olivia to think.

They'd continued talking late into the night, the kitchen a fug of smoke, their bums numbed by the hard chairs. In the end Olivia had stayed over, Dun remaining awake in her armchair – too excited to sleep. It was on, they'd decided and Olivia had liked the plan – if worried about how they'd manage to pull it off. Dun's obsessive mind was buzzing with ideas and detail. Their first step would be for Olivia to organise – getting Dun work at Graeme's house on the day of the party.

Dun would deal with the planning and organising of the rest – in fact she'd already done one of her tasks – her washing line was up.

CHAPTER 15

Belfast

The organisation had had a bad time of it in the last few months. Kevin and Sam had seen two major arms shipments seized, and a large cache of explosives unearthed. Neither believed in coincidence, and they had been ruthless in their search for the informers. Punishments went up, and the results paid off.

They had the bastards, all four of them, the touts. One they had shot immediately, he was the more fortunate, left to die in a ditch near his home. The remaining three had felt the full force of Sam's fury.

There was too much to lose. Before the leaks they had believed they had a secure unit working. Now the reality was that they had been had, sold out – not something either appreciated. Never mind how the other men felt about it, Kevin had been so angry he had given Sam free rein. He had the three of them in the lockup and as much time as he wanted. He used it well. Afterwards, his own men had been slow to talk; considered 'hard', even they'd been shocked. It had taken real bottle to watch, and when it was over there had been a rush for the door, one man retching helplessly – trying to clear the smell from his nostrils. Inside the lockup was carnage; what had started out as a Sam 'special', had soon deteriorated into butchery.

All three had been kneecapped, quickly and quietly, with a gun. They were under no illusions as to what would happen to them in the lockup, over the years it had become infamous. Their only hope was that their dead mate had been the example, and maybe they'd get away with their lives. Sam's skill at kneecapping was renowned and even recognised on hospital orthopaedic wards. He had done so many that he could, by altering the angle of the gun, either wreck your knee joint forever, or do damage which, with luck, might mean you would walk again one day. Small comfort, but some at least. They all knew him as one of the coldest bastards around.

Sam had lost it when the last guy to be `capped had freaked out, watching and smelling his mates, seeing what was coming his way. As Sam approached him, the smell hit him.

"He's shat himself," he screeched – he loathed the smell of shite; it brought all sorts of memories back. He kneecapped him hurriedly and messily, hating the stench, angered by it.

The men would never have been recognised afterwards, even if they hadn't been burned. Sam had taken his baseball bat to them, beating every part of their bodies until they were a bloodied mass. He had finished with their heads. Their own mothers couldn't have known them, those lumps of pulp. He'd been drained, spent by it, and stank of what he had done – blood and faeces this time, not to mention the rest. He had crossed a line, and somewhere inside himself he knew it.

Kevin was sent for, Sam's helpers unable to deal with the situation, numbed by the carnage. Within minutes he was there, with a back up car and a can of petrol.

"Wrap him in this, and get him in the car – quick." Kevin ordered, tossing one of the men an old blanket. To the other man he gave the petrol can, and the order to torch the lockup.

Within the hour the lockup was destroyed, and Kevin was dealing with Sam in a safe house nearby on the estate. Often used as a meeting place in the early days, it had new tenants now, but with the same willingness to help the

CHAPTER 15

organisation. Just go round the back and knock. Sam had passed through their home numbly. Everything he had on had to be got rid of, preferably burned. Kevin's driver had been sent to Sam's house to bring a complete change of clothing, especially shoes. By the time he arrived back Sam was cleaner, sitting in the kitchen in a blanket, under some control. Kevin handed over the bin bag full of bloodied clothing and the man left again, this time for the local hospital. They had a contact who worked at the incinerator site at the back of the hospital – he liked his cash bonuses for services rendered.

The families of the dead men knew the score – one body had already been found, the others never would. There would be no 'Missing Persons' form filled in, those who had betrayed had paid. Touts were scum. On the street it would be said that one was dead, to make an example of, and that the other three had been `capped and banished to England. Who needed to know more? Kevin, having dealt with the practicalities, then had to confront Sam.

The pair of them had sat in the kitchen, talking quietly for almost an hour. Kevin, and those above him whom he had contacted, didn't doubt that the punishment fitted the crime – but the method was too extreme. Their organisation, like the others, however big or small, needed credibility more and more. Extremes like these would do serious damage to their image. Sam was in for a sudden career change – he'd done a grand job over the years, but... Kevin needn't have worried about how to raise it with Sam – the guy was in shock – receptive and detached, simultaneously. That was Sam's last night as enforcer, he was moving up again, but first would have a break with his wife – he'd been through a lot lately.

Kevin had taken him home, Stella waiting for him at the door. For once he was happy to be mothered, fussed over, able to be a bit small. He had slept a dreamless sleep, getting up late the next day, drained and exhausted.

The loan of a house by the sea for a week had been organised, Kevin calling in to give the keys to Stella whilst Sam slept. Over his breakfast he had considered the holiday, deciding in the end that a week would be too long, a few days would do. Stella understood his need to be back in the city. He had his first new job coming up in a fortnight – Graeme Ward.

CHAPTER 16

Meetings 2003

It had been Olivia who had come up with the answer – her friend Dun. Graeme had been relieved and had left it up to his wife to make the arrangements, preferring not to be in the house when his mother arrived. He wasn't sure whether the women confided in each other, whether Olivia knew what a mess they were in – best to stay offside, he decided.

"Eleanor, this is Dun," Olivia said in her most calm voice, and waited. Her daughter-in-law had pulled herself together and greeted Dun pleasantly enough, shocked by the woman's appearance. Graeme had said she was a hard worker who didn't have much to say – but she looked so hard and sullen.

There they stood in the large kitchen in Putney, Eleanor putting the kettle on in order to have something to do, uncomfortable in the silence. Olivia Ward didn't often play the matriarch; it was a card to be used rarely and effectively, like right now.

Olivia knew well Eleanor's aversion to having strangers in her home – cleaning or not – she found it invasive. Graeme had gone on at length about it, and for once she was in complete agreement with him. There should be help in the house on the night of the party; as for afterwards, she didn't care. She had played the game as skilfully as her son – getting what she wanted without him even realising it. He had been the easy one to work on, seeming more distracted than usual, but when she'd announced over drinks at her house that she had the answer to the problem, he had given her his full attention, unusually for him.

"I've got the very person to help in the house, she's quiet, hardworking, and best of all she's 'one of us' – if you like".

"Yeah? Who's that then?" Graeme had responded, sitting up in the chair.

"You know my friend Dun – well you've heard me talk of her anyway – she would be just right, Eleanor wouldn't find her in the way at all, and coming from our part of the world she'd fit in more." Olivia trotted out, as rehearsed with Dun the day before.

They had both reckoned that as Graeme rarely listened to much his mother said, (less since she turned seventy), so the need to provide a plausible explanation for Dun's wish to be a domestic lessened. Added to which was the bonus that obviously things were dreadful between son and daughter in law – Eleanor looking drawn and drained, Graeme not himself at all.

So now Dun sat, squat and silent, drinking her tea as the other two chatted. Olivia had told her to let her run it – it might be her son's house, but this was very much her show. Eleanor had asked Dun a couple of innocuous questions about hours and rate of pay and had been happy to leave it at that.

"Is Christine coming?" Olivia had asked, as they were finishing off their tea, Dun a still presence at the end of the table.

"Yes, we heard a few days ago, she is definitely coming and bringing Nick as well – it would seem that it is all back on again, according to Graeme."

Both women smiled, Nick was a delight to have around, witty and easygoing, with the quick Irish banter they loved.

"Och that's great, I'll give her a ring later in the week," said Olivia smiling.

Dun at this point had stood up and asked for the loo. Eleanor had taken her through to the cloakroom and Olivia had waited, knowing that she would be back speedily for a

Chapter 16

quick word.

"Is she all right Olivia?" asked Eleanor seconds later, waving her hand towards the hall. "She doesn't say anything, never mind 'much' does she – or is it me?"

Olivia shook her head, answering quietly,

"No she's very quiet, but totally reliable, believe me, she's fine," as Dun re-entered the room, solid and pointing out the time- they would miss their bus if they stayed any longer.

The necessary noises made, they had left soon afterwards, Eleanor watching them go off down the drive together, an incongruous sight. Olivia slim and elegant, and Dun looking like something out of a documentary on the homeless.

She'd heard of Dun often enough, but couldn't say that meeting her had made much of a difference. Still, if Olivia rated her, and would be there to iron out any problems on the night, she would go with it. Graeme would be pleased, but more importantly Olivia was happy. When she and Eleanor had spoken by phone it had been made clear to her that the request to employ Dun was of major importance to Olivia.

She hadn't queried it; apparently the woman needed money and was proud, and it was rare indeed for her mother in law to ask her for anything. After Graeme's latest escapade they had become a little closer, she hadn't told Olivia the detail, but it was what she hadn't said that had made the difference.

★★★

The car bringing Mark Bateson to the meeting with Commander Drake had driven swiftly inside the warehouse. Doors closed quickly, and he was escorted to the

Portakabins at the far end, aware of being watched.

The man had been a surprise – Mark had imagined the hard-bitten detective in the grotty suit with attitude and blinkers. Drake was smooth, well dressed and supercilious. The gossip that Mark had gathered on him was limited; apart from being very sharp, he was well connected in Whitehall and in the county set. For this current campaign he was being given free reign, and total secrecy. He had chosen his small team carefully, checking backgrounds and weeding out those with any Irish connections.

"I need to be certain that your minds are completely focused on the job and not being affected by any political or sentimental shit," was how he had addressed the team at their first meeting.

"We will be approaching this task with a completely different attitude. Forget what you think you know about Ulster – the IRA, the UDA, whatever. We are after major criminals hiding behind their political fronts. My goal is to catch them as you would anyone else, not getting embroiled in any of their mind fogging nationalist/unionist games. Too much time has been wasted in the past trying to understand and untangle situations that are beyond us. We don't understand the game, never mind the rules – so instead we concentrate on what we do best, catching criminals – any questions?" Drake ended, looking at the ten faces in front of him, knowing there would be plenty.

Drake had strong views on what he wanted to get from this team. He had personally briefed and tested each of them, and considered them trustworthy. All understood the plan, keeping out the political factors would simplify the goal, but being able to do that would be more than tough. Mark's visit to the warehouse that morning was the start of

CHAPTER 16

another thread in the web that Drake was weaving.

"Good morning everyone, and a swift introduction to our visitor, Mark Bateson," was what greeted Mark at the doorway.

"He's the Whitehall chap who's going to help us build up a picture on one of our current interests, Mr. Graeme Ward. His job is an irrelevancy – it's his social contact with Ward that we hope will give us a lead on the their latest operation. Currently we've heard that it may happen in a matter of weeks – welcome Mark..." Drake stopped and gestured towards the doorway.

Mark had been a little nonplussed by the introduction, but came smoothly up to the front and shook hands with Drake, who knew that he had momentarily caught Mark off balance and been pleased at the petty win. Compared to the usual formal Whitehall meetings Mark attended, this was informal and incisive – blunt even. Drake encouraged his team to come forward with their questions and opinions, dealing ruthlessly with those he felt were straying from the main point. Mark had been told that he would not be given more information than necessary, but would be required to give anything, however minor, on Ward. He found the questions came thick and fast, without allowing him time to wonder at their relevance.

He described his relationship with the Wards, how their first meeting with their children at the mini rugby had resulted in a loose friendship that had lasted fifteen years. Graeme's obvious increase in wealth, the variety of his business contacts and his weakness for women were the major areas covered. As Mark gave the info, Drake added notes to the display boards behind. Photographs and titles, lines linking names, it had been strange to see Graeme's up there.

"Right, that's your lot – I'm off to have a few words with Mark in private. Look at what we have now, and get started on the Belfast link first." With that, Drake took Mark's elbow and steered him to the far side of the boards. It was a thin partition wall leading to a minute office. Drake closed the door and pointed to the spare chair – Mark sat as Drake went behind the desk to his chair.

"Would you like a nip?" Drake enquired, holding the whiskey aloft.

"No, I'm fine – bit early for me," Mark answered, preferring a coffee.

"I think better with little nips, keeps me sharp," Drake had replied, pouring himself a double. He sat and looked for a while at Mark, sizing him up before speaking.

"This is a one off that few people know anything about – even within the Cabinet it's restricted info. The place is like a sieve, as you know – hence the 'Anti terrorist' label for this little set up. Frankly there are too many in power who have links with the people we're after. Even you – eh?" Drake had paused to faintly smile at Mark.

"What you've given us today is useful, and with more to come we could improve our odds considerably; we are trying a different tack, which just might work. In a nutshell I'm treating them all the same – criminals who have got away with it for too long. September 11th made this operation happen – we've got America alongside us now, giving us names that previously they'd have passed over as insignificant, or worse, even sympathised with." Mark had nodded his agreement, he'd had the experience of being blanked in the past when trying to get info. from some US sources.

"Given better intelligence – which we are now seeing –

Chapter 16

and a concentrated effort, we could make a serious difference. We know that both sides are sweating, feeling the pinch with regard to arms and materiel. They have the money, and there is a mountain of stuff available from the former Eastern bloc, but it's hard to get it through – seizures of shipments are up. We believe that the next arms activity will use the old route, from the States, and that your friend is involved." Drake stopped to have more whiskey, waiting for Mark's reaction.

"I find it hard to believe that Graeme is in on this – it seems so unlikely considering how his brother was murdered, and it's a hell of a long way from his usual building and glazing businesses. He certainly doesn't need the money," countered Mark, already having doubts about his friend, and wishing he wasn't.

"Sorry chum – his name has come up too often in the last few months to be insignificant. We have him on film in a London hotel, meeting an interesting guy from Belfast. This guy gets more interesting the more we discreetly poke into his background. The FBI has even come up with Ward's name in connection with someone over there. There is no way that your friend has got into this by accident, it's not feasible." Drake had stood up at this point and had waited for Mark to join him.

Standing up, Mark faced him across the desk, aware that his time was up with the man; Drake obviously felt he had done enough.

"Now you're clear on what's needed from you – and you know enough about what we're up to. I want to hear from you on a weekly basis- unless there is serious stuff going down, in which case ring the 'office' number I've given you and I'll see you immediately. Right, that's it for the time being. Good to have met you, and remember me to Fiona, won't you." Drake's hand was outstretched, and as Mark shook it, a knock on the door interrupted them.

Mark felt that it was prearranged, but was glad to leave anyway – he needed a coffee and time to think before his meeting with Eleanor Ward.

Drake was happy with how things had gone. Mark's information was valuable, especially this forthcoming rugby party at Ward's. The man would come up with more, despite any links he had with Ward. His loyalty to the Service came first – Drake was sure. It had been amusing too to meet the poor sod who had got stuck with Fiona Carswell. He knew her big brother, had boarded with him at Wellington College, had commiserated with him as little sister turned into the original party girl. These days she was invisible, a bit of a hermit sunk in a bottle by all accounts.

Drake rang his uncle in Whitehall to report on Mark Bateson as Mark was being driven back to the office, then left for an early lunch at the Royal Thames Yacht Club, Knightsbridge. He might have to site his office in a dump, but it didn't mean he had to eat there. His driver Thomas was his own 'man' as Drake had never learned to drive – had never wanted to.

CHAPTER 17

Both sides now 2003

Opening the drawing room curtains flooded the room with sunlight, reminding Eleanor why she'd fallen for the house in the first place. Light and airy, it welcomed people in, and she had made it her room. Uncluttered and elegant, it reflected only her taste, Graeme's ostentatious, golf- trophy look banished to the other side of the hall.

Today Olivia was coming for lunch and Eleanor was keen to have everything just right. The women didn't often get together without Graeme, and Eleanor was glad that he'd be unlikely to do more than just drop in – if that. She tried to spend as little time as possible with him, steadily detaching herself emotionally – and it was getting easier to do.

His business seemed hectic, he was rarely in and she was making use of the time to think about, and for, herself. Taking time and taking stock of what her life consisted of.

It was galling having to admit to herself that it wasn't much. She'd given years away pandering to Graeme, pretending not to notice his other women. Years of ridiculous compromises to keep the peace; of accepting her place on his mental list of what was important to him. She knew that she featured close to the bottom – well below his business, their children, his mother, rugby, and golf – perhaps alongside his sister Christine. She could say that she'd been a good mother, but that time was gone, their independence established, her children had their own lives to lead.

She was glad that her own parents were dead, not here to see the mess that the marriage had turned into, just as her father had so wisely predicted, and she had so arrogantly ignored. Regretted too that she had in some way let them down by accepting the snide digs about her father being English. – by being almost apologetic. Perhaps it had made her try harder to be a 'good wee wife' – whatever the sad reason, it left a sour taste in her mouth – she'd sold herself out.

Take Olivia's visit today, she thought, moving into the kitchen. In over a quarter of a century, and all that that entails within a family's history, she could count on one hand the number of times that she had felt included by her. She respected Olivia's intelligence but had never been allowed to get to know her. Held at arm's length, watching the real warmth switch on for those whom Olivia considered 'close family'. No matter what Eleanor did, there was always the barrier – not being one of them, being different. Even the misfit Dun was closer to Olivia than she. She'd wondered often how many others felt it – this not belonging to either tribe, in a country where everyone was in one, no matter how tenuous the link.

Standing at the sink she remembered Olivia's reaction to Graeme's call, telling her that he had proposed to Eleanor. So long ago, the words never forgotten, they summed up the situation.

"Mum, Eleanor and I have something to tell you, and you're the first to know," Graeme had started happily. Olivia had cut in immediately, stopping him from continuing.

"Aahh Graeme, don't spoil my Christmas now," she had said, unaware that Eleanor was listening in.

She'd been so naïve then, believing Graeme's assurance that Olivia would come round to the idea of them together. It'd never happened – she got respect for the four healthy grandchildren and keeping Graeme happy – but that was it.

Cool and polite to each other, Eleanor had stopped trying to get any closer – it was a waste of time, and she had

Chapter 17

wasted too much already.

Yet it was Olivia who was helping her now with the party. Willingly coming over to wait in for deliveries whilst Eleanor was out, happy to polish the silver, check the china and glass. The lunch today was by way of a thank you from Eleanor, she appreciated the effort. In fact when she thought about it, now that she no longer cared about Olivia's rules regarding what constituted 'real Northern Irish people' her attitude had changed. This lunch was one where Olivia wouldn't be calling the shots – Eleanor intended to speak her mind.

"The bus was late and then the traffic was unbelievable," Olivia announced as Eleanor showed her into the drawing room.

"Oh, this looks very nice my dear, all organised, and I've kept you waiting – I am sorry," she continued as she settled into the wing chair.

"Don't worry about it Olivia, everything's fine – anyway, what would you like to drink?" Eleanor asked, standing by the tray.

"Gin and tonic please – I've gone off sherry, it just knocks me for six."

Eleanor brought the drinks over and sitting on the chaise-longue opposite raised her glass to her mother in law.

"Good health, and thanks for all your help – it really made a difference. I feel that apart from the guests everything should be fine!"

"And to you dear, and you know I was glad to be able to help. It occurred to me though, will you be putting many up on the night? Is there anyway I could be of help there?" Olivia asked, expecting the refusal, but needing the information.

"Oh no, that's all taken care of, we're only having Jack Barnes to stay, and Graeme's booked the Tower Hotel for his new Belfast business contact — but thanks for the offer anyway. Here, let me help," Eleanor stood up to move the little dishes nearer to Olivia.

"I've done all that can be done in advance. The rest will be fresh food, so now is my calm time until the day before, when the cooking starts. Oh, and Graeme has hired tables and chairs — he's decided that small groups would be better. They're being delivered on the day. You know the kind — naff gilt with horrid nylon 'velveteen' seats." Eleanor's bitchiness was a surprise.

"Do I take it that things haven't improved between the pair of you then?" Olivia asked gently, looking closely at Eleanor.

Actually thinking how well she looked; the clothes were different certainly, but it was much more than that — there was an air about her.

"You can say that again. It's not something that could be easily resolved — even if one wanted to — another gin and tonic?" The daughter-in-law was coolness personified.

Inside, her own mother's genes wanted to explode and shout — 'what an absolute bastard your son has been' — outwardly she was her father, polite to the end.

Olivia nodded to the offer and thought that it must be really bad if Eleanor was on her 'one' trip. It had always been a signal of who she felt she was — obviously it was the reserved English today. Graeme had made a right mess by the look of things.

"I'm sorry to hear you say that — I know it's not easy for you. He's a law unto himself, always has been," Olivia offered to Eleanor's back as she poured the drinks.

Chapter 17

"Tell me Olivia, does he take after his father?" was Eleanor's response, handing Olivia another large gin and tonic. She hadn't known her father in law well, but enough to get the flavour of his views on her. She was the daughter, however 'nice', of an Englishman, his son should have married one of his own, not her.

Olivia took more than a sip, and decided to go with Dun's view after all.

'Bloody talk to her, be honest. We need her on our side, bring her round a bit if you can, without telling her too much, eh ?' had been the advice.

"Well, I suppose he is in a way," Olivia began, taking another sip. Eleanor did likewise, but her drink was almost pure tonic water. No way was she going to miss any of this. Mr. Ward senior in her view had been a bullying, racist oik – saved only by Olivia's inherent calming, cultured influence.

"My husband was a good provider for the family, but not what you would call an easy man to get on with," said Olivia cautiously.

"He couldn't stand me, could he?" Eleanor came back swiftly, not wanting a side step.

"No, that's true, he didn't like you – but then it wasn't so much you – more where you came from, who you were," Olivia answered truthfully, if uncomfortably.

"And you weren't too keen either, were you?" Eleanor asked quietly.

"True. I wasn't. But understand me when I say that neither of us was being personal." Eleanor looked at Olivia with total disbelief written all over her face.

"Not personal – how on earth could it have been anything else! Go on, admit just for once, that you and your family have had it in for me since we met – it's too late to

105

make a difference, but it would be so refreshing to hear the truth." Eleanor held Olivia's eye, and for once it was the latter who looked away first.

"Eleanor, it wasn't like that, there were all sorts of reasons for what went on. I mean, your father in law had had a dreadful business experience with an English partner who cheated him – he never got over it, it coloured how he saw them."

"So I pay for a business failure, and for having an English father – Olivia you must admit it's simple bigotry. You were just as bad, so what reason did you have? Eleanor was pushing it along; it felt good to finally open the nasty boxes

"That's harder. Give me a small top up Eleanor." Olivia was glad that she'd had a smoke with Dun before leaving. She was less nervous about dealing with what was coming; it seemed easier to simply talk, not to hide any more. She waited until Eleanor was back with her drink before continuing.

"I never thought you were right for each other, I thought that Graeme should marry someone from our set, as you know. It makes it easier if you're from the same background – you fit in more and you do tend to think alike."

Olivia had changed, Eleanor thought. This was the truth as she'd always known it inside herself, but had never got anyone to own up to it. She felt as though she was tying up loose ends.

"And of course, unlike the girls from your cosy little set, I came without the money and with the impertinence to believe that I was anyone's equal. Fatal mistake with your lot eh?"

Eleanor was less cool now, Olivia thought. She has forgotten and forgiven nothing for years – but then would

Chapter 17

you blame her?

"You know that we wanted Graeme to marry Sheila – her father was in business, and she came with a house, and yes, her father wasn't English – there, that's the truth. But also true is that I've grown to respect you, you've given me beautiful grandchildren and have worked hard to make my son successful and happy – not an easy task".

At this, Olivia stood up. Eleanor instinctively recoiled, dreading some fake show of affection. She needn't have worried; Olivia had moved towards the window. She needed to think for a moment before speaking.

"Before we go on Olivia, excuse me for a moment, I need to see what's happening in the kitchen." Eleanor left the room and Olivia breathed out – honesty was hard work.

On her return Eleanor found Olivia back in her chair.

"Something tells me that lunch is going to be an irrelevancy today," Olivia started with, looking at Eleanor's face.

"Perhaps it's as well. You asked me if Graeme took after his father. At times he does. He has the same way of having to be top dog, of getting his own way – but if you're asking me did his father carry on with other women the way my son does – I have to say that I honestly don't know.

I never felt suspicious, never even considered that he might. If he did, well, I was never humiliated the way that you have been by Graeme. You look surprised – he is my son and I love him, but it doesn't mean I have to like what he does. You were very good to me when Tom was murdered, something which to my shame I've never acknowledged. Graeme was grasping and greedy – as if owning more would make him more….." Olivia stopped, shrugged her shoulders, and finished off her drink. Eleanor was impressed.

Erect and calm, Olivia felt better inside, and it showed. She looked at her daughter in law, an intelligent and attractive woman, and regretted toeing the disapproval line. Eleanor had proved herself time and again to be loyal, but it'd never been enough for them. In her head she thought what a bastard her son was.

"It's funny Olivia, I've wanted to hear this from you for so long, and I'm glad that you've been honest – it now makes what I have to say easier. I'm going to leave him – I don't yet know when or how, but this farce is over. This time Graeme will not be able to fix it – I refuse to go through any more of his hoops. You're the only person who knows – and I intend to keep it that way. I'll do this wretched party and then decide when." Eleanor's face was sad but defiant.

"Well you don't surprise me – part of me has wondered when, not if, you'd have had enough. He's a fool, but no one can tell him anything – and he certainly isn't going to change, no matter what he says. You couldn't have done more for him – indeed you may have done more than I could have, had I been in your position." Olivia was forthright; the gins had really kicked in.

"I won't say a word about what you intend to do, Eleanor. In fact I'm touched that you've confided in me – God knows I've given you plenty of grief over the years – and I sincerely hope that no matter where you go you'll stay in touch with me. Strange to ask considering how it has been between us, but I do mean it – it won't be easy to leave Graeme, he doesn't take rejection of any sort." Olivia's voice had genuine concern in it.

"I hear your warning and it's something I'm thinking about very seriously. Part of me feels awkward saying this to

Chapter 17

you – he is your son after all – but for that very reason you'll understand. I'm afraid some days when I think of the steps I have to take. He'll go absolutely mad when I tell him – I'm not exaggerating when I say he may not want me but he believes he owns me and he'll bloody prove it if necessary – it's scary..." Eleanor paused, not sure whether to say more.

"Has he ever hit you?" Olivia had to know, her son was turning out to be a right one, and she really wanted to hear it all.

"No, he never hit me, only the wall just beside my ear – it was enough I can tell you. No, I don't fear assault so much as his own special intimidation. He'll use anything to get at me I know that, but I will get through this – maybe in bits and broke – but at least as an individual, not a bloody doormat." Eleanor felt good at spitting the words out – she also knew that Olivia, as a woman, was empathising.

"Well I meant what I said – you'll be welcome in my home, regardless of Graeme. I've learned a lot about my son which has hurt and dismayed me, not just recently, but since Tom died. I realise how much I needed Tom to act as the go between, to help Graeme and me get along. You've filled that gap to some extent, but Graeme and I have difficulty recognising each other sometimes – I feel I don't even know him these days." Olivia was stating facts, Eleanor was nodding.

"I will stay in touch when it happens – and thanks for your honesty. Now, what do we do about this lunch – it's entirely up to you. Come on into the kitchen and decide what you'd like – it's just about edible." Eleanor led the way into the kitchen, Olivia trailing behind.

"Do you know what Eleanor, I've completely lost my

appetite – it's like I've already got too much to digest already. I'm tired dear, I'd just like to head off home – and for once you may get me a taxi." Olivia looked drained, and Eleanor agreed.

She called the cab company from Graeme's study, booking two cabs – one for now and one for an hour's time.

"That's it, they'll be round in a few minutes – and remember it goes on Graeme's account."

I won't forget – why do you think I've taken the bus all these years !" Olivia's attempt at a smile was more of a grimace. It incensed her son that she refused his offer of transport, it made her feel in control.

Eleanor understood, and was glad that she hadn't told her about the VD from Graeme's tart – it definitely would have been too much for her to take. Olivia got ready to go, saddened but relieved at having been so honest. She felt that Eleanor had enough on her plate and was glad that she hadn't told her about Graeme's new business partner.

They said goodbye minutes later not touching each other at all, yet closer than they'd ever been. As the taxi pulled away, Eleanor hurried upstairs to get ready. She had to get out of the house in case Graeme appeared.

CHAPTER 18

The List

Olivia got the taxi to drop her off at the bottom of the Walworth Road. She rang Dun from the call box by the library, wanting to go over straight away to the flat. Dun hadn't gone to work that day, taking a 'sickie' to give her the time to discreetly do her shopping.

"Yes, come on over, I'm not long in – and you're earlier than I expected. I'll meet you in the yard – there are some kids hanging around on the stairs looking for bother. See you soon." Dun's telephone manner was always brisk and brief.

Meeting up minutes later, Olivia was glad of the escort. The kids had such flat and closed faces, reluctant to allow passage up the stairs, their empty bottles and aerosols around them. Stony silence as they checked the two women out.

Dun never took her eyes off them as she manoeuvred Olivia past – turning on the half landing to check no-one was moving. At the flat a new heavy lock had obviously just been fitted on the front door, and Olivia was surprised that once inside Dun bolted it top and bottom as well.

"I know, it seems a bit over the top – but those kids'll need money in a while, and they'll do anything to get it. Currently they're off their faces, but by early evening it'll all kick in. It used to be their big brothers on the staircases, pissed and sniffing – but they've moved on to better things. They're now crack heads – mad and dangerous bastards – with their dealer on the third floor. So yes, things have got even rougher round here. Tea or coffee?" she asked, putting the kettle on.

"Tea please, and if you've got anything in the cake tin – I haven't actually had lunch," Olivia replied, sitting down at the table. The window in the kitchen had another lock fitted, its packaging still on the table next to Dun's bag of shopping.

"So tell me, how did it go with Eleanor then – how come you didn't get lunch?" asked Dun as she skinned up on the work surface.

Olivia recounted her visit and her friend nodded approvingly.

"I told you, be honest and see the difference. You might feel wrung out by it, but you'll be better for having done it – and I bet Eleanor was surprised." Dun had plonked the tea and a slab of fruitcake in front of her. The tea slopped on to the plastic cloth – Olivia shook her head as Dun picked up the dishcloth. She'd rather have a puddle than the rank grey cloth that wiped everywhere and cleaned nothing.

"Ah Dun she was… in fact… we surprised each other. All the time she was talking I was thinking that I don't know her. Not as an individual, always as Graeme's wife – and what a job that has been for her. Yes, you were right – but I just find it so hard to hear from all quarters what a nasty piece of work my son is." Olivia's anger was on the rise, Dun could feel it.

"Well, she's doing the right thing, leaving him, I would. Mind you, thank God she isn't cancelling the party – not when I'm this far on. Here, I had these copied for you – you can see what kind of a man we're dealing with." Dun gave Olivia the brown envelope full of copied press clippings, all about the punishment beatings and the murders – all still unsolved. They were her collection, tracking Sam's career, recognising his style and cruelty. She didn't tell Olivia they were hers – she let the

CHAPTER 18

assumption stand that she'd got them from the library.

"I'll take them home with me Dun, if you don't mind. I don't feel able to handle much else today, and I'd rather read them in the morning when I'm fresh." Olivia left the envelope on the side.

"Tell me, what about your shopping – did you get what we needed?"

Dun smiled, she had indeed and hadn't worried about concealing her purchases – either way it wouldn't matter who knew what she'd bought – it would be too late by then.

"Yes, I got it all – I only had to go up to Camberwell Green in the end." Dun answered, lifting the bag off the table. It wasn't heavy, just a few everyday DIY items – Dun unpacked the bag, storing its contents under the sink.

She didn't tell Olivia that she had also been to see the dealer on the third floor – her order for liquid Ecstasy would be in by the end of the week. She felt her friend had enough to worry about already.

They sat and talked of the following week, Dun reassuring Olivia that it was all in hand, trust her – and she did, implicitly. It all made sense and seemed so just and right – if long overdue. Finding out so much about Graeme had made Olivia relive her mental video of Tom – and added more heat to her hatred for his killers. That was nothing compared to how Dun was feeling – she was high with the anticipation, savouring the planning, and empowered by the thought of revenge.

In the early evening she walked Olivia home, all the way, too restless to stay indoors. She could feel the waves building up inside her – great surges of energy and worse. Olivia didn't notice, tired out and thinking of

Tom, she just wanted her bed.

As ever, the honesty was less than total, the games still continued.

CHAPTER 19

St. James' Park

Eleanor was shocked when she saw Mark, the bruising and scratch marks on his face still livid, with huge bags under his eyes and a thick lip.

"My God – what happened?" she asked, sitting down on the bench beside him.

"You got here quickly – thanks for coming." Mark touched her hand, and she noticed the knuckles were grazed. He'd been beaten up and was still in shock she reckoned.

"Yes, Olivia had to leave early so when I got your message I knew I could get away quickly. But tell me, what's this all about?" She didn't move her hand away.

"My dear wife has lost it entirely. I got attacked last night trying to stop her from harming herself. I've never hit a woman in my life, but I came close to it I can tell you." Mark's voice was unsteady, it had been a shocking experience, he'd realised that if she'd had a gun she would have shot him, and herself.

"Fiona did this to you – your wife did this!? Eleanor was astounded, appalled. She'd considered a mugger, but Fiona!

"Yes, I'm appalled too. So is everyone in the street – she threw most of my stuff out of the drawing room window. It was a nightmare – the entire place is trashed, she has burned papers, photos – probably the deeds to the house. I've no idea what's missing, I've had to pull out of work today – Christ I couldn't even make a coffee at home – there isn't a whole piece of crockery in the place." Mark leaned forward, his head in his hands. Eleanor began to stroke his back, deciding what to do.

"Come on, I know just what you need. It's minutes away, and if you're embarrassed about how you look, don't be –

you've been mugged." Eleanor pulled his hands away from his face, and made him stand up.

Tea at the Ritz – the best idea she'd had that day, smooth and soothing. He relaxed gradually, taking comfort from the traditional, oblivious to the tourists. It was all so calm and civilised.

"Now talk to me, tell me everything that happened." Eleanor spoke quietly, and Mark began.

"She'd been out for lunch which had stretched into cocktails and beyond. A neighbour found her trying to fit her key into the front door at about 7pm. He helped her in. I didn't know any of this when I got home at 10pm and at first thought we'd been burgled. The door was open, lamps had been knocked over, the sofas slashed and the bookcases overturned – and that was only the start.

I was panicking – thinking of what `they' could have done to her – and then I found her. Slumped behind the bathroom door, with a broken vodka bottle in her hand. She'd a few minor cuts on her hands, and a deeper one on her knee. I thought she'd passed out as I couldn't get her to answer me at all – so I bent down, took the bottle out of her hand and bang – she hit me with the heel of her shoe which I hadn't noticed in the other hand. Far from being comatose – she was beyond any control. I don't know who she hates most, herself or me.

Tiled bathroom floors are lethal with vodka and broken glass everywhere – then add Fiona going berserk. Every time I tried to hold her down she would bite, scratch, kick, spit. I'm covered in bruises – if she'd been a man I'd have simply punched hard, but – well I couldn't, could I?" Mark stopped to drink some tea.

"God, this is dreadful – how did you get her to stop?"

CHAPTER 19

Eleanor asked, trying to picture it.

"Caught her with a bath sheet and then managed to wrap her in it. I got her out of the bloody bathroom and rang for help."

"And where is she now? In hospital?"

"No – I rang my father in law and he came to the rescue – anything to try to keep it private. He and her brother loaded her into the car and took her down to Wiltshire where he has a second home. He's had to do this before, take her away, get the friendly doctor and the private nurse in and…. hey presto! – a new Fiona in a week."

"But surely that's just a temporary patching up – how does that help her, or you, for that matter?" Eleanor couldn't see the logic.

"No. It doesn't make sense I know. The Carswells will never admit that their daughter is a complete drunk with a serious psychiatric problem. It's always the same, the cover up, the smoothing over – but this time they're going to have to face it. I can't deal with this any longer, she needs professional help – not me as her emotional, and now physical, punchbag." Mark's hands were fiddling with the cup and saucer, Eleanor felt so sorry for him.

"I've really had enough of her – do you know when all this started, this really nasty vicious behaviour? When Chris was born – and he's twenty now! I could handle her drinking – it wasn't so bad then, looking back – but what we've sunk to over the years is sick and nasty. She had a dreadful time at his birth – emergency caesarean because he was being strangled by the umbilical cord. The surgeon acted to save Chris, and it was all a total panic. Fiona was never the same afterwards – post-puerperal psychosis the shrink called it. The Carswells called it a touch of the 'baby blues' – and you can guess whose opinion counted. Since then, if I'm honest, it has been down hill all the way – she believes that it's everyone else who has got it wrong – especially me." He stopped and signalled to the waiter. Before Eleanor could speak, he added,

"This was the best of places to bring me to – I'm feeling semi-human again. Now I want to add my bit. Let's have champagne."

She couldn't say no, she didn't want to. She wanted Mark to unwind, to be able to be listened to as he had done for her in the past – and she adored champagne.

"I'd love some – I've been on tonic water whilst Olivia had very large gin and tonics – so I believe I deserve the treat, thank you." She smiled at him, leaning back in the chair.

"I'm so glad you got a mobile – I know how much you hate them – but today I really needed to reach you and it worked didn't it?" Mark had actually been amazed that she hadn't got one; surely everyone had one by now.

"Yes, it worked – eventually. I'm completely useless at retrieving messages – and I can't see the numbers either!" Eleanor admitted happily.

"I've never wanted one for the simple reason that I couldn't bear Graeme to be able to reach me wherever, whenever. He would love it, and I would feel completely controlled by him. These days, however, I'm quite glad I've got one – especially at a time like this."

The champagne had arrived and they had toasted each other, silently. He could see the concern for him in her eyes and was grateful. She was such a contrast to the hate filled Fiona; he could feel himself calming down.

"Anyway, let's put my troubles away for the day and hear about what happened to you – how come you only got the

CHAPTER 19

tonic?" He teased, trying to move them both on.

"It was lunch with a difference. The food is untouched in the kitchen, but the air was cleared in Putney!"

"Go on – I thought this was just a quiet little lunch for the pair of you – not fireworks," said Mark, trying to sip champagne with his thick lip.

"I know, but it was like we'd both reached a point where something had to be said. She is angry and unhappy with Graeme, that was obvious, and it just made it easier for me to speak my mind about him and some old family stuff that hadn't been resolved. It made a change to have some honesty, believe me." Eleanor was feeling the bubbles inside.

"What has he done to upset her then?" he asked, knowing that normally Olivia would not openly show her displeasure with Graeme, believing it to be disloyal.

"Partly it's what he's been up to lately. She doesn't know the details, but she now knows that I'm not going to stay- that I've decided to quit after I do the rugby night dinner. She said that she understood why, and I believe her. She also said something about hearing bad things about Graeme, not just from me. That was all she would say on that, but then she actually apologised for being such a cow for the last quarter century – it was pretty amazing really." Eleanor paused to drink, Mark watched her closely, catching her eye as she put the glass down.

"We were both trying to be honest – but there's so much history between us that trust is still difficult."

"In other words, like most people, you were still holding back – so was she by the sound of it."

"You're right – who is ever totally honest?"

If Mark felt uncomfortable with the comment, he didn't show it. Eleanor, in her head, was checking all the things she withheld. Currently the worst one was venereal disease – she dreaded ever having to mention it, cringed at the thought of her GP knowing, wondering, even gossiping in the surgery. She drank more and watched the glass being refilled, again. They were both feeling the kick, and were going with it.

"Anyway, she knows where I stand with regard to Graeme – and astonishingly after I'd said my bit she asked me to stay in touch with her, regardless of him – and you know how much that means."

"For someone who has only tolerated you over the years, it's a big thing to offer – Graeme won't be pleased." Mark's understatement made her nod.

"Precisely. It's unheard of where they're from – mother sticks by son, no matter what. That's why I know that there is much more to this than just his treatment of me. Mind you, she's been absolutely super with helping me out for the party. She even offered to help with putting someone up if necessary. I was surprised by that, but didn't need it anyway."

"Have you got many staying over then?"

"No, most people are either London based or have a flat here. I've got to put up an old friend of Graeme's over from the States, and the only other one will be in a hotel."

"Is Graeme going to impress him with something like this?" Mark asked, suggesting the Ritz.

"No, he's in the Tower, so to speak! " Eleanor giggled, Mark was happy. She went on,

"I've been told that he's small, like a jockey, with the social skills of – I don't know what – but Graeme has warned me that some people won't understand all he says, and that he wants him to feel really welcome. It's all to do with some new business in Belfast that he's setting

Chapter 19

up." Eleanor finished, fiddling with her glass.

If she'd been looking at Mark she'd have noticed the change in his eyes. He'd got the information that Drake wanted – fine- but it was more than that. He was falling for her. As if on cue, his mobile vibrated; quickly checking he switched it off – he could do without the Carswells right now. He didn't want this to end, the bottle was empty, but they had only warmed up.

"Look! It's all gone. We can't drink without eating – and you can guess the rest...."

Eleanor felt the same, it was early and this was something she didn't want to end.

"Go on then, tell me about the wonderful little place you know."

"Well, actually, it's a stroll from here, and it is wonderful – provided they haven't lost their touch – shall we give it a try?"

"Why not – but first excuse me for a few minutes." Eleanor wasn't going anywhere without checking her makeup.

As she headed off to find the cloakroom, Mark efficiently settled up and rang the restaurant to make sure that a table was available. Although they knew him well, he didn't want anything to spoil the evening. He needn't have worried, it was a quiet night and early, with a large party coming in much later. He asked that the champagne be at the table and rang off with a smile. It hurt his lip, but he felt better inside.

Eleanor was quite a long time in the cloakroom. She felt great, and it wasn't all down to the champagne. Being with Mark excited her, made her feel younger, and it showed in the mirror. She took her time retouching her eye makeup, catching a glimpse of her old self in the reflection, brighter and happier. Mark waited patiently, uncaring about the curious glances. Eleanor had got it right – he had been mugged – in more ways than one.

"Ready to go?" he asked her as she came towards him with a smile.

"Yes, finally. Now tell me where we're going, I can walk only so far in these shoes!"

Taking her arm they left the Ritz and headed down to Piccadilly Circus, turning into Regent Street, and almost immediately into Jermyn Street. The restaurant was visible, half way down on the left. Eleanor was delighted, she'd seen it before when buying Graeme's shirts in the shop opposite, but had never been.

"So, is this near enough for you? It's an old favourite of mine, have you…?"

"No, I've often passed it, " Eleanor cut in, " it's one of those places I'd always meant to try, but never did."

She half wondered if Graeme used it – but decided on entering that it was too quietly discreet for his taste, or lack of it. The thought made her giggle.

"What's the joke?" said Mark, looking at her, thinking how good she looked when happy.

"Oh, a mixture of champagne and feeling free," came her answer.

Mark was glad, he felt likewise. He had never brought Fiona here keeping it as somewhere he could dine in peace.

The meal was superb, and if the waiter disapproved of them drinking only champagne with it he didn't show it. Mark and Eleanor were doing and having what they wanted, finding out how pleasant dining was without the demands of their respective spouses. They talked about everything except their domestic problems, both trying not to let them in, unwilling to allow the mood to be soured.

Chapter 19

It was over coffee that it all changed.

To Mark's horror, the party the restaurant had spoken of arrived and contained Drake, smoothly shepherding his young female companion into the restaurant. They had obviously been celebrating. Knowing that Drake would spot him as soon as he'd taken his seat, Mark acted swiftly to prevent him from coming over to their table.

"Damn – it's always the same when you want no intrusions – there's a colleague I've needed to arrange to see and haven't – would you excuse me for a moment?"

Eleanor watched him approach the group, touching the man on the shoulder.

She couldn't hear what Mark was saying as he had his back to her, but she could see the reaction.

"Good God Bateson, been in a scrap? You look ghastly."

"Not now. I need to have a word with you, in private."

From relaxed, Drake's smile had stiffened, and his eyes passed over Eleanor quickly.

"Indeed. Call me in two hours, here. I'll make my excuses and see you then," with that, he turned away and Mark came back to the table.

"Everything sorted?"

"Yeah – it's nothing important – just another thing that got left out today. I abandoned everything and fled, and on reflection it was the best thing to do. It's impossible to pretend that nothing has happened – but equally I know that for the time being I have to keep going. Today was the day I stole for myself – I'll face it all tomorrow. You must understand that one."

"Oh yes, and I think we've done well over dinner, we've avoided the nightmares, but only just. I've got one last effort to make, and I'll do it well because I hate doing things badly, after that I don't intend to have anything to do with Graeme. He can talk to my lawyer – I mean it. What about you?"

"Well currently I'm avoiding my father in law who has had the temerity to leave me a message suggesting it would help Fiona if I went down to see her in a few days – she's feeling dreadful and wants reassurance! I'm too angry to speak to him now, but when I do it will be in town, just the two of us – then I'll deal with Fiona. I have to work it out carefully over the next couple of weeks – but yes, like you – it's time to stop the façade, make a new life." Mark finished his coffee, looking at Eleanor.

She knew what he was thinking, and didn't want him to say it – let things be, she willed him, don't add to the pressure. Part of her was afraid to think beyond the next few days.

"Where will you stay tonight?" she asked, as he stifled a yawn.

"Excuse me, I think I'm beginning to slide – I had little or no sleep last night, and it's all catching up with me. I'm staying with an old friend over in Pimlico for the next couple of days, and then I'll go back home." He signalled for the bill, noting that Drake's party was in full swing with glasses being raised for another boisterous toast.

"What about the damage?" Eleanor couldn't help asking.

"Ah… Eleanor's practical side coming to the fore!" He tried to tease, but the bitterness followed.

"Oh, you won't believe what the Carswells – or rather their money – can do when their precious daughter goes off the rails. Daddy has sent his housekeeper in and has hired a team of cleaners for her to terrorise. Naturally everything will be replaced, no expense spared and I will

Chapter 19

have a pristine home in days. As if that will wipe out what has gone on – they really do believe that if you throw enough money at it – it'll go away."

"Yes – Graeme has the same view, but not the style," Eleanor commented grimly, thinking of some of the ghastly peace offerings in the past, hidden from sight in the cupboard on the landing.

"Anyway, it's the last time that I'm going along with their capers – and yes, like you, I too am a bit afraid. Shall we go?"

Mark had felt Eleanor pulling back, and had understood. He wanted to get closer to her, but instinctively knew it was more than they could handle.

Eleanor meanwhile, was now admiring his quiet way in dealing with people – ordering food, paying the bill, whatever. The contrast between his discreet handling and Graeme's loud hectoring was incredible, and the result was infinitely better all round. Watching him across the table only made her realise how much she had been missing a soul mate first and foremost.

"You've placed me in your debt now Mark – I shall have to return the favour and take you to where I eat on my own – I'm right aren't I? You've never brought Fiona here have you?" Mark nodded his agreement.

"Mind you, my haunt is certainly not as salubrious as here – but I've used it since the children were tiny – you can let me know when you have a 'window of opportunity'!

Eleanor had brought Graeme to the table in their minds, and they both laughed – the phrase conjured up the man at his most pompous.

They left the restaurant tired and happy and went towards the Circus to find her a cab. Drake watched their departure, deciding he would probably have to miss his pudding and Christ would he have a few words with Bateson later. Ward's bloody wife – what was the man thinking of?

The man in question wasn't thinking straight, and was aware that he had just over an hour before he met Drake. Having said a brief farewell and watched the taxi head off with a mellow Eleanor, he decided to clear his head with a brisk walk. Down as far as the Mall and back brought him round, with a double espresso helping even more. He rang Drake punctually.

"Yes, hold on. I'll take this outside." Mark could hear the sounds of the party and Drake moving out of the building. At this rate, he thought, they could speak in person.

"Right, I'm here, where are you right now? Good… just what I wanted. Come back to Jermyn Street and meet me – quickly." Mark joined him in minutes.

"Here take these and go and let yourself in. Thomas will look after you and I'll join you as soon as I can." Drake was holding out a set of keys, and was pointing across the street from the restaurant. Mark looked bemused.

"I keep a service flat – number 8, and Thomas looks after me. Go on, I'll follow when I've settled the crew, he knows you're coming."

Mark had noticed the old Mansion apartments alongside the shops – trust Drake to have a little bolthole like this. As Drake re-entered the restaurant, Mark crossed the street. He didn't have to use the entrance key – Thomas was already there, waiting.

Once inside, he was unaware that he was close to the heart of the city. Quiet and luxurious; he sank into the old Chesterfield while Thomas got him a drink. He was thinking

Chapter 19

of how best to explain things to Drake when the door of the apartment opened, and he heard the bustle of his arrival.

"Well – I can't say that I was delighted to see you, but I will be fascinated to hear the explanation. Thank you Thomas." Drake sat down, glass in hand.

Mark waited until the door had closed and they were alone.

"I'm not going to go into all the grubby detail of what has happened to me – suffice to say that Fiona Carswell is lucky not to be in a secure psychiatric ward. She is out of control and this is what it looks like."

Drake's eyebrows went up, but he stayed silent. He didn't doubt Mark; it was common knowledge that Fiona was on the slide, despite the Carswell family's efforts to keep it quiet. He was due to lunch with her brother the following week and would check out how serious it was.

"Also, what you saw in the restaurant was a friend giving me support – someone who knows me and Fiona, and who came to the rescue when I asked her to. Eleanor Ward is my friend – that's all."

In his head Drake thought this was a load of codswallop – what he had seen was more than that, definitely something burgeoning. Mark was hoping to leave it there, and Drake eyed him over his glass.

"You know, the more we find out about Ward, the less savoury he becomes. I am relieved that yours is a simple friendship with his wife – anything more would be seriously inadvisable, professionally of course, and for the good of your health as well." Mark was grateful for the break, but alert to the warning. Drake went on,

"I understand from our American chums that Ward's old friend has confirmed his flight to London – he's coming soon, this deal is about to happen."

"And I know where he will stay – he's the only guest to stay at the house that night," Mark quickly volunteered.

"Really. What about our little Northern Irish friend – where will he be?" asked Drake.

"The Tower Hotel – I think Graeme has a company account there, but I'm not certain. I gather that Graeme is keen to make the man feel welcome, he's a new business partner – and that's all I have gleaned so far." Mark finished his drink, and Drake could see the exhaustion taking over. The man was done in, he needed rest – Drake pushed the little button and Thomas entered.

"My friend is about to leave, would you see that he finds a cab at the Circus, thank you."

He stood and waited for Mark to struggle to his feet, then escorted him to the door.

"Thomas gets cabs quicker than most, he'll see you off. That was a useful little chat, and do hear me – be very careful where and how you tread. I shall call you in a couple of days – see how you are, eh?"

"Goodnight, and yes, I will."

Thomas was waiting on the pavement and the two men walked to Piccadilly Circus. Mark sank into the back of the cab, heading off for Pimlico and peace. Thomas returned to the flat and joined Drake with a drink in his hand.

"That's him gone – was it useful?"

"Certainly it was Thomas, your discreet surveillance paid off. I want to know where and when they next meet. I need to know what Bateson gets up to. Cheers."

The ex-Para raised his glass to Drake in response.

"Cheers – sir." Close they might be, but Thomas knew how to handle Drake – deferentially.

CHAPTER 20

Dun has fun

She woke feeling great. Her sleep pattern had changed; she catnapped, unable to switch off for long. Waking with a start and instantly alert, she could feel the excitement inside her, surging up all the time. So much to plan and check, check and plan. She loved the excitement as her obsessive planning paid off. Today she would see Flash – for the next item on her list. Not that she kept lists for long; once dealt with she burned them in the sink, every scrap.

It was only five in the morning so she had time enough for a smoke and coffee. He wouldn't be there much before seven.

Flash – no one knew his real name – was the man with the meat. Top quality, out of his garage, courtesy of the bent chef across the river in the five star hotel. She'd known him since coming to the estate, tipped off by a neighbour who wanted to curry favour with her.

"Stupid bastard," she muttered as she made her coffee.

Still, it meant that she – and subsequently Olivia – ate some of the best meat in London, at a very special price. Today though wasn't a meat-buying day – Dun had different needs. Flash was always respectful of her, she was much stronger than he was – but more importantly he could feel the madness in her. She made the hairs on the back of his neck stand up when she was going off on one – he'd tried describing her to his mates in Smithfield Market.

"She's solid and sullen, with a rage in her that isn't connected to what's actually going on round her. Fucking mad she is, with a strength that would impress you lot." The meat porters didn't believe him of course, they'd never seen her 'lose it' like he had.

Flash's name had nothing to do with how he looked or

behaved. It was how he'd come to sell meat in the first place. In his heavy overcoat with cuts of meat hanging inside, he used to come into the pub near the meat pie plant on the Walworth Road, offering a quick peek, with cash deals later out by the toilets.

These days however, he'd moved up and on – he had a ten per cent cut on the choice meat order for the hotel, dropped off Friday lunchtimes, sold out by the evening. The chef got his money and Flash still made a good profit. His garage was the business – clean and organised, with a large fridge and new sink unit illegally plumbed in, a butcher's block, his battery of knives and choppers above and the huge mincing machine, all secure inside his metal security cage. Like most people on the estate he had no compunction about ripping other people off, but guarded his own stuff violently – if necessary. He and Dun shared similar views on that – why involve the police when a thump and a warning did the job in minutes?

"You're a bit early Dun – there'll be nothing till late morning," Flash had said in answer to her knock on the door.

"Oh I know that Flash – I was heading over to the Old Kent Road to pick up some gear that's due in off the Dover run. How's it going with you – business good?" Dun had no worries about Flash grassing her up, they were all up to something.

"Not bad, but I'm doing more of the 'wash and go' than I really like – a lot of work for not much in return. But still, I'm making a crust. Coffee?"

Dun accepted his offer and went on into the garage. She needed to know how Flash dealt with what didn't 'wash and go'. He'd never sold her any of it of course – it was for the

Chapter 20

tossers – people who'd eat anything provided it was cheap. Out of date, condemned meat, washed and repackaged, with the really bad bits trimmed off – and there was plenty of that.

"What happens to the stuff that doesn't clean up enough, even for your thickest punters – don't tell me you mince it?" She asked over her coffee.

"Nah – that's pushing it. I used to be able to slip it into the dump and leave it to the rats. Now would you believe it – the place is bloody crawling with people – and rats – like some third world country. Sifting and poking – it's a business alright. No, these days I use the river – what I put in will be gone in no time. It works – but it's a longer drive than it used to be."

"Yeah, that's true, more posh stuff going up by the day – they'll soon own the river on both sides." Dun's reply echoed the local's view on developments that benefited the 'haves', pushing their opposites further into their sink estates, fuelling their jealousy and anger. She couldn't care less about it.

"Too right – mind you, I hear the pickings are even better."Flash was referring to the quality of the stolen stuff being sold on the estate – top of the range, and plentiful.

They talked more over their coffees and a smoke and then Dun left, having given nothing of herself, but happy with what she'd gleaned. Within another hour she'd done her deal at the transport caff, and was back home, weighing her cannabis to make sure she hadn't been ripped off. It was a good deal in weight and quality; Dun was pleased. She'd need to be relatively mellow to sort out her next item on the list – transport.

★★★

Dun has fun

It wouldn't show up in a large Jameson's – colourless and odourless, how could he spot it – how could anyone? She wasn't sure about the length of time it took to work though. That and the transport – they were the things that were nagging her.

An earlier attempt to reach the Greek had failed; she'd left a message for him at his brother's minicab office, but had heard nothing. He was her choice of driver – Olivia's offer of letting Graeme organise it was out of the question, she needed her own type of taxi. Nico was a driver for all sorts of people, rumour had it (he certainly never confirmed it)… from the fringes of organised crime, to the quick domestic flit. He was silent and busy, able to choose the jobs he took. It was never just the question of money – if he didn't fancy what you were up to he wouldn't get involved. Dun reckoned she knew exactly how to get him to do the job, all she needed was a brief chat. Whatever he chose to charge her didn't matter – Olivia would pick up the tab, indeed had already been giving her cash to pay for 'expenses.' She decided to visit the minicab office at lunchtime, wait it out if necessary. She skinned up, perched at her kitchen table, working out exactly what she would tell Nico. She wasn't worried – he would already know who she was, and that she was no timewaster. It was all going well, and the buzz she was getting from it was like a huge surge in her head.

CHAPTER 21

Putney planning

"For God's sake Graeme, leave it alone, I'm in the middle of doing it now!" Eleanor's exasperation cut into the silence that had hung in the kitchen.

"Look – I'm only trying to help, no need to bite my bloody head off," he had retorted, but had stopped poking through her lists.

"Why can't you just let me get on with it, like I always do? Or have you decided that it's another thing I can't get right? If that's the case, you can take over – go on let's see you try – it would be a first!" Eleanor was spitting the words, banging her mug on the work surface.

"Look dearie…." Graeme's cut in stopped her – his patronising put down applying the brakes on her current rage.

"What did you call me? 'Dearie'?! – Don't ever use that one on me again – I'm not the dumb cluck you take me for. Try it out on one of your little tarts, not on me – not ever again – Christ – every time I look at you do you know what I think? – Go on, guess. You can't even guess, can you? I think and rage, Graeme; rage at the shit you've given me over the years, rage at the fact that my life, since I met you, has been a total waste – how the hell did an intelligent woman put up with this for so long – it really takes some beating. The children, our children, are what have kept us together, that's all! " She was glaring at him, hating what she saw, but hating herself more for having put up with it, for having acquiesced. She felt like a tart herself – monetary gain for services rendered, where was the difference?

Graeme was regretting having come into the kitchen in the first place. He'd only wanted to check that things were on track – but dealing with Eleanor was now completely unpredictable, likely to turn into major confrontation any time – he considered her hormones and changed his tack.

"Sorry Eleanor – I didn't mean to wind you up. Let's just deal with the party and we'll take time out afterwards to sort out the mess. We can work something out, get away for a few days on our own – come on now – don't let us fall out over this as well." He tried, watching her across the kitchen, hoping to God that she'd calm down.

With only days to go, he was as tense as hell with little fuse left. He hated not being able to control it all – too much at present was out of his reach. The shipment was en route, the players were all ready and he was stuck in a designer kitchen in Putney trying to reason with someone he barely recognised.

Eleanor had moved across to the Aga and was returning his look, arms folded – it didn't look promising he thought, pulling out a chair at the old refectory table and sitting down heavily.

"You always see things with a price tag don't you?" She began,

"Always thinking that you can buy whatever it is you want. The business deal, the other women, and me – always me."

Graeme groaned inwardly – he knew that he'd be there for the duration. This was the start of the loop – insoluble arguments going back years, with no apparent logic, but with perfect recall. He never held on to the shit, was able to just let it go and move on. Not so Eleanor – she was driven by her idea of justice, fairness. He thought it naïve rubbish now, but when he'd met her he'd admired the spirit and the principles – such a perfect contrast to him. Right now, however, he wanted to shake her.

"All I was trying to say to you was, that in a week or so,

Chapter 21

I'll take you somewhere – your choice even – and we can spend time talking about all the things that are getting you down."

He almost sounded sincere, Eleanor thought – almost. She put the kettle on for coffee.

"I couldn't count the number of times I've heard that. The reality is that I actually believe you, get ready and book my choice, and then you cancel it – pressure of work. Then miraculously at the last minute we end up on a late flight to bloody Northern Ireland again. Not so much a break, more of a change of sink. Try again Graeme – I don't believe you anymore." She leaned forward to emphasise each word.

"Och come on Eleanor, that may have happened a few times, but think of all the places we've been able to enjoy – come on – what about our trip to Thailand – hardly County Antrim – eh?" He'd hardly finished when he wished that he could retract it – he'd forgotten the 'difficulty'.

"Nice one Graeme – you've obviously never been left sitting alone in a bar in Bangkok whilst your so-called husband goes upstairs for a 'massage' have you?"

"Oh, not that one again – how many times can we go over the same bloody history – how many times can I apologise? You just can't ever let anything go – and yet never seem to remember the really important things I've done for you. Like bloody moving over here for starters." Graeme was narked, Eleanor was glad to see it – his fake calm irritated her immeasurably.

"Our moving here was down to both of us, let's face it. Go on – it wasn't just me that had to get out. For whatever reason you too wanted out – it has just always been easier to blame me. 'The English in her,' as you have so often described it to your drinking buddies. 'She feels more comfortable over there' – like I'm some sort of oddity. As if I'd forced you to leave your homeland – whereas we both know damn well that you were just ready for the bigger pond, much more lucrative and with your contacts – success guaranteed," she snapped at him.

"Huh – you don't seem to mind enjoying what I provide for you – what my hard work has earned – do you? "

"Graeme, we've been over this – it was always you who had to have the trappings, I was the one who wanted less show, more of a relationship. But you don't agree, and never will. All that matters is the money, never mind how hard you have to push, who you have to bribe – you'll get what you want. I really see you as a bully – with just a veneer of charm and fake style."

She said the last bit with regret in her voice, it had been so different when they had first got together.

As she held his gaze she cast her mind back – how did it get to be decades? Where had it all gone? A 'dance' at the local tennis club – soft drinks and an appalling band; being walked home by the confident young Graeme, so full of ideas. Her delight at being chatted up by him had moved on to the worry of how to end the evening – this was the bit she'd never done before. The awkward kiss by the front gate as her father opened the front door. She had been so innocent, and so had he, for all his bluster. They had grown up together she had thought, and she'd trusted him implicitly. Now, though, she'd looked at their marriage coldly – without the sentimental haze – and once that happens, it can never be the same.

"Thanks for the vote of confidence Eleanor – it's good to know where I stand in my wife's opinion. I've never bullied you in your bloody life – believe me, if I had, you'd

Chapter 21

remember it."

"But you have, and I do – I remember all of it Graeme, every last bit – believe me," she was calm facing him.

"You have a wonderful knack of twisting everything, of glossing over…."

"No, not twist Graeme, more remember – do tell me that the 'wall', for example, didn't happen – go on, I'm listening."

He couldn't, and she knew it. They'd spent half the night at the local casualty department after he had broken two knuckles punching the wall just beside her left ear. She had been petrified of the violence in him – no matter that the blow had not connected with her face, the intent to frighten had been palpable. Even now, years on, she could remember the sick taste in her mouth and the shaking of her legs. Unbelievably she had driven him to the hospital and had listened to his version of how he had damaged his hand – without a word. It was the first time that she had realised how confined the space in a car is, how close one has to be – she had smelled his anger coming through his aftershave, his breathing through his nose as he tried to get a handle on his rage.

"That's all a very long time ago Eleanor, and it has never happened again has it?" His voice was low and level, hating to be reminded of it.

"To me it was a rare moment of truth Graeme, and we both know that no matter how long ago it was, nothing takes away from the intent, your intent – to scare me, pull me back into line, teach me a lesson – whatever. Cutely it also gives you the genuine claim that you have never hit a woman in your life – Christ!"

"It's actually something I never talk about, try not to even think about – you know that, don't you?"

"Yes, I know that, but also know the reason – it doesn't fit with Mr. Ward's smooth image. It's all right to screw around, that's just how you are eh? But hitting women – no, that's beyond the Pale, isn't it?" She moved across the kitchen, putting things away.

"Anyway, I've no idea why I'm even bothering to talk to you about it now – to you it's water under the bridge – you wish I'd shut up and deal with the here and now – you do, don't you Graeme?"

Looking at her he gave a half nod, uncertain whether a denial would be better, and deciding, very wisely, that honesty might pay.

"Yes, I thought so – plus ca change eh?"

Eleanor's little smile was a cold one, Graeme's French was atrocious – seat-squirmingly awful. Now and then she liked to remind him of it, score a point.

"Right then, let's deal with the here and now. You talk, I'll listen," and she sat down at the far end of the table, waiting.

Graeme was surprised by the halt, the switching off of her rant, it wasn't like her – normally once she started it could go on for hours. But then how could he comment on 'normal' these days? They hardly saw each other – since the STD she had withdrawn from him, creating her own space in their eldest child's bedroom. They left each other messages, polite little notes on the fridge.

He carefully placed his personal organiser on the table and began. Eleanor pulled out her notebook, this she could deal with. They were a team when it came to entertaining – probably the only area in their lives where they truly connected. Graeme would have agreed – had he ever given

Chapter 21

it serious thought.

Eleanor only noted the basics as Graeme pedantically went through his lists: the champagne, the wines, the tables and chairs – and the special Bushmill's whiskey at the end. To her it was straightforward, she had all her facts ready for any question from him, it was how they worked – he flapped a bit, she calmed him, both able to work together.

"And my last one is our hired help – this Dun woman. You've said that she's a bit of a rough diamond – but she's alright isn't she?"

Eleanor considered her answer carefully, knowing that whatever picture her husband had conjured up in his mind of Dun would be far from the reality – knowing too that he'd have found a way of not employing her had he ever clapped eyes on her. For Olivia's sake she made the issue seem trivial.

"She's fine for what she'll be doing, she won't leave the kitchen – and your mother has it all in hand anyway. They've even sorted their own transport – Olivia rang earlier – so you can cross that off the list as well. Christine has also rung – she now wants to stay overnight with us, which I've agreed to, of course."

If Graeme had views on his sister's change of mind he kept quiet – there was enough going on without raising dust over her. Eleanor was running that end of things, and would make it work. As for the domestic help, well if his mother and wife were happy...... He had bigger things to worry about.

"And that just leaves my menu – I've printed you a copy. Here you are – if you want to talk to me about it you'll have to leave it until this evening. I'm on my way out for lunch and won't be in till later." Eleanor stood, handing him the copy.

As the kitchen door closed behind her Graeme began to read.

"You bitch," he murmured. It was entirely in French.

CHAPTER 22

Belfast recalled

Graeme sat on at the table finishing his coffee, the menu lying where he'd tossed it. He could hear the sounds of Eleanor moving around the house in a hurry. He didn't feel like going anywhere and couldn't be assed to try speaking further. It was sad that it all seemed so black to her. Sure, he'd been a bad lad in many ways, but he did love her – he thought. He had loved her in the beginning, back in Belfast, but that was a different matter – another life.

Their families were so different, would never have met socially had it not been for Graeme's chance meeting with Eleanor. A tennis club dance, up off the Newtownards Road somewhere – not his scene at all, but the visit to the school friend's house had stretched into the evening and he'd agreed to go 'just for a laugh'. He'd felt out of step – he hadn't known anyone other than his friend, who was the life and soul of their group, busy and confident. The group had fortified themselves with a quick drink filched from home, and were on good form, eying the phalanx of girls lined up on the other side of the pavilion. Their muttered comments about the girls' attributes, or lack of them, fuelled their fake bravado. They had smoked their B&H's and held their Cokes coolly, safe in the certainty that no girl would dare cross the floor to speak to them; it just wasn't done. The game could only start when the boys made the first move, and they had, moving as one, homing in on their pre-selected targets.

He'd had no competition over his choice – the others were keener on the blondes. For him it'd been the dark haired one on the edge of their set, obviously not fully one of them, and much more aloof, who appealed to him. God

141

he'd felt so awkward as they'd had peeled off into pairs leaving him with Eleanor.

There'd been quite a good band he thought, and an attempt to dim the lights had plunged the area round the tea urn into near darkness – the place to aim for, Graeme had been told. Any girl willing to go there was up for a 'feel', was potentially 'fast'. It hadn't been like that for him. He and Eleanor had talked for hours, braving the cold of the verandah to be able to hear each other, oblivious to the rest. He had wanted to walk her home, hadn't wanted it to end; he remembered wanting to touch her hair, how he hated his own ginger frizz – not that there was much left of it these days – and had he really kissed her? It had been an awkward peck as he recalled, perfectly punctuated by her father opening the front door. It was the start though, and he had pushed to see her the following day, arranging to meet in the city centre for coffee.

He could see her in his mind, choosing the venue, in a hurry in case her father came to the door again.

"I've got to go in, he'll be out in a minute. Look, I'll meet you tomorrow, at the Linen Hall Library, at eleven – okay?"

"Where?!" he'd never heard of it.

"Oh you know, opposite the City Hall – beside the Gramophone Shop," and she'd left him, running up the drive and in the door, just pausing on the step to wave quickly. He had walked away so happy, couldn't wait for the next day.

Unlike him he had been at the meeting place early – normally he rarely surfaced before midday on a Saturday, oblivious to the sounds of Tom and Christine getting ready for their rugby and hockey matches. He'd plastered down his hair as best he could and had shaved – unnecessarily, but

Chapter 22

it had felt the mature thing to do – now all he had to do was wait. Posing outside the shop, inwardly anxious that he might be stood up, he was greeted by friends and acquaintances passing by, on their way to shop and have their coffees in town.

"I'm sorry – the bus was late. You must have thought that I wasn't coming," she had blurted out, a bit out of breath from rushing.

"No, no. I knew you would come," he had lied, the twenty-minute wait having been hell.

"You see, there's the Library, look," she pointed at the worn steps flanked by the old handrails, its brass nameplate shining.

"My father's a member and used to take me there when I was little. He says they've got an amazing collection, but my main memory is the warmth of the open fire and the old squishy armchairs – great on a wet afternoon!"

"Sorry Eleanor, it doesn't ring any bells with me – I've never really taken notice of it before, I never regarded going to a library as much of a treat! Now – where would you like to go for a coffee?"

"I've no idea, I only know the one my mother and I use, so you decide – please."

He had, and they had sat for hours in the Coffee House talking quietly and ordering carefully, aware that money was tight.

"I've just finished at St. Malachy's – can't wait for the results to see whether I can get into Queen's," he'd told her the night before – "Economics – not too stressful – what about you?"

She hadn't given him a complete answer;

"I'm hoping to read French," was as far as she had gone, adding that he'd have to wait for the rest.

143

"So, come on, you're going to give me the whole picture," he teased, and she did.

"It's not going to be what you expect," she started.

He'd already decided that her reluctance the night before had been because of religious differences. It was always the way, it defined life in the Province – which foot did you dig with, Catholic or Protestant. She already knew that he was Catholic – St. Malachy's was one of the best Catholic Grammar schools in Belfast, but he had no idea with regard to her.

They both lived in nice middle class areas, religions mixed to a degree, the Catholics making their way up the financial ladder and moving into previously Protestant middle class bastions.

"I'm a boarder at the Dominican Convent, Portstewart – do you know it?"

"What – the place that looks like Colditz, up on the rocks?"

"That's the one, sea crashing on the rocks below and us freezing above. My father was keen for me to experience the discipline of a convent, keep my mind on studying, not partying – it's a fee-paying prison really – I've got two more years to go and then – freedom! I'll get into Queen's and will make up for lost time!"

"So did your father's plan work?"

"No, not really, I'm an only child and hate being away from home – most of term time I spend wishing I was back here, hating the place. I can't stand being locked up with the other ninety five."

"What ! There are only ninety five pupils in your school?"

"Boarders yes, and then a few day pupils. It's tiny – my

Chapter 22

Latin class consists of four – a nightmare if you're bottom of the class like I am!"

"God – I don't envy you. Wouldn't your parents let you move back for your 'A' levels, let you do them at a day school here?" He was disappointed that she wouldn't be around during term time.

"No – my father is a quiet academic with very strong views – he thinks that there's nothing better than the Spartan life style and endless learning – he won't hear of it, so I'm stuck with the nuns for two more years. The joke of it is that I'm not really Catholic at all – I only got in because my mother is, and knew the Mother Prioress when she was little".

"Hold on, you've lost me there. I need help!"

"Why do you think I didn't try and tell you this last night? My father is English, my mother is Northern Irish – she's Catholic, he is…a Baha'i

"You've really lost me now – what's that when it's at home?"

"It's a nineteenth century religion – believing in the unity of all religions and all mankind – sort of peace, love and help others regardless – type of thing. I find it very gentle and caring compared to what passes for religion here – so much hatred and distrust."

"Do they have a church here in Belfast?"

"Not as such – my father and I used to go to meetings in a house in Eglantine Avenue – off the Lisburn Road. All very low key and non-judgmental – I don't go any more, after the heavy-duty nuns in term time I come home to have fun. My mother understands, but my father doesn't – it has a lot to do with being an only child."

How they talked that day, from family to religion, from

dreams to disasters – walking round the city centre in the late afternoon, Graeme trying to extend it into the evening.

"Come on, why don't you phone home and tell them you won't be back till later – that you'll be in by ten," he had pleaded, thinking that ten was ridiculously early.

"I can't – really I can't. I'm not allowed out more than one evening a week, and I was late last night – he won't hear of it, I know. I've got to get the next bus home and even that won't guarantee that there won't be a row." She had stopped to speak, holding his hands and looking up into his face.

"Oh, come here," had been his reply, pulling her into his arms and hugging her.

"I'm not trying to make things difficult for you, I just don't want you to go." He murmured in her ear, both of them trying to ignore the shoppers and workers hurrying past. She hadn't pulled back, had stayed in the embrace, hugging him in return – loving the warmth and strength of him.

"C'mon then, let's get you on the bus. No point in winding your Da up – but I've got to see you again soon – I'll phone you tonight and we can work something out."

She'd thanked him for understanding and they had hurried round to the City Hall to wait for her bus. That was when he'd really kissed her, standing in the doorway of Hogg's china and glassware shop, gently and slowly, neither caring who might see them.

As the bus pulled away he stood on the pavement waiting to see if she would look back – She had! – and had hurried round to catch his bus up the Lisburn Road on a little cloud.

It really had been the first and only time that he had

Chapter 22

experienced the thrill of falling in love with someone, a silly grin breaking out for no reason as he thought of her, a happiness on the top deck of the bus as it eased its way through the traffic at Shaftesbury Square. As he walked up Derryvolgie Avenue he was happy – with an innocence about him that immediately alerted his mother, Olivia.

The Wards meet Eleanor

"I think our Graeme has got the bug," Olivia said to her husband, as she finished off kneading the dough on the board. She always made the wheaten bread, it was Martin's favourite, he liked to watch her make it, taking the time to talk over the day's business, warm in the kitchen.

It was always the same, Saturday afternoon, with the football results on the radio, bread in the oven.

"What makes you say that? I don't see any change in him; does what he wants when he wants as always," came his grumpy reply.

"No, of course you don't – you're always on his back about what you think he should be doing, and miss the obvious – have you really not noticed how he is? Forever on the phone, going out to meet her – he's not being like himself at all. Our Graeme is infatuated – Tom tells me her name is Eleanor, but as yet I haven't been told officially." Olivia put the bread in the oven and came to sit beside him at the table, hoping to keep the peace, wanting Martin to talk about their eldest son.

They were a comfortable pair together, Olivia making it her business to ensure Martin's domestic life was as stress free as possible. He expected it anyway; just as his mother had done for his father, putting herself second, being a proper wife and mother. Olivia was happy with it; Martin ran the building business, she ran the home – and the children.

Right now she had to try to bring Martin round, to soften him with regard to Graeme. The pair had not spoken since the row over his 'A' level results, avoiding each other as much as possible. Graeme had obviously not worked hard enough, they were poor compared to what he could have

Chapter 23

come up with — she knew that. He had scraped into Queen's thanks to heavy support from the school. She'd resolved the problem, but not the underlying mess.

"You can say what you like Olivia, but you know yourself that he's a chancer, always on the look out for the easy option, the quick effortless solution. He's had it easy, that one, turns on the charm and waits for it all to happen. If he'd ever done a day's work in his life he might understand economics — the real ones. Now I'm supposed to fund him for years while he wastes more of his life playing at being a student. Why in the name of God he doesn't come in with me I'll never know — he could be running the business in no time."

Martin was unable to accept that Graeme wouldn't consider joining the family business. Even after the disastrous summer of employing his son as a brickie's mate, with the rows and mutinous aftermath, he just couldn't see it. They were totally incompatible — Graeme refusing to accept that he had to start at the bottom — he was the boss's son, so why should he? Meeting his father's diametrically opposed view, 'You start as I did, at the bottom. You prove yourself and I'll move you up, and the men will respect you.'

"What's to respect Da? Let's face it, we're not exactly talking McAlpine here, are we? I mean, little building jobs with a work force of five — maybe six when there's a rush — and premises which look like Steptoe's!"

"Yes, well that's as may be, but it's kept you warm and fed hasn't it? Small thanks I get for the effort though."

It was unpleasant all round, everyone in the house affected by the endless antagonism between father and son. Olivia had done her best; talking to Graeme whenever she could, calming Martin by absorbing his disappointment in his son.

"I do know what Graeme can be like – but I don't forget the good in him. These days he just has a way of instantly putting your back up, half the time he doesn't even know that he's doing it. I know that you don't want to hear it, but he's very like you – strong and opinionated – not a bad thing, but difficult when there are two of you at it, full tilt!"

"Och I know Olivia. He just gets on my wick. Knows nothing, knows it all. You know, the other day I wanted to belt him one – the way he talks to me, as if I'm not quite with it. I would never have dreamed of speaking to my father like that, I can tell you."

"I know, Martin, I know. Your father and you as a father now, there's no comparison. Couldn't you just accept that Graeme is turning into a man, trying to be one by testing it out on you, and at the same time can be the small child? He does appreciate all that you've done for him, but like most kids doesn't necessarily show it the way you'd like."

"You can say that again. He appreciates it so much that he helps himself to anything he fancies, never bloody asks – acts as though it's his by right – god he's an arrogant sod sometimes. He's taken all my golf balls again, and left me with a collection of rubbish – and when I tackled him about it he looked at me as though I'm some sad old duffer!"

It was true and Olivia couldn't dispute it, Graeme had to be right, had to win, every time. Exactly like his father, he had the expectation of success but unlike his father he had the health and energy to back it up.

"Who's a sad old duffer?" Tom called from the utility room, dumping his rugby kit on the floor and coming through to the kitchen.

Chapter 23

"Come on, own up – hiya Ma," bending to kiss his mother, nodding at his father.

"Och, nothing son, just having a bit of a rant here, whilst your mother tries to pour the oil on the troubled waters – how was the match, did you win?"

Olivia went to make more tea, and to check the bread as the two of them talked. Tom was such a contrast to his brother. Whereas Graeme was greedy for everything, pushing all the time, Tom was the complete opposite – so laid back and easygoing, pleased to get a result and consequently finding fewer problems – sometimes it was hard to believe they were related. Physically too they were dissimilar, Tom resembling her side of the family – 'tall, dark and handsome' as his doting aunts would call him. True, and with hair that his sister Christine envied – dark and sleek. Graeme and Christine took after the Wards, short and stocky with curly ginger hair and, especially in Graeme's case, the temperament to match. Tom had been the placid baby; he ate and slept and smiled his way along, whereas Graeme had fought it all and slept little, screaming his way through his earliest years.

Looking across the kitchen at the pair of them at the table she could see Martin's face relaxing as Tom chatted away, making his father begin to smile with his descriptions of the players. The tension was easing out of him, soon he would offer Tom a beer as they enjoyed the craic. With Christine due back soon, it would be one of their better evenings, Graeme wouldn't be in until late, by which stage his father would've gone to bed. It was better that way, the row could be postponed until the morning.

Sad but true – she did her best to act as a bulwark between the two, but she herself could not understand

Graeme's attitude at times, and currently found him even more secretive than ever.

"Has he taken your car again?" Martin was still on Graeme's case, but she could tell that it was waning.

"Yes, but only because he's got to get to the other side of the city and it would take two bus rides each way – you know how I don't like him out late hanging about on his own – you never know." She knew that that one would work, but caught Tom's eye to back her up just in case.

"Yeah, she has a point there Dad – the buses are always late and it's not funny when the pubs are out and you're on your own, waiting. Doesn't have to be because you're Catholic, could be just that they didn't like the look of you. I told you what happened to Patrick."

"That was bad, but really he should've had more sense than to go to near the Shankill – no matter how good the band was meant to be," Olivia cut in. "Simple common sense – I mean how daft to put yourself at risk of a kicking for the sake of a band."

She'd seen the youth; had been shocked by the broken arm in its autographed plaster, his face a multi-coloured mass of bruising. He'd been an easy target for the locals – like they said, they could tell he was a Teague, an f'ing RC by the look of him. Madly musical, Patrick wouldn't accept the sectarian boundaries. Olivia agreed with the principle, but feared the potential risk.

She was the liberal one in the marriage, live and let live, just be careful and you'll be alright. They never had any trouble where they lived; it was an area that was predominantly Protestant professional, with a sprinkling of well-to-do Catholics. All had their gardeners and cleaners, their holiday homes by the sea or lough, and the golf club

Chapter 23

membership. You could nearly forget the rest if you wanted, protected by your status, but somehow it always seeped in.

For Martin it was always there, the distrust and resentment – the bitterness that the better contracts never seemed to come his way, always ending up with the Protestant firms. It was getting worse in his opinion, the divide was widening. Graeme had argued with him that it was more likely to be his lack of marketing skills, his out of date ideas that put him at a disadvantage – but Martin knew better.

To his mind he knew how this city worked – the Brits made sure that the Prods kept power, the Prods got all the best jobs, and he was one of the Teagues fighting his way up, against the odds. Sometimes he envied the Jews in Belfast – convinced that they had their businesses and their lives better protected, insulated from the eternal RC/Prod battle. He didn't dislike Protestants – he just couldn't bring himself to trust them.

The Brits however, were a different matter entirely – a simple, inbred, immovable hatred. He carried the reminder in his wallet, the only photo he ever cared about and which had shocked Olivia when she had been shown it.

It was a small black and white picture of three people standing in a row outside a white cottage. At first it seemed the one in the middle had moved, is blurred somehow. It's only when you get closer that you see it for what it is – a horrifying charred body, held upright by the two on either side of him. 'It' was a he, but resembled the Mummy in the Belfast museum – black and shrivelled. They were Martin's family – his father torched by the infamous Black and Tans, held up by his brothers while their mother grieved inside the farmhouse. It had been an unjustified attack on the

The Wards meet Eleanor

Ward's farm by the British, a murder which turned a family forever against them. Sullen and laden with resentment they'd sold up and moved to the big city, Belfast. Martin was the success of the family, the only one who made anything of his life – but he never forgot where he was from and why.

His children mixed with everyone and anyone, his wife had seen to that, diluting the mix, pushing them away from the past. He knew she was right to do so, he wasn't that blinkered, but it wasn't for him. Of course he was able to mix but that didn't mean he wanted to. Look at how open minded he had been over the children's education for heaven's sake. In a place where your school labels you for life, he had compromised. For Graeme it was St. Malachy's but for Tom it had been the Methodist College – with Christine pushing to go there later.

Tom's pleas had been heard; having easily passed his eleven plus he had persuaded his parents, using all of his charm, to let him go to Methody, for the rugby. His mother had backed him, disliking the Catholic school's small mindedness over a sport. Martin had caved in, and hadn't regretted it, – watching his son on the wing was a real delight. If there were problems being a Catholic at Methody Tom kept them to himself. His was a sunny life compared to his brother's.

"Right, you two, I need to set the table, we'll be ready to eat soon." Olivia came towards them, cutlery in hand. They didn't have to move far to the old armchairs by the range – like most builders Martin's own house was always next on the list, and the long promised Aga had yet to materialise. Olivia had grown used to the wait, she had an ordinary cooker, and keeping the range meant that she could have an old sofa and two armchairs round it, making a warm snug in her huge kitchen.

It too was yet to be finished, the bare plaster showing where the scullery, pantry, and walk-in larder had once been. Martin had reassured her that when his men did come, it would take less than a week to complete. She didn't go on about it, business had to come first, and more importantly Martin's health was a worry to her. He'd aged these last few months, tired and grey with a lack of energy that he put down to being 'under the weather'. She wanted him to see the doctor, but so far had met with little success.

"There's nothing wrong with me. I'm not traipsing round to waste his time and mine – a few days by the sea would do me more good than anything else. That, and our Graeme behaving himself for a change," had been his response.

She left it there, but now across the kitchen she could see the worry lines deep in his face, his eyes baggy and tired, slumping in the chair.

"Tom, go and get your father a beer, they're in the utility room, still in the box – they'll be cold enough out there!"

Tom had scarcely got up from the chair to do her bidding when they all heard the car in the drive. Seconds later Christine arrived in, shopping bags to the fore, her face full of being the one 'in the know'.

"I met our Graeme – I mean I was nearly home when he pulled over, he's forgotten his wallet, and he's on his way…."

"He'd forget his head if it wasn't screwed on," was as much as Olivia got out before Graeme appeared in the doorway, with a girl standing awkwardly behind him.

Typical of Graeme, they had all thought for different reasons. Christine and Tom were delighted, their sibling nosiness hungry for something to tease him about. Martin was struggling to get up from the chair, not best pleased at being disturbed from his relaxation. Olivia smoothed her hair and moved towards her son.

"Graeme, don't stand in front of her, come on in dear, I'm Graeme's mother, and this is his father, his brother Tom, and Christine whom you've already met. Would you like a cup of tea or something?"

"Hello Mrs. Ward, Mr. Ward, pleased to meet you, hello Tom. No, thank you, I'm fine really," with a blush and handshake all round, she was in the room.

"Sorry, this is Eleanor – Eleanor Clarke." Graeme came out with, awkwardly for him. He'd persuaded her to come in, assuring her that she'd be welcome, she hadn't wanted to, but he had won.

CHAPTER 24

Eleanor meets the Wards

"No, really, they'd love to meet you, and I want you to meet them – please. C'mon, just for a few minutes and we'll be gone, promise."

"Och Graeme, couldn't I just sit in the car and you run on in? I'm not sure this is such a good idea really, it's all a bit soon. I mean it's not that long since we met and it's all been a …."

He had kissed her then, wanting her to agree with him. Stopping the words he had leaned across to open her door.

"C'mon, Da's a bit of a moan, but you'll rate Mum, and Tom's a gas – they'll love you, believe me."

Now standing in their kitchen she wasn't so sure. Self consciously smoothing down her skirt, she'd shaken hands with them all and had sat down on the sofa as invited. Well not so much an invite from Mr. Ward, more of a 'point and follow' exercise.

Mrs. Ward was warmer, and she was much more 'trendy' than Eleanor's own mother. Wearing slacks and a jumper, with some lipstick on, and with her hair loosely pinned up so that strands came down, she looked much younger than the father. Eleanor was glad that they sat together on the sofa, that way she had a more friendly face to focus on, but was acutely aware of all eyes on her.

"Tell me, Eleanor, are you going to Queen's too?" had been Mr. Ward's first question.

It was obvious to all in the room that Eleanor was several years younger than Graeme, and all knew that it was just a mask for the opening sortie

"Oh no, I'm just starting my 'A' levels, two more years to go – and then Queen's, hopefully. I'd like to study French and then maybe teach." Eleanor answered in a soft voice. Tom, curled up in a battered leather armchair, caught her eye and grinned conspiratorially. Parents – they have to find out don't they?

She knew that this wasn't going to be as brief as Graeme had promised; Mr. Ward was now alert and obviously deciding to make conversation. Mrs. Ward was continuing to offer refreshment – now a Coca Cola no less. Graeme remained standing behind her, out of sight. Declining all offers she perched on the edge of the sofa, waiting for the next question. Looking at Mr. Ward directly she was ready when he asked:

"Where are you at school then for these 'A' levels?"

"I'm a boarder at the Dominican Convent, Portstewart. I'm due back next week, worse luck." She meant it, she hated the place, hated the idea of having to leave her first real boyfriend.

"Ah, I know it well, used to see it from the window of the hotel there – do you remember Olivia, the one by the harbour where we stopped for tea that time – after the golf at Portrush – the Carrig was it?"

"The Carrig-na-cule – my parents take me there for tea when they come to visit." Eleanor came in with as Olivia began to speak:

"Yes, I do – the convent dominates the town, doesn't it? Up there on the rocks it overlooks the whole sweep of the prom and town, and then you have the open sea on the other side. It looked great when we were there, in the summer, but I'd imagine it's pretty grim in winter though?"

"Grim is the word; it's freezing and the food is atrocious."

"But I bet the nuns tell you that it is all good for the soul eh?" Mr. Ward came in with, and she could tell at once that

Chapter 24

he was all in favour of the strict convent life she so loathed.

"Oh yes, well you know what the Dominicans are like…" she began neutrally, aware of Graeme leaving the room, running up the stairs to his bedroom.

"Strict but fair I say, strict but with kindness – and they do great work you know, great teachers the Dominicans," pronounced Mr. Ward, whilst Eleanor groaned inside, she knew what was coming next.

"You can't beat a convent education in my opinion," which spurred his daughter into action, to Eleanor's relief.

"Och Daddy, you just love the idea of all that control; he wanted me to go to a convent you know, some place miles away, but I just couldn't bear the idea of not being at home, never mind the rest. Do your brothers and sisters board as well?" Christine had stopped one line of questioning, but the new one didn't help Eleanor much. It always caused a reaction.

"Actually, I'm an only child."

True to form she thought as she read their expressions. Christine and Tom were sympathetic, Mrs. Ward was selecting a gynaecological reason, and Mr. Ward was itching to ask why. She was so relieved to hear Graeme, standing up the minute he came into the room.

"Right, we're off now, I'm taking Eleanor up to the Student's Union for the hop, her last chance to hear some good music before she goes back. Can I use the car please?"

Eleanor watched the eye contact between the parents, and knew that Graeme had pitched it carefully. She wasn't surprised when his mother smoothed the way.

"Och that'll be alright – won't it Martin? Just be careful eh?" Olivia's appeal came quickly.

"And no drinking mind. And not too late either, right?" he replied, standing up to say good-bye.

Eleanor couldn't wait to get out, she didn't want to face his next question, who her parents were. The religion would be a minor problem compared to her father's nationality. For the moment she wanted Mr. Ward to remain ignorant, knowing that once he knew her father was an Englishman, he would see her in a completely different light. She pushed the thought of being disloyal to her father out of her mind, and said her thanks, like any polite convent girl would. She agreed with his mother that she would be sure to come round again, liking her warmth. Mr. Ward was pleasant, happy enough with his idea of her.

Driving down to the University she was quiet, aware that her whole body was tense. She could feel Graeme's relief; he was pleased with her.

"See, I told you it would be fine, didn't I? Never worry about the rest – we can work it out bit by bit. Trust me, we can. Now, shall we stop at the Eg for a quick one?"

She relaxed in the busy bar, the Eglantine, full of students out for a few jars. Watching Graeme work his way to the crowded bar she stood near the door – one day she'd be one of them – free and having a ball.

CHAPTER 25

Olivia, past and present

"I see my life in two clear segments, Dun, before and after. I might look like an older version of what I once was, but it's just a front, like yours." Olivia spoke quietly, comfortable in her chair, in her home. She had invited Dun over, refusing to take no for an answer. She needed to talk, to let her friend into her thoughts before it all started; there would be no time afterwards. She knew that Dun was uncomfortable and ignored it, her need to be on home ground taking precedence over inverted snobbery.

"You told me about your worst nightmare, your lobotomy; you told me that I could never understand how much you had been through, that I had never been as far down as you. You're right in one sense. I never had the brutal medical treatment you suffered, but I have been to the blackest holes just like you. Go ahead, smoke if you want, I don't mind."

As Dun lit up she went on, leaning forward:

"I'd known for months that Martin wasn't going to live long, we both knew and we were able to prepare ourselves, as best you can. Even though you know that death is near, you always hope that there'll be a bit more time. We got nearly a year in the end, and I became a youngish widow with three children and debts. I grieved, God how I grieved, but it passed with time, and I got on with my life. We all did, with Graeme giving up his university education to take over the business, keeping the family. There was always hope in us, always talk of the future." Dun was watchful as Olivia stood up and moved to the mantelpiece, restless.

"But then, just when you think you can handle it, that maybe it might even be getting better – Bang! It's all blown apart, finished. You get wakened by the police to be told that your son is dead. Two bullets in the head, and do you have anyone who could come and stay with you?

I couldn't take it in at first, thought that it was a mistake, but of course it wasn't. My beautiful son was waiting for me to identify him in the morgue – and I couldn't even do that. Graeme did it for me, I just folded, became a robot. I would sit in his room for hours, touching his things, smelling his clothes. Anything to bring him back to me – I made his room a shrine, never letting anything be moved or changed, but it was never enough. How could anyone do that, why Tom, why anyone? You know how bad it had become in 1975 Dun. "

Dun knew well; sectarian murders, even a show band had been targeted. The atmosphere tense, expectant and murderous.

"Well it finished me. You saw how I was when I met you first; I could barely function, and was so full of medication that nothing got through. That was how I wanted it, how I needed it in fact. I didn't care anymore, nothing mattered, hurry up God and let me go – I could see no reason to continue living. Part of that has stayed with me; like you I learned to play the game, keep the rules enough to get out and stay out, but nothing gets me out of the hole that was Tom. It stopped for me then, and any hope I ever had of seeing someone brought to justice over his death died a long time ago." She was shaking, and Dun couldn't bear it.

"You and a lot of other people Olivia; what has gone on in our country for years is going to continue, you can see it coming, can't you?"

"God – you're so right. I'd thought that this time we'd see an end to it, but it's like we're warming up for a new round.

Chapter 25

The next generation of terrorists who will run rings round our government yet again. More bloody innocents will be killed, and only the names will have changed. I truly don't care about the future, there's nothing to hold me anymore. My children have their own lives; I just want to go now having left a mark, an angry scratch on the surface, but one that will make me feel that at least I put one of them away – so much for peace and reconciliation – eh Dun? Hardly the act of a good Christian is it ?"

Olivia wasn't looking for any reassurances Dun was relieved to hear. Her only friend's calm announcement was the perfect depressive's flat detachment, which matched her own mindset. Part of her had had the feeling that Olivia might pull out, go all moral on her. Relieved, she began to skin up.

"Och Olivia, you know how I feel. I've nobody who'd give a shit if I lived or died – apart from you. You're the only person who ever tried to understand me, all the bits of me, never let me down. You've given me your friendship for the best part of twenty eight years you know – for me they have been the calmest times in my whole pathetic life, you know that don't you?" Dun asked, passing the spliff over. As ever her friend coughed as she tried to inhale, and they both smiled; it was part of their unlikely history.

"I know too that if your Tom hadn't been murdered, we'd never have met." Dun came out with, catching Olivia off guard.

"It's true though, isn't it?" Dun asked, waiting for her friend to agree before continuing:

"I can picture you in your big fancy house, your golf club friends, your holiday home by the sea – Christ! I bet you even had accounts at the big shops didn't you, a cleaner, a gardener? Thought so. I'd have been the cleaner at the golf club. Someone you nodded at, and remembered to tip at Christmas, that would have been the sum of it."

Dun had got up and gone over to the butler's tray and was pouring the whiskey, Olivia giving her a nod.

"You're right Dun, absolutely right. I never appreciated how easy my life was, how cushy. Up until Martin's illness we hadn't had much to complain about, even after that my lifestyle didn't change much – it was just like you said, good clothes, nice homes – all the trappings of a middle-class matron in Belfast.

After Tom went though, I saw everything with a frightening clarity – none of it was worth a damn. I couldn't communicate with anyone beyond a 'yes' or 'no', not even Graeme or Christine. Sometimes I'd just curl up in Tom's old chair in the kitchen, he always loved it, trying to sense him with me. I'd do it for hours, holding him in my mind's eye, shut off from everything. I ran away in the end, ran away to London where no-one would know me, where I could wait out my time. Bit like you Dun, in a way, isn't it?" she asked, taking the whiskey from her.

"Neither of us had much of a future that's true, or much hope. We've survived these years, got through a chunk of life propping each other up. I couldn't have hacked it if you hadn't appeared, I'd have been back in the ward on a Section or worse by now; and you – well, there were quite a few times when I wondered if you'd top yourself, if you'd take the short cut. I'd have understood- well, I say I would but..." Dun shook her head; it had been a real fear for her.

"Yes, there were times, especially birthdays and anniversaries, trying to come up with a reason why another day would be worth the effort. Just black and hopeless, with

CHAPTER 25

the top off the pills, and the whiskey bottle opened. They did pass, but the underlying pain is just the same, like yours. You gave me the only friendship that I can actually handle, the one that is for real; I don't trust anyone else, they've always let me down, always. Cheers."

It was a cheerless toast, Olivia's face showing the strain, looking so old. Dun was moved; she brought out the best in her, made her feel valued. She'd make it happen for Olivia; she'd never let her down.

"Cheers Olivia, and God bless the cleansing station!" Dun's glass went up and Olivia joined her, clinking glasses and even managing a small smile.

"Yes, to the station and our first meeting. That was a horrendous place; to this day I've never told anyone about it. In fact I can't believe that I actually went there."

"No, it was hardly your sort of place and yet you weren't the first 'nice' type we'd had you know." Dun commented, adding;

"We'd regularly get social workers, nice middle-class do-gooders, needing de-lousing. They found it a shock too, I can tell you. They had clients, just like your neighbour, who were crawling with them, and just like you they'd pick them up during a visit. For whatever reason you did the right thing that day, our treatment worked; a lot of people would get stuff from the chemist but wouldn't follow the instructions properly, ending up far worse off."

"Yes, that was what I'd been told. But mainly I just remember the panic I was in, wanting someone to look after me like they did in the clinic. Fix it, make it better – like a child again. That and feeling so bloody lonely, for all that I wanted to be alone. When I heard your accent I had to say something, for some reason I was afraid to let the moment pass." Olivia looked at her old and battered friend and nodded to her.

"Maybe it was all meant to happen," was Dun's answer, finishing her drink.

" I mean, you were off your face that day," she went on; "God knows how much crap you'd taken, but it was clear to me that you were a long way from home, in every sense of the word. You were doing things that the old Olivia, the Belfast 'lady' wouldn't have dreamed of, or couldn't have imagined! Mind you, am I glad that you did – and now I'll make bloody sure that you get your revenge. There's nobody else who will, we both know that." Her voice was bitter; right then she'd have walked on water for Olivia had it been possible.

Olivia left her chair and topped up their glasses, touching Dun on the shoulder as she passed.

"Dun, I'm much more like you than you can imagine. I went to pieces when Martin died, but after Tom's murder – well I'd say I fragmented then, and the bits never fitted together again. I felt it in you, and you recognised it in me too – two broken people pretending to live life. A daft game, if ever there was one. Now… well we're going to do it, we're going to have our say before we go. I'm not backing out of it, yes I know you thought I might, but you were wrong. I wanted you here today to thank you for helping me get through the years, but most importantly to thank you for what's about to happen." Olivia was gesturing to Dun who wanted to interrupt.

"No, let me finish. I need retribution, and afterwards, well, that's my ticket to freedom. I have it all planned but I wanted to tell you, not to leave without warning. You knew it anyway, didn't you?"

Chapter 25

"Yes, I guessed, but that doesn't mean I like it," was Dun's quiet answer.

"It's my choice, my life, and for me, it's going home – at last," Olivia finished. Dun could see her determination, and knew there was no point in arguing. This was something they'd often talked about; Olivia even joking that, knowing her, she'd get the dosage wrong.

"Just don't get it wrong Olivia, make certain that you do it right. I'll not be around to help, you know that," she warned.

"Yes, I know, and yet I don't know what you have planned for afterwards – are you going to tell me?" Olivia knew her question would probably get the same treatment earlier ones had got.

"No, I'm not going to say because I honestly don't know what will happen. That's the truth Olivia. It's impossible to sort that one out until I've finished the job. Once that's over, well, it could go either way, you know that." Dun's face was so open Olivia had to get to her feet.

"Oh come here Dun, come here," holding out her arms to the small child that was her friend. Dun got up and silently the two women hugged each other for the first time. Dun feeling the thinness of Olivia through her jumper, shocked at how frail she was. For her part, Olivia was realising the strength and hard muscle in Dun. After a moment they each pulled back, Dun breaking the silence first:

"Come on, it's time for another drink before I go."

"No, no more until we've eaten. You've time to eat surely? I've made us a real Ulster tea – well as close as I can make it." Olivia was moving towards the door.

"Oh go on then, bring the bottle," she added as Dun

picked up the glasses.

Dun followed her through to the kitchen and sat down at the table while Olivia got busy.

After their meal they stayed on at the table, smoking and talking. Dun had, as always, eaten quickly, not wanting to talk until she had scraped her plate noisily. Olivia had picked at hers, tired and drained by the day.

"That was brilliant, thank you," said Dun, on finishing her man sized portion in minutes.

"I've got to head off soon to check out our taxis," she added and Olivia was jerked back to reality. This was a change; previously they were only using one on the way back from Putney.

"I've decided that I want the guy to take us there so that later he won't have a problem picking us up on time. It's pricey, but I feel safer; something less to worry about. Did you remember to get the cash?" With only days to go Dun was on top form with her lists.

"Yes, it's upstairs. Do you want it now? Hang on, I won't be a minute," Olivia replied and went to fetch it.

"I wasn't sure if two was enough, so I took out five, here," she said, coming in through the door and holding out a wad of notes. Dun took it, counted five hundred, and tucked them down the side of her boot, inside the sock.

"That'll be plenty. Once I've taken the taxi charge out of this, I'll use the rest to get my clothes tomorrow. Can you meet me at East Street market in the morning, help me sort out the clothes quickly – say about 10, on the corner of the Walworth Road? Good. Okay, now I've got to go." Dun pushed back her chair, Olivia went to get her jacket.

Within minutes she had disappeared down the street, heading for home. Olivia turned off everything and went to bed, not caring about clearing up – it'd all still be there in the morning.

CHAPTER 26

Christine's meeting – Galway city

Dagmar Mann stood at her window in Ely Place, watching her next client through the slats of the blind. She'd been Christine Ward's therapist on and off for years; trying to help her move on and see a future, not just the past. She watched as Christine gathered her bag and locked the car, walking confidently towards the entrance.

Dagmar turned away and sat down to scan her case notes and finish her cup of tea. She liked this client; generally Christine would open up quickly and use their hour together productively – well that was what she hoped anyway. The receptionist buzzed her – she had ten minutes.

Christine Ward always presented well at the clinic; it was hard to tell if things weren't right with her, she had a wonderful mask, a knack of putting on the show that hid the real side of her. Today she looked attractive in a long denim skirt and navy blue jumper, her long curly auburn hair loose. She looked younger than she was, and could have passed for late thirties, until you saw her up close; it was the eyes that gave her away. When she was down they seemed to change colour from hazel to near green, becoming hooded and wary – old eyes.

She sat, pretending to read the magazine as she waited, preparing in her head how she would use her time. At 80 Euros an hour she found it expensive, if useful.

She hadn't always been like that; like her brothers, Graeme and Tom, she'd had a happy childhood, wanting for nothing. Looking back on it she realised just how lucky they'd been and just how swiftly they had all disintegrated and scattered afterwards. That was why she was here today

Chapter 26

in Ely Place. She felt overwhelmed by it all again, and with the pain came the anger, the dangerous anger. She used the counselling infrequently, it was her final safety valve. Better the expense of a therapist than the pills, she felt. She'd tried them all over the years, finally realising that treating the symptoms wasn't getting her anywhere.

"Just go through Miss Ward, first door on the left," the receptionist had chirruped in the bizarre singsong voice of constant repetition.

Christine tapped on the door before entering, and was welcomed by Dagmar. She liked the large German, felt safe with her. She never felt awkward about starting; she used their sessions to dump and didn't care where the personal information ended up – just that there would be some relief, a bit of insight into her nightmares.

"Let's start with how you are, Christine. It's been over three months – how have things been?" The voice was gentle and warm.

"Take your time, there's no hurry here."

"Well…I've dumped my bloke, or rather he's had enough of my depression and has dumped me. I suspect my mother is planning to kill herself, and as for my brother Graeme – God!" Christine's hands finished the sentence for her.

Dagmar wasn't surprised to hear about the end of the relationship. Christine was unable to sustain or develop any relationship beyond two years at most. It followed a pattern; this one had lasted longer because Christine had wanted him to accompany her to some important family do in London. Now even that was off, and she suspected Christine was looking for a way out of attending at all.

She had re-read her summary of Christine's case notes before seeing her. Only girl, two male siblings; one a successful businessman living in London, other shot 'in error' by a paramilitary force in the North in 1975. Father died of heart disease when she was a teenager, Mother a chronic depressive since the murder of her son, also living in London.

The mother's breakdown had been severe; her withdrawal from her remaining children, Graeme and Christine, damaging them both.

In Christine's case she had fled to Eire, choosing an alternative life style on the west coast. She'd bought outright a tiny cottage on the edge of Kinvarra, close enough to be with people, far enough out to keep them at bay if she wished. Her life was completely simple, it was all that she could handle. As long as she had enough to live on she was content; food, heat, shelter and the everlasting Morris Traveller.

The artistic side in her developed over the years – doing Batik prints in a studio over near Lisdoonvarna paid little, but gave her great satisfaction. Dagmar had seen her work for sale – Christine's picture of a hound from the ancient Book of Kells now hung in her own home. No hippie tie-die that; the modern copy of the work was powerful and vibrant. Colours that she wouldn't have associated with the Christine Ward she knew.

"Let's start with your relationship..."

Christine's initial outbursts were always the same, the pent up anxiety resulting in the dramatic blurt.

"I don't want to go to London without Nick, he moved out of my place in Kinvarra over a week ago, and won't return my calls. I've tried every which way to get hold of him, but nothing. Graeme, the brother from hell, is hovering; I can feel him getting ready to give me the 'family

Chapter 26

must attend' lecture about his bloody party, using Eleanor as his mouthpiece. I don't think I can play the 'face ache' game, I really don't."

Christine had strong views on socialising 'Graeme style'; his London friends were anathema to her with their expensive posing and superficiality. Their women were even more alarming; over made-up faces set like masks with eyes that priced everything on your back and more importantly, your jewellery. The brittle empty chatter as they coldly checked you over – Christine had nothing in common with them. She bought clothing when she needed it, never 'lunched', and didn't need her BMW changed every year. She knew how they saw her – had overheard some of the comments.

"God! Isn't she an odd one, that Christine? I mean you'd be hard pressed to see they were brother and sister. I always find Graeme easier to be with than her, you know what I mean?"

"Oh, I do, I do. She's a bit 'holier than thou', tries to make people feel guilty about just enjoying the good things in life."

The others had agreed, and Christine had been relieved. To have been likened to Graeme would have upset her much more than any catty comment. She despised her brother and his lifestyle – his greed had corrupted him. She was amazed that her sister-in-law had stuck it for all these years. The man was an arrogant sod, with a contempt for women that would take your breath away. Christine had never forgiven him for what had happened after Tom's death.

Following her mother's decision to leave Northern Ireland, she and Graeme were jointly given the family's holiday home on the Antrim coast. Graeme could never share anything – any fool knew that – but Christine had been surprised at the speed of his move to get her share.

Tom was barely cold in his grave, their mother was in pieces and Graeme wanted his own way, at his price. Her own brother had stitched her up, had assumed that she would never work it out. How cocky was that? He'd thought that he'd got away with it, never realising that she had signed the house over to him at his price for the sake of peace. She knew full well that he had done her out of thousands.

That was how he was, that was Graeme – money and power before everything. At that moment she had wished that it had been he who had died, not Tom. He'd even managed to wind their mother up by laying claim to family pieces that meant nothing to him, everything to her. There was no way she was going over to London without support.

"Nick and I were friends first, lovers second. Sometimes I wish that it'd stayed that way, it seems we talked more, understood each other better – were real friends. Trying to live together has been a disaster for us. He wants more than I can give him, or anybody else for that matter."

Christine paused to drink some water, eyeing the 'No Smoking' sign; she needed a cigarette badly, knew too that her therapist smoked.

"Don't even ask, Christine."

"Just wishful thinking," she answered, putting her glass down.

"So Nick has left and won't respond to your calls." Dagmar prompted.

"Because I wouldn't give him an answer. I couldn't give him one. I don't need or want to formalise what we have.

Chapter 26

He wants marriage, no less." Christine sounded almost indignant.

"You know what I'm like," she went on. "The minute that stuff starts up I want out, want to run. Only this time, this one beat me to it. Part of me says that it's better like this; I was conning him, he deserved better – someone whole. The other part of me misses him so much that I ache with it."

The voice had dropped, the mask had slipped – she wiped the tears away with her hands.

"Then there is the question of my mother. You know that there've been times when I couldn't afford to come to see you. It was hard enough making ends meet – you were the luxury I couldn't afford. Well…as of this week, according to my bank, I could afford to come and see you every day if I liked. My account has been credited to the tune of 25,000 Euros, and there's only one person in the world who would do that – my mother. I believe it's her way of getting ready to go, putting her affairs in order."

"Have you spoken to her lately?"

Christine's reply was a shake of the head as she dug out a handkerchief from her bag.

"No. I've only spoken to Eleanor. Mum is vague and withdrawn again, she always promises to 'phone me back, and then never does. This time I think it is deliberate; more avoidance than forgetfulness. She sounds like she did not long after Tom died, but with an edge to her. ."

"Do you believe that she might harm, even kill herself?" It was the question that Christine had gone over for days.

"I don't believe my mother wants to live much longer. She loathes the idea of senility, and fights off her arthritis with anything and everything just to keep mobile. I feel that if anything changes in her physical balance, it'll be enough to make her want out. She is not the mother I knew when I was little – that person was killed when her son was. I've never been able to fill the gap that Tom left, I was always Daddy's girl, and we both knew it."

She could see them all as a family: Tom and her mother close as always, she twisting her father round her little finger, and Graeme on the edge of it all, watching. In the background was Eleanor.

"There's another thing about going to London – Eleanor. I said that I'd spoken to her, well at first that was to sort out where I could stay, with or without Nick. He and I had planned to stay at Mum's, but then when he left, I couldn't face telling her that I'd made another mess in my life…so I used Eleanor. What was odd was that she was so accommodating, so willing to help me out. I didn't have to go into detail, she just took it on. God knows why – I've never seen her as anything other than Graeme's doormat, and have probably let my feelings show."

"Even when you first met her?" Dagmar asked, knowing that Eleanor had been around the family before Christine had lost her beloved father, and had also been friends with Tom.

"No, it wasn't like that in the beginning. I liked her when she first came, both of us were schoolgirls, but she was going out with my big brother. It was the only time in his life that Graeme wanted people to know what he was up to – to approve of her. It's taken me a long time to see how it was, and how impossible his wish was."

Christine was moving into an area she had never fully talked about before, hadn't wanted to. Dagmar was pleased that another door was being unlocked.

CHAPTER 26

"Go on…." she prompted, "tell me what it was like.."

"Well she was an only child and loved the buzz of our house; brothers and a sister and all that goes with it. She came across as cool and slightly reserved, but with a real sense of life just tucked away underneath. I only saw her during the school holidays when she came home from the awful school her parents sent her to. She hated being away from home, but had no choice in the matter. I think she felt that I had many of the things that she would have loved: day school, home life, close family contact and some sort of a social life – certainly from what she told me I believe she lived each day in the convent marking time, wanting to go home.

"It was that self-possessed coolness that hooked Graeme. I saw it as her shield, thought she was pretty lonely really, but he saw it as something different. Don't get me wrong, she wasn't little Miss Meek – I mean she played Camogie for a start!" Christine's voice showed how impressed she was – Dagmar had to ask why.

"Camogie is the female version of Hurling. Do you know what Hurling is?- Have you ever seen it played – or seen the Guinness ad on telly even?" Christine asked.

"Of course I know what Hurling is – but this other game, no. I cannot imagine girls playing this game, it is so violent."

"Well she did, and she loved it. She told me that the Mother Prioress of the convent was going to stop it because of the number of injuries, but that she was against it – she loved the danger and the speed. It took away the frustration of being locked up all the time. She regarded hockey as a tame game, and netball for incompetents. I liked that bit of her too; used to show her my bruises after a hard hockey match, and argue the point with her. She was strong underneath it all, but had this need to fit in, blend in – a shame really. Especially when Graeme stopped being starry eyed, and saw how he could use it to his own advantage. Sorry, I need the loo, Dagmar."

Christine stopped and picked up her bag, both of them knowing that she would stand outside the front door for a few minutes, get her nicotine hit and come back. Dagmar was happy to let her have a break – she'd stop the clock and wait.

Outside the door Christine was sifting her thoughts and memories, smoking hard. She was feeling uncomfortable about where this was going. There was more than a touch of guilt in her as she stubbed her cigarette out and went back in.

"Anyway, she was great to start with, and then it all changed." Dagmar raised an eyebrow, Christine shrugged.

"Oh it was a typical Northern Ireland farce really. Eleanor Clarke was welcomed into our home, not just because she was big brother's boyfriend, but because we liked her. She would come over on a Saturday night for 'tea' – which as you know in Ulster is a huge meal, and be with us as a family."

"She was different from Graeme's other girlfriends, she made him think and even try hard. That bit was really good, and she and Tom got on really well too." Christine paused.

"So, at the beginning it was good, and then?"

"It had to come out some time, and when it did it was over for Eleanor as far as my father was concerned. At first he heard that she went to a convent – that made her alright in his eyes, nothing better in fact. Then we had to deal with the fact that although she went to a convent, she was a

Chapter 26

Ba'hai. That threw the old man, he hadn't a clue what it meant – all he wanted to know was whether it was Catholic Ba'hai or Protestant Ba'hai!" Christine's humour was black, so was the memory of her father's behaviour.

"But that wasn't the end of it – it was quite a while afterwards that the rest came out. I think Graeme believed that if Dad got to know her first then he might be able to cope with the fact that her father was English, a Brit. He went absolutely mad when Graeme told him – nearly a year later, I think it was. They rowed really badly. Dad could cope with Brits in the outside world, but not within his own family. He couldn't move on that, and neither would Graeme move with regard to Eleanor. By that stage, although he hadn't told us officially, he was planning on marrying her. Mum was going nuts about the fact that we didn't even know her family and all that stuff. Tom was clear – he liked her, and couldn't see why there had to be a problem."

"And you, Christine, where were you in this?" Dagmar pushed gently, aware of how thin the line was with her.

"They were both a pair of innocents really, when I think of it; nothing happened between them until after they were married. That's hard to imagine in this day and age, but that's how it was."

"You Christine, where were you – which side did you take?"

"That's the bit I don't much like Dagmar; it's not something I'm proud of, but I did what I felt was right at the time..."

"And afterwards it didn't feel so right?"

"Yes. Looking back I made a choice to keep my father happy – it was wrong. I sided with him, even though I didn't really agree with him, his appalling bigotry. It sounds inexcusable now; but at the time he was ill and I thought more about his happiness than Graeme's. So…it meant that Eleanor and I didn't really move on from there…"

"You followed your father, and what did your mother do about Eleanor?"

"Need you ask? Mum was polite, but never let Eleanor get close after that. She wouldn't have upset her husband at the best of times, but now that he was ill she became fiercely protective of him. Nothing was allowed that would upset him – what a joke that was! Graeme and he never really got it sorted, not properly; I think Eleanor was the last straw for both of them." Christine's words couldn't convey how bad it had been.

"So, she was excluded…"

"Except by Tom; he used to meet her in town sometimes for a coffee and a chat, he felt sorry for her. I was sorry too, but not sorry enough to do anything about it. We weren't fair to Eleanor Clarke – all of us, bar Tom," she said, "and now, there she is; willing to help me without hesitation, still propping up that bloody brother of mine, and dealing with a mother in law who has never let her in – yes, I do feel guilty about Eleanor." She was nodding as she leaned back in the chair.

"Do you intend to do anything about this feeling?" Dagmar asked.

"I should, and I have thought about it – it's a bit late though isn't it?" She asked, knowing full well what the answer would be.

"Is it really too late ?"

She was tired as she drove out of Galway city, over the Wolfe Tone bridge and past the docks, keen to get back to

Chapter 26

her cottage and light the wood-burner. The session had been good – Dagmar helped her put a different perspective on what had gone on, and at the end had left Christine to choose, as always. However, this time her choice would be the one that made the difference, it would be her own.

CHAPTER 27

Drake sits tight

The increase in information in the last week had been phenomenal. The FBI had come up with the goods, and Drake was in good form for once.

"Right everyone, pay attention," he called out in the Portakabin, waiting for his team to stop and listen. They could see he was pumped up about something, and moved towards his end of the room. He waited until all noise stopped before speaking again, running his eye over the lot of them. They had found the wait frustrating; the weeks of meticulous work displayed on the boards would come to little unless the action took place.

"The good news is that the ship left Boston on schedule; the FBI have monitored the whole thing and are certain that the goods are on board," he let the ripple of pleasure go round the group before continuing.

"And the bad news is?" came from the back of the group.

"More of the same for the time being." He knew there'd be a groan from them, they'd been cooped up for too long.

"All right, I know you're frustrated with the wait, aren't we all? But this is the time for double-checking everything; for making sure that we have not missed a bloody thing. I do not intend to let some piece of shit wriggle out of my grasp on some damn technicality, all because we missed something. Cover every angle on our targets, imagine that you've got one of their barristers on your tail, because you will have when we catch the buggers!" Drake spoke from experience; hours spent in the dock under ferocious cross-examination, despair over the cases where an elementary mistake let a barrister find the chink and end up with an acquittal.

CHAPTER 27

"How long are we looking at now, sir?" The question came from the front, the leggy blonde with the deep voice. She was smart and gorgeous, teacher's pet, and teacher loved it.

"I believe it's a matter of days, Louise, days," he answered, thinking she had legs that went on forever, that she was young enough to be his daughter, and wishing that his celibacy rule during an operation was negotiable.

"I'm pretty sure that by next week it will all be over for them. The FBI are in constant touch, we've got the London end under the microscope, and Mark Bateson will be on the spot. No-one will be picked up until we've got every major player in place. I'm due to see the Minister later today, and Mark Bateson in…" he paused, looking at his watch, "under an hour. Anything else?" Abrupt as ever, but always on 'receive', Drake waited. After a short pause, he couldn't wait for them to ask.

"Where does the Minister stand on this one? That's the question that I can sniff in the air right now… Have we really got carte blanche? Can we believe that these bastards will get what they deserve? That we'll get real support? I believe we will team – otherwise I wouldn't be pissing about in a dump like this! I mean, look at me – would I?"

His hands indicated his Savile Row suit, the hand-made shoes, his classy understated style – having played to the audience he enjoyed their chuckle. They trusted him; he only hoped that the Minister was worthy of his trust, one never knew who was in cahoots with whom these days. He might have clout in some places; in others he watched his step.

His team was on side, he knew who they were. The Westminster lot – well that was different. How many of them had Irish grannies? How many had been supporters of the 'Troops Out' movement in their youth? That was what worried him. The place leaked like a sieve.

"I'll have more information by tomorrow morning – meanwhile get on with it here. If anything changes you'll be told via Thomas." Drake indicated his driver waiting by the door. Thomas was more than a driver, they all knew that – everything about him yelled army, and heavy duty with it.

Drake left quickly – he had to get north of the river to meet Bateson and would be lucky to make it on time, the traffic was a nightmare. Thomas was as good as any black cabbie at finding the back ways through the mess and they were only minutes late pulling up outside the pub.

"Come back for me in an hour, Thomas. I will have had enough of this place by then," Drake murmured, looking at the façade of the pub. The 'Duke of Wellington' had seen better days, but it was off the beaten track and convenient. He wouldn't sit down in there, Thomas thought correctly; it was a chewing gum on the seats and sticky floor place for sure

"Yes sir," he replied, holding the car door open as Drake emerged. He hero-worshipped his boss, regarding him as a real bloke despite being a toff. He watched as Drake entered the pub, waiting until the doors closed behind him before driving off.

Mark Bateson was at the bar; apart from him, the clientele consisted of a woman on the fruit machine in the corner, and two men from a local building site with their pints.

"Hello – ah! You've got them in already, well done," said Drake, eyeing the smeary glass with distaste – at least the whiskey would act as a disinfectant.

"Hello, and sorry about this place. I haven't been here for

Chapter 27

years – shall we sit?" Mark replied, handing Drake his drink.

"Cheers.. why don't we perch over there," Drake suggested, steering him towards the window with a shelf for their drinks. The place was filthy and stale-aired, the lingering smell of deep fat fryers and dirty ashtrays blending together.

"I've been sitting all day, need to let the circulation work a bit. You look much better than the last time I saw you – how is it on the domestic front?" Drake asked, already knowing that Fiona was back in town. His lunch with her brother had been very productive, if expensive.

"Thank you, I do feel much better. As for my dear wife, she is back and we are trying to sort it out – but you didn't want to see me about my marital mess..." Mark answered, looking directly at Drake. He wasn't going to be drawn further; his home life was like walking on eggshells, he hoped that he'd be able to hold it all together until after the party. Right now he wanted to focus on the job.

"No, you're quite right, I didn't. I just needed to have a quick word about the 'social event of the year'. Drake's voice was intentionally blasé; he had only wanted to meet Mark to check him out in person, to spot any potential waver. He went on:

"I intend to act only after you have ensured that the deal has been done. We want to be able to hit them simultaneously, that way we get them all. There is a hell of a lot riding on you on the night, Mark, a hell of a lot. Like a refill?" Drake had finished his drink, and was ready for another; Mark declined, and Drake went to the bar to get his own.

He could feel the tension regarding Fiona and hoped that the man did have a handle on it. He was somewhat reassured, however, by seeing him in person. Thomas had reported on the frequency of the meetings between Mark and Eleanor Ward, noting their increasing length and venues. He even had a wager, modest of course, with Thomas betting they had done it, and Drake not convinced at all. He would win the bet; he could spot serious hesitation from fifty yards, and Mark and Eleanor both suffered from it. Thomas wouldn't bet on the boss pulling Louise though – he could spot a dead cert easily.

Drake paid the unfriendly barmaid, reluctant to pick up his change off the dirty bar surface.

"Keep the change," he nodded to her, wondering 'where do they find them?'

As he arrived back at the window, Mark spoke immediately.

"I know what you're thinking Drake, and you needn't worry. I've got my mind on the job, despite the rest, believe me." Drake shook his head.

"Actually that wasn't what I was thinking. I have no doubt that you'll be on top of the situation, and that however bad things are between you and Fiona, it won't affect your job. What I was thinking was, what about the situation between the Wards? Will that one hold until afterwards?"

"Absolutely. Eleanor has told me that she is determined to make the party a success, and I believe her. She says that she and Graeme have little contact other than over the arrangements, but also that he is tense beyond belief over business – that figures ! – and is forever having to go out to 'meetings'. She actually believes that they are meetings, unlike in the past when she knew it was a cover for seeing a tart. No, the Wards will both work to make sure that the

Chapter 27

evening is a success, I'm certain." Mark spoke with confidence, Drake watched him over the rim of his glass as he finished his drink.

"Good. That's what I wanted to hear. Now, can I drop you anywhere?" he asked, seeing Thomas standing in the doorway.

"No, I'd rather walk it from here thanks. When do you want to see me again?" Mark was not fazed by the abrupt halt, like many he saw it as Drake's way, nothing personal.

"I don't, old chap, I don't." Drake smiled, holding out his hand. Mark shook it and queried:

"You don't?"

"No. I like it kept simple. I trust you, and I also trust you will contact me should anything untoward happen – all options covered I think. Now, I must go – take great care Mark."

With that he left, and was out through the pub in seconds. Thomas was ahead with the door already open; he climbed in and leant back.

"My God, what an absolute dive, totally disgusting – straight home please," were his comments, as the car started.

"Were you happy with the man, sir?" Thomas asked, eyeing him in the mirror.

"Yes. A couple of reservations, but in the main, yes. Bateson will deliver alright, if only to prove me wrong. The Wards are sound enough to get through the 'do' according to him. As I know for sure he's getting that info directly from Mrs. Ward, I think I can take that as a certainty. Currently I am moderately happy. Any calls?" Drake enquired.

"Yes sir. Miss Henshaw 'phoned to confirm dinner this evening, I have arranged to collect her at 8pm." Thomas was happy to inform him, knowing how pleased he'd be.

"Oh that's good Thomas! Dinner with the lovely Louise, the perfect antidote to a meeting with the Minister," came Drake's answer, as he closed his eyes. Thomas smiled and drove on, glad he hadn't gone for that bet.

CHAPTER 28

Dropping in

"I was over this way on a bit of business, and thought I'd drop in and see how you are," Graeme announced, as Olivia opened the door to him. She'd been dozing in the sitting room by the fire, content after dinner; peacefully considering whether she would bother with television.

"Graeme, how nice to see you," she answered, offering her cheek. This was not what she had had in mind for her evening. She led him into her sitting room, wishing he'd telephoned first.

"Come on in, I was just about to have a whiskey – would you like one?" She asked, going to the tray.

"A wee one would be grand, thanks. How are you Mum? I've rung you a few times but you're never in, or you don't answer. Everything alright?" Graeme asked, settling into the chair she'd vacated to open the door to him. It annoyed her every time he did it; he knew perfectly well it was her seat – she was always surprised at how petulant he could make her feel.

"I'm fine dear. A little tired, but nothing more than that. I've probably been asleep and not heard the 'phone. I find I have little naps that I don't remember starting!" she replied with a smile, handing him his drink and sitting opposite him. He looked tired and strained, even in the soft light of the lamps that made her sitting room so cosy.

Graeme took his glass and had a sip. His mother had aged in the last few months; even he couldn't miss it. She moved differently too, with less determination and more resignation; like she was accepting of her age.

Olivia settled herself with her drink, and waited. Graeme was playing with his glass, gazing into the fire. It was she who broke the silence, not comfortable with it.

"Everything ready for the big day then? Eleanor certainly seems on top of it all, she's really making such an effort, isn't she?" Unable to resist raising the issue, it was her way of not letting Graeme take control of her evening.

She was tired out these days; a heaviness inside her, along with a total intolerance for time-wasting. This middle-aged man was apparently part of her; this bent businessman, about to get involved with terrorists, was her son. Sometimes she found it hard to believe that she had given birth to him, he was so unlike what she'd hoped he would be. Of course she loved him, the consequence of a happy union; however, the resulting adult had never failed to disappoint her she realised. Love and dislike; that summed up their relationship for her.

"Yes, well, apart from the last few bits and pieces, we're all set. Eleanor has it all under control, like you said. It should be a grand evening all round." Graeme looked up to answer her, making his voice sound confident.

In fact he was sick with anxiety over it. Never mind the dreadful atmosphere between him and Eleanor, the phone calls from Belfast had been increasing, their tone shifting towards a subtle menace as time went by. Everyone was tense – he couldn't relax, couldn't even enjoy a woman these days. Frustrated in every sense of the word; he couldn't wait for it all to happen, and yet was dreading the day.

"It should indeed. I'm looking forward to it, it's been a long time since you gave such a big party. Normally when it's rugby it's just you and the lads, with massive hangovers the next day." Olivia wanted her son to say something to redeem himself.

"Well, it's about time that I did then, obviously! Seriously

Chapter 28

though, I owe hospitality to a few business contacts, and wanted to give them the personal touch as opposed to the posh restaurant. Then there was the rugby crowd, and the old friends, and suddenly the numbers got bigger. But sure the house lends itself to a party, and like you said, Eleanor does it all with real class," lied Graeme.

Olivia nodded; she could understand the hospitality side of it, the need and responsibility to give it. That one went in with the breast milk, along with the old F.H.B. rule – family hold back – so that the guest should have the best; but the rest of it saddened her, his glib lies and smooth patter.

"Well Dun and I will be there early to help, don't worry," she churned out mechanically, draining her glass.

"Get me another one will you dear, I'll call it my nightcap," was the best she could muster. She didn't care how much she drank, or smoked, it was irrelevant now.

Graeme got up to pour her another drink, surprised at how quickly she had knocked the first one back. She had always enjoyed a drink, but tended to linger over it; he had never seen her anything more than tipsy – and that was a rare event.

"Thank you dear," Olivia said, taking the glass from him.

"Aren't you having another?"

"No – I'm fine with this, don't want to lose my licence, do I?" replied Graeme, picking up his glass.

That bit was the truth alright; he had become paranoid about the possibility of being pulled over by the police, of drawing attention to himself in any way. The risk was too great, and anyway the alcohol didn't work, it didn't stop the worry in the pit of his stomach.

"That's not like you Graeme, you've always tended to sail

a bit close to the wind where driving is concerned." Olivia commented tartly, recalling the time he'd pranged his car whilst drunk, hiding it in a friend's garage to avoid getting caught. She'd been disapproving, sympathising with the other driver, and had rowed seriously with him about it. He knew what she was referring to and it irritated him to have it dragged up again. What was it with women and their elephantine memories?

Olivia watched him, could read what was going through his head, but was surprised by his angry response.

"In the name of God, does anything ever get forgiven and forgotten in this bloody family of ours!" He shouted at her, looking at her impassive face.

"I'd be grateful if you would refrain from raising your voice, Graeme. There is no need, my hearing is fine," she said coldly, becoming increasingly angry with him. He shouldn't have come, she wasn't up for playing games. Holding his gaze, she decided not to let it pass for the sake of peace.

"You never could take anyone's advice, be it on a moral issue or practical help. Never – and as for taking responsibility for your actions, for being able to accept that you got things wrong – well!" She shrugged, shaking her head.

"Christ! Who was it that kept the family when Da died, eh? Who gave up university to build up a crappy little company? But that doesn't count anymore in your eyes. All you can see is that I'm not Tom, that I'm not what you have in mind for a son. That's the bloody truth of it, and you know it!" He came back at her, voice lowered as much as he could. He was shaking with the intensity of his feelings, the bitter injustice of it all.

Chapter 28

The atmosphere was electric in the room; Graeme found it too hot and small, he wanted to get up and pace around. His mother had flushed cheeks, remaining erect in the chair she was seething inside.

"How dare you. I've treated you and Christine equally, as my children, whom I love," her voice unsteady.

"Ach, the great equality story again. How many times do you think I've heard it now, fifty? More? I don't know, but I'll tell you now that it's a lie; I know it, you know it, and Christine knows it. We understood Da's death, it made sense to us, and we all tried to fill the gap after he went. We had been prepared for it- we knew that nothing further could be done for him.

Then Tom is murdered and Christine and I soon find out that not only have we lost our brother, but our mother too. Oh don't shake your head at me, you know fine well that after his death you went away from us emotionally and never came back.

We've talked you know, Christine and I, talked about feeling guilty for being alive when Tom isn't. Wondering which one of us you'd have missed least." Graeme stopped.

He couldn't go on to describe how shut out he'd felt by his mother. Didn't want to say that it started when Tom was born, how jealous he had been of his little brother. His world had changed and he hated it: hated the amount of attention lavished on Tom, unaware that he had received the same, if not more. Christine, well, she was the girl, that was alright. Then Tom is dead and within days is a saint. A saint forever; perfect in her eyes; he could never compete with that. He had done his best though, offering what he could, knowing that she didn't want him.

"Graeme, leave it alone, don't push this further. I did

what I could for the pair of you – I didn't give a damn about property, belongings, they were an irrelevance. But you two, you were all that was left, and I did my best. In bits maybe, but there's no handbook for parenting, you can only do the best you can," she pleaded.

She didn't want to hear what he was saying; she knew that there was some truth in there that she'd rather not go into. Like most mothers, she tried not to show preference; obviously she'd made a mess of this one.

"Yes, let's leave it alone when it gets too near the truth. Mum, you always preferred Tom, and we all knew it. His death changed all of us in every way, nothing was ever the same, try as we might to pretend otherwise."

That was a statement, and Olivia nodded, in acceptance. What was the point now in denying it?

CHAPTER 29

Fiona's back in town

'Fiona looks great,' her father thought, as she got into the back of the Rolls to join him. She'd had the best of everything, and it showed; whatever the 'shots' were that she'd had, they had done the job. She looked like his daughter again – fresh eyed and alert, beautifully groomed and chic.

"All set darling?" Carswell asked, taking her hand for a moment.

"Yes, Daddy, I'm ready," said Fiona, as the car moved smoothly off down the drive and through the gates. They were on their way to London, back to Islington

She was nervous about returning. She hadn't seen Mark since that night, and her attempts to talk to him on the 'phone had failed.

Part of her problem was that she couldn't really remember a lot of what had happened: the drunk's amnesia after the drunk's destruction leaving her unsure of the detail. She knew that it had been really bad because of how her father had been towards her afterwards. There had been a change, a shift in how he treated her which had come as a shock. She'd always played at being 'Daddy's girl' – it had worked well for her, all of her life. Not anymore though; as soon as she was sober enough, her Daddy had turned stern and firm, not at all what she'd wanted. His new doctor had been a nightmare too; he'd been awful about giving her a 'little something' to help her, pushing her instead towards a bloody shrink who didn't even approve of any drugs. Despite herself, she had improved; but inside, all she ever thought about was how to get her hands on some alcohol – her body was screaming for it.

"Don't worry, Mark knows you're coming and is going

to try to be there to meet us. I thought perhaps it would be better if I was there to help at the start," she heard him say.

"Did you speak to him?" She asked, having tried the night before without any success; he had ignored her messages, again.

"Yes, I had a quick word with him last night; he's incredibly busy at present apparently, but was pleased to hear that you are so much better – and you are, Fiona. You look fantastic." Carswell had had more than a quick word with his son in law, they had talked regularly during Fiona's stay. He had developed a lot of respect for Mark, for his ability to cope with his daughter.

"Huh, I doubt it. He has avoided having anything to do with me," came the whiney response.

It irritated her father to hear her tone; everyone had done their damnedest to sort out her mess, dropping everything to deal with it. He was swift to stop her continuing;

"I think he needed to have some space, to let things cool down. He's a good man, Fiona, who has put up with some pretty dreadful behaviour on your part for a long time, and don't you forget it." His voice was firm; he'd been on a very steep learning curve with regard to his daughter, finally having to face reality.

It had started the night when he had gone to fetch her; he'd never seen anything like it. She was a total wreck, a sodden heap of alcohol, blood and rage. The damage to the home had been shocking, but money fixed all of that easily. Not so easy to fix Fiona, to listen to an honest doctor's description of what he had tried to ignore for years.

'She's a chronic alcoholic, who cannot survive if she continues drinking at this rate. Her liver will pack up – it's inevitable. Drink to her is almost as important as oxygen,

Chapter 29

she believes it allows her to function. The next few weeks will be crucial for her, and her support system must be in place otherwise she will slip, no question.'

'In my opinion alcohol is one of the most addictive of substances, as bad as any Class A drug. She is a junkie, Mr. Carswell, and also has deep seated psychiatric problems which I believe are to do with the birth of her son. She must be helped on both fronts, one is not enough.'

He had heard the man, and though upset, had at once arranged to meet with his son-in-law. Taking him to his club for dinner, he had first apologised for pestering him to visit Fiona. Mark had been appreciative of his gesture, and had allowed himself to be gently pumped for information over an excellent meal.

It had been a detached discussion for him; despite revealing dreadful rows and recriminations Mark had been able to distance himself emotionally. He felt sorry for Carswell in a sense, but hadn't forgotten, either, the man's utter refusal to be told anything in the past. He would help but wouldn't be cajoled into continuing the farce. It wasn't the time to say it, he would wait until Fiona was more stable; meanwhile, they both shared the common interest of trying to save her from herself.

"I'm sorry Daddy, I didn't mean to sound so pathetic. I'm just anxious about meeting him, you know; I am trying really hard, I never want this to happen again." Fiona was back-pedalling, seeking a way to soften him up. She was glad the chauffeur couldn't overhear her, it would make her feel a little uncomfortable.

"That's better," said her father. "I know you're apprehensive, but you don't need to be. Mark wants you to get better, to help you get there. We all just have to take it slowly, darling, one day at a time, and I do know how hard you've been trying, I'm proud of your efforts." Fiona basked in his approval.

After half an hour she couldn't wait any longer.

"I'm afraid I'm going to have to have a pit stop Daddy, I drank far too much tea this morning. Don't care if it's the dreaded service station!" she added, as Carswell spoke to the chauffeur.

Minutes later she got out of the car, watched by them both as she hurried towards the building. It was hard to believe her prognosis; she looked so well.

"Well James, we've done it again – but God, was it a close call," said Carswell quietly. James had been with him on every one of Fiona's disasters; from lifting her, wrapped in blankets, as she clawed at him, to cleaning up her sick and mess – he had dealt with it all.

"It was indeed, sir. Let's hope she can keep going," James replied, knowing already that it was doomed.

The two men were comfortable together. After years of sharing each other's company there was little they didn't know about each other. Carswell had employed James when others wouldn't, his compulsive gambling making him unreliable in their eyes. Carswell had given him the chance, and miraculously he had held on to the job. Looking after Fiona was something few would do, but he saw it as a paying back for the odd times when he slipped. He understood addiction better than Carswell, had felt the sweat of aching want.

Meanwhile, Fiona hurried along to the 'Ladies', past the inevitable 'floor washing in progress' sign, and locked the cubicle door. She dumped her bag on the cistern, quickly unzipping it. The crack of the seal breaking on the

Chapter 29

miniature was a joy to her. She swallowed the vodka, coughing as it went down. Oh the kick, the sheer pleasure of the warmth hitting her. She opened another, and happily stood in the filthy graffiti'ed space.

She had had to work so hard to get the stuff, it had cost her a bloody fortune to bribe James. She kept her distance from him; he was the chauffeur, she was the boss's daughter, and she liked it that way. She didn't like the closeness of the relationship between her father and James. In fact she didn't really like her father getting close to anyone other than her and her brother.

She had been glad when her parents had divorced; aged seven, she had decided that her mother wasn't worthy of her father. In her little head it made perfect sense, but she never said it out loud, something told her it wouldn't be right. Like with her brother, when he'd told her to keep their little games in bed a secret, that it wouldn't be right to let anyone know, she had understood.

"But Daddy, my Daddy," she whispered to herself, opening another bottle. She half giggled at her supply of miniatures; they'd cost 200 quid! but it was worth every penny – of Daddy's money.

She idolised him, his strength, and his achievements, even his smell. He was the perfect man in her eyes, how could she ever have thought that someone as insignificant as Mark Bateson could come anywhere near his level?

Four minis later she emerged, warmed up, checking herself in the mirror, glad that the moronic public were few in number. Avoiding James' eye, she got back into the car.

"Better?" asked her father.

"Ohh, much, thanks Daddy, much," she replied, and it was true, she felt wonderful.

James drove them the rest of the way, aware of the silence in the back. He had to have the money, had to pay his gambling debt. She had to have the drink.

True to his word, Mark was at home, watching for the car from the drawing room window. He hurried out to meet them, helping to bring the luggage in. The bustle of arrival covered the awkwardness, helped them over the first hurdle.

"Thank you James, I'll call you when I'm ready to leave," said Carswell, as the final bag came in.

"Very good sir, " and the chauffeur was gone, glad to get offside. He didn't envy Mark one bit; Fiona Carswell was a nasty piece of work in his eyes. Rude and spoilt, with such a bitter spiteful side to her, she was bound to blow it, again.

"Tea or coffee?" Mark asked them as Fiona looked around the kitchen; everything was different, new and smart.

"I'd prefer a cold drink actually; tonic and ice please, Mark," came her demure answer. She knew that every trace of alcohol would have been removed from the house, her little stashes uncovered and thrown out. It didn't worry her much; she had enough supplies for the day.

Her husband busied himself with their drinks, looking healthy and well, making small talk with her father. She took her drink and went through their home, room by room. It all looked perfect, so cool, stylish, and sterile. There was no warmth in the place, no evidence that anyone actually lived there. She checked out the flower arrangement in the drawing room; large and expensive, it was of course from her father. No sign of anything from Mark, but then what did she expect?

Their bathroom had been re-tiled. As she stood in its doorway, she had a flashback, a sudden unpleasant picture of herself on the floor. Turning off the lights quickly she closed

Chapter 29

the door on it and looked round their bedroom.

'Mark doesn't sleep here', she thought, as she ran her eye over the room. Nothing of his was in evidence and she immediately knew where to look. Down the corridor to Chris's room, and there it all was; the books and the reading glasses, the pile of magazines beside the bed, and the smell of his aftershave in the bathroom.

'Right. At least I know,' she thought. In some way it took away some of the pressure, she'd had no idea how they would be able to share the home, never mind the bed. Tour completed, she went to find them.

"Thank you for the flowers Daddy, they're beautiful," she said, on entering the drawing room. Carswell smiled at her, trying to look relaxed, but Mark was watchful.

He knew she wouldn't comment on the changes, the replacements – she never did. In her mind she'd just trashed a few things – why dwell on it? He'd never succeeded in getting her to take any responsibility for the damage she did. As long as the Carswell chequebook was available to her, she did as she pleased. After all, his salary wouldn't even cover her annual credit card bills, as she reminded him often.

He'd spent as little time as possible in the place; coming home to sleep, leaving for work early. Now as he watched his wife across the room he felt nothing other than tension. He hadn't got her anything to mark her return; what was it a return to? It couldn't be more of the same, and they all knew that. As he watched her he had to admire her style, she was playing the scene perfectly. The father still had a lot to learn about his daughter.

Conversation was laboured; there were few safe topics and Carswell's departure later made little difference. Each had their reasons for not wanting to start the inevitable discussion, and Mark was delighted to leave the room to take a 'phone call.

When he came back he found she had gone to the bedroom, leaving the door ajar. He could see that she was unpacking.

"Oh, there you are," he said, standing outside in the corridor. "I've come to see what you'd like for dinner; I've got a few bits in from M & S – I didn't have the time to go anywhere else, but…"

"I'm not particularly hungry, thanks Mark. I was thinking of finishing this and having a long bath. You go ahead, I'll come and find something later." Fiona replied quickly, not wanting them to try and eat together; Mark was relieved, he felt the same.

Fiona had stopped laying out her things to look at him; she was exhausted by all the tension, and sad that they had come to this; polite avoidance or drunken violence – some choice.

"Okay, I'll go and let you finish. Enjoy your bath," and with that, Mark quietly closed the door and left.

She finished off quickly. Running the bath slowly gave her time to check what had been found, or missed, in the hunt for her drink supplies. It was like a perverse game of hide and seek between them. He had done well this time; he'd probably been helped by Daddy's bloody housekeeper she thought; everything was gone, nothing remained;

'Shit!' she muttered, as she went to the bathroom and fetched the glass. Methodically she poured four miniatures into it and sat on the end of the bed. She could do without the tonic and ice. Tomorrow she'd check out her best hiding place – Mark's study.

CHAPTER 30

Figures

"It must be like winning the bloody lottery," Dun announced, "everyone a winner, so long as you're one of them."

"What have you got there?" Olivia asked, sitting in the corner of Dun's kitchen. They'd just got in from shopping up the Walworth Road, the kettle was on and Dun had been scanning the newspaper while she waited.

"It's a piece in the paper about the Bloody Sunday inquiry. The whole thing is turning into some kind of fucking farce – forget about what it's meant to be doing, all it ever does is waste money. You were out of date, Olivia, about the charges bloody lawyers make. Have a look at this!" Dun brought the paper over, and the two women read on.

"How can something like that cost over a hundred and twenty million pounds?"

"Where does it all go?" Their questions came out simultaneously.

The article shocked them; like many they knew the inquiry was still rumbling on, with major games being played all round; it was a disgrace. How expensive a one they hadn't known – like most people.

"Well it says here that over fifty per cent goes to the lawyers – sixty million pounds for services rendered, and they hope to be finished in a few more months! After more than six years of being paid about 1,500 pounds an hour, you'd bloody hope they would!" Olivia was disgusted, it seemed an obscenity to her that so much money was being made out of misery.

"I reckon they'll drag it out a bit longer, who really wants it to end?" Dun asked her, pouring the tea and passing Olivia her mug.

Olivia couldn't answer, she was thinking about what Graeme had told her at Christmas.

'You wouldn't believe where some of my old friends have ended up. They've landed the job of a lifetime – part of the legal team on the inquiry. Compared to them, Mum, I'm some poor lad scraping a living. They are just creaming it, they can charge whatever they like. Two of them reckoned that when it's over they'll probably retire.'

He had been so impressed; she was depressed. It seemed so immoral to her, and yet she hadn't even tried to change her son's attitude.

"Who indeed, Dun. When it stops, what will they do?" Olivia asked.

Dun shrugged; in her head it wouldn't make sense to stop anything so lucrative.

"It won't. When they finish this one, there'll be another inquiry to start up, you'll see. Sad people, trying to find out the truth, will be conned all over again, and the legal bods will make another fucking fortune on the back of it. It's the way it is over there; one way or the other, high or low, real money is being made out of the Troubles. People in that set-up will not want it to end – why would they?"

Dun's thoughts were with Sam Hudson; he could never revert back to what he once had been, an agricultural worker on the minimum wage. He'd had the good life for too long, had forgotten who he was. He couldn't live without the trappings that terrorism had brought him. Christ, he'd worked hard enough for them.

"Come on, let's finish off the morning on a happier note. You're right Dun, it all sucks, as you would say, and I don't want to spend any more of our time on it. Go and try on your outfit. Let's see if we've got what we needed." Olivia

CHAPTER 30

cut in, taking their mugs to the sink. Dun was happy to agree; passing her spliff over to Olivia, she took the bag and went off to change. Minutes later she was back, looking respectable if not conservative.

Olivia had totally ruled out any idea of making Dun wear a skirt. She had chosen black trousers, and had accepted that Dun could only wear a black tee shirt on top; she had biceps and bulk that made working in a long-sleeved top impossible. The long white apron, from waist to mid-calf made it look smarter.

"That'll do nicely, Dun. You look the part, but we'll have to sort out your hair as well," she said, pleased at how they'd done. Shopping for clothes with Dun was a nightmare, but this morning she had really made an effort.

"Yeah, it's not bad, but I'm not having my hair touched. I'll wash it, but that's it. I fucking hate those places, they always make such a song and dance over my scar." Dun sounded hacked off, and Olivia knew when best to leave it.

"Sorry Dun, I forgot, it doesn't matter at all. You do what you like on that front," adding:

"I mean, in the great scheme of things it won't count for much will it!!" The laugh was forced; she felt the whole thing was surreal.

Part of her couldn't really believe that she was finalising the planning of a murder, that within a matter of days she would be a killer; it didn't feel like that to her. She felt bemused by it all, carried along by Dun; and in another way, driving Dun to satisfy her own revenge. In her old world, she'd have been living like so many elderly Ulster matrons; an early round of golf in the morning, lunch with her cronies, and a rubber of bridge in the evening – respectable and law abiding.

But that was her problem, she didn't have any respect for what was going on, she was sick of it, and sickened by it all. Let them get on with it, she was going soon and was glad.

"Hey, c'mon, Olivia, we're going to sort it. We're both just completely wound up about it all and we don't have to be, I'm telling you, we don't." Dun came over to her, placing a heavy hand on her shoulder.

"Listen, I've picked up the last of the stuff I need; there is nothing more for us to do other than turn up, then I'll do exactly as we've planned. You know what you have to do and when. We're going to make our mark, we're not going to be stopped." Her squeeze was as gentle as she could make it.

"Oh don't worry Dun, it was just a momentary lapse," replied Olivia;

"A bit of my mind is buzzing with the 'what ifs?' and another bit is just so calm about it all. I believe we're in the right here fundamentally. I mean, 'an eye for an eye' sounded right to me when I was little, it made sense. That sort of thinking got buried along the way, covered up by endless politically correct notions. The result is that there is no justice, not for people like me. So, I am ready, believe me." She touched the hand briefly, as Dun moved away.

"There is one thing though, that I want you to know, that you have to accept. It's what I want. "

"Hang on," said Dun, "let me change out of this first," not wanting to hear what was coming next. Olivia waited patiently.

"Now, sit down and let's get this over with," she said, on Dun's return.

"I have, as they say, put my affairs in order. I went to see Jack Solomon and have made my new will. It is all very simple, and as I wish it to be; Christine and you are my sole heirs.

CHAPTER 30

"No, don't interrupt, this is important. I have already sent Christine some money, and she will have my house. You will have the rest of the money, and certain items from the house, that I know you would like. If not, flog them! I won't know, will I?"

"You know I don't want anything, Olivia," Dun tried to cut in.

"That's not the point, it's what I want you to have. It'll be enough to help make things a bit easier for you, no matter where you might be. Just accept my wishes, please." Olivia asked gently, and Dun agreed. She didn't bother asking her about Graeme.

CHAPTER 31

Thursday

"No, I can't make it at all today, I've got deliveries coming and I really need to be here to check. Any chance of lunch tomorrow?" Eleanor asked hopefully.

With Fiona back in town Mark had been preoccupied, so brief on the telephone that she couldn't really tell how he was; she needed to see him for herself.

"Yes, as early as you like, and we'll go to my little Italian haunt, you know, Charlotte Street?" She was delighted to hear him agree, and even more pleased when he'd added that he was missing her. Ringing off, she went back to work, feeling great.

She loved entertaining; getting the house ready this morning was a pleasure for her. Despite the politics of the party, she'd enjoy making sure that her guests would get the best hospitality possible. Methodically working through her lists, with Graeme out of the way, she was in her element. Useless at reading a map, or even finding the car in a car park, this was what she excelled at.

'I love being in control of it all,' she thought as she went back into the hall.

Currently the storage area, it was stacked with various containers. All checked, she'd started moving them through to the kitchen when she heard Graeme's car in the drive.

'Oh blast.. he's early'

"How's it going ? Need a hand ?" He called, as he came to find her.

"No, it's fine – once I've done this lot. That just leaves the tables and chairs – which you're doing tomorrow morning….." Eleanor gave him time to nod but not speak.

"So before the food arrives, I'm going get started

CHAPTER 31

on clearing the dining room," she added, wishing she'd been able to do it earlier.

"Hang on," said Graeme, "Jack's due in, and I thought we'd all eat.. .."

"No chance – dinner's informal tonight. I've far too much to do, and anyway Jack likes nothing better than a meal in the kitchen with old friends," she told him firmly. Graeme let it go, retreating to his study.

She'd already prepared bedrooms for Christine and Jack Barnes, glad that Christine would be the first to arrive. Her call the day before had confirmed that it would be just her, no man. Eleanor had felt the sadness in her voice, and had responded gently.

'No, you just come when you're ready. It'll do you good to get away from Galway for a few days. Let me know when your flight is due in and I'll have a driver waiting for you. No, it's no trouble, Christine, just get on the plane.'

Christine's reply was a muffled agreement, she would be early; Eleanor could tell she was in tears.

'Alright then, see you tomorrow', was all she could say before the line went dead.

It'll be alright, she told herself; they'd have a chance to talk before Jack arrived, with any luck.

Jack Barnes was due in at Heathrow at 7pm, that was Graeme's next task and it was hours away. He knew that there were plenty of other things that he should be getting on with, but it was impossible to settle to anything. Moving round his study, half-heartedly putting papers away; his mind was on the plane over the Atlantic, the Liberian registered ship off the west coast of Ireland, and as for the Belfast contingent... He shook himself, the mixture of paranoia and adrenalin racing through him was as close to being on speed as he'd ever know.

***

Fiona too was in a study, only unlike Graeme, it wasn't hers. With Mark safely off to work she was able to poke around in peace.

'Let's see how thorough they were then,' she muttered, as she went over to his desk. She snooped periodically, like most insecure wives; the careful checking of suit pockets and desk drawers, wallets if possible, and the credit card statements. They were all part of being a wife, Fiona style.

'Not quite so smart, Mark,' she said, as her fingers found her emergency bottle behind his desk. She left it where it was, so pleased he hadn't found it. Pulling out the chair she sat down at the desk, and tried the handles of the drawers.

It was in the bottom right one that she found them, folded away, the receipts. She knew it couldn't be work, those were always sent off for re-imbursement. These dates were for when she hadn't been in town, when Mark had been too busy to take her calls.

'Christ! He's got another woman, he must have; he's having a bloody affair!' She exclaimed as she read each one carefully: the dinners for two in places she'd never heard of, the items from Liberty's, it was all there in order. Replacing them exactly as she had found them, she closed the drawer and left the room, shocked and in a hurry to check his other stuff. She couldn't find anything in his room despite going through everything meticulously, but she knew she was right. What she'd always imagined in the past was real now.

Chapter 31

'I need to get hold of his mobile, I need to know,' was her decision, but achieving it would be tough; Mark was being caring towards her, but was so wary.

'He treats me as though I'm some sort of patient or relative that he ought to take care of,' she thought, and she was right there too.

Mark was playing a holding game, keeping it all together for the next few days. He no longer saw her as a woman he'd had to have, and marry; that person had died long ago. He was being kind, and they both knew it.

★★★

For Dun, however, it was such a good day; she'd managed to sleep for more than four hours and felt rested. She hadn't been using her bed lately, preferring her chair in the sitting room, feeling less vulnerable there. It was the undressing for bed that made her feel unsafe, ever since she was tiny. That was when the bad things had first started happening to her.

'Let's not go there,' she told herself; too charged up to let those memories come back, it was better that she keep the important ones to the fore.

'Just keep your mind on the job; don't start losing the fucking plot now,' came the mutter from behind her hands as she rubbed her face awake.

Her excitement was building as the day got nearer, sometimes she had difficulty in holding it all together as it grew bigger inside her head. She could feel it, like a heavy lump pushing for space in her skull. Her pacing helped, as it had so often in the past; with arms wrapped tightly round herself she would walk the tiny

Thursday

flat, round and round, giving herself a good talking to for most of the night.

'Killing's different, it makes it clean,' was her claim. She'd found it'd worked before.

CHAPTER 32

Friday

"Oh Mark, I'm so glad to see you!" Eleanor hugged him on the pavement regardless of who might see them. The traffic crawled past, inching out on to the Tottenham Court Road.

"God, have I missed you! How are you?" Came his smiling answer as he held her close.

"Oh I'm a mixture of efficiency and chaos. What about you?"

Mark laughed and pulled her towards the door of the restaurant.

"Come on, let's get a table and we can swap notes," was all he would say.

Mark could see that Eleanor was at home in the little place, greeted by the owner as she entered, they'd been quickly seated and drinks ordered. She'd laughed at the flattery as he made a show of pouring their wine. As he retreated, Eleanor and Mark toasted each other.

"I've been coming here since the kids were little, you know. This was one of the few places that would welcome me, infant and buggy. It's simple and good food, and Paolo always tells me that I haven't changed a bit in over twenty years, which is definitely a bonus!"

Mark watched her, admiring the woman; he loved seeing the change in her when she relaxed, the life in her face. He reached across the table and took her hand in his.

"I know which bit of you is in chaos, Eleanor. It doesn't need to be a problem, it really doesn't."

"I don't think you do Mark." She looked up at him.

"Try me," he said, withdrawing his hands and lifting his glass. This was their first chance to talk privately since it had happened.

FRIDAY

"It's something that we have to talk about, and for me it's much more important than any party or my domestic crap," he added. He'd been worried about what it meant, that perhaps she didn't feel the same way after all. Eleanor shook her head as if reading his mind.

"No, it's not what you think, you're wrong. – Listen, I just didn't know how to tell you – still don't. It's all such a mixture of emotions and embarrassment…"

"Embarrassment?!" Mark nearly raised his voice. "How could you possibly have felt embarrassed?"

"Yes, don't laugh, it's pretty real for me. I panicked that night when you suggested that I stay overnight in Pimlico. I was worried about everything; my age, my lack of experience in bed…."

They both recalled the evening; it had gone so well with dinner and talk, with a late coffee and brandy in Mark's temporary home. They'd had the place to themselves, and Mark had tried so hard to get her to stay the night with him. From the close warmth of the sofa, where they'd been curled up together, it was yards to his room but it might as well have been miles. She had withdrawn completely on him, leaving soon afterwards in a taxi, apologising as it drew away. He'd been left wondering what had gone so wrong, whereas she had sniffed throughout her journey home, miserable.

"You're unbelievable Eleanor, how could you have thought like that? I've been worried that perhaps I'd got it wrong, and yet didn't want to believe it. You know how I feel about you – you do… " Mark was deadly serious – Eleanor came clean.

"It wasn't just those things, there was something else and I didn't want to disgust you," was her opening, and Mark

Chapter 32

listened as she told him, feeling her pain.

When she had finished he wanted to thump Graeme Ward; instead he leaned across the table and kissed her.

"Eleanor, stop worrying about it; it's something we can check out soon and put your mind to rest – and I'm really glad you've told me. I just wish that you'd been able to tell me earlier," he said softly.

"Oh I know, I wanted to Mark, but there was never the right time – God, is there ever a right time for that sort of news !?"

"True enough. Well right now, strange as it might seem to you, I feel happier than I've felt in days. I thought it was going to be much worse, that you don't fancy me…."

Eleanor looked at him, full of relief and shaking her head at his comment.

"No… you know that isn't true Mark. I've never played around in my life; this is no silly game for me, I want to be with you, even if I am nervous." Her eyes confirmed the words and Mark beamed. Nervousness he could handle, given time.

Their food arrived and they ate, drank, and flirted outrageously with each other, relieved and happy. It was so innocent and silly, in sharp contrast to what they were each going home to deal with.

"I feel like a kid sometimes, wondering what you're up to and will you phone or not, what's happening with Fiona, will you sort it out. It's a revolving list, and .."

Before she could say any more Mark cut in:

"I've got a similar one about you, Eleanor, but my list just lost one worry, and that has helped. Like you, I don't play games or mess around, it's a huge step for me too, but one that is long overdue. Fiona and I were dead long before any of this. She only wants it to go on because she's safe, looked after. Frankly it could be anyone doing the caring – by the end of the evening she doesn't even know who I am half the time. I've already told her father that I'm leaving and it's final." Mark paused, Eleanor was obviously surprised to hear what he'd done.

"How did he take it?" she asked, "I mean when I told Olivia about not staying with Graeme, she was remarkably okay about it."

"Because she knows what you live with, and Carswell knows what I live with. Neither of them sees the whole picture, but what they have seen helps them understand how bad it is. Between us we've put in a lifetime of clearing up after their children, one way or the other. He understands why I want out, but obviously would prefer me to stay. It wasn't the easiest of meetings when I told him."

"I can imagine – but it's done now and that's a start. Come on Mark – life starts after this bloody party – and I can't wait…" Eleanor smiled at him, squeezing his arm.

"How's it all going anyway? You're nearly there – this time tomorrow it'll be the rugby, and then…"Mark shrugged.

"And then it'll really kick off," said Eleanor;

"Actually, I think I'm doing quite well; I have two contented houseguests, I've got the house the way I want it, and will start my cooking later when I leave you. I've also cancelled my hair appointment because I'd rather spend the time here with you, and I have no idea what I'll wear tomorrow night – but apart from that it's all going to plan! What about you?" She smiled up at him, finishing her drink.

"Well, Fiona and I co-exist in our super smart home.

Chapter 32

She's apparently seeing a therapist; we are polite and civilised, and I know that she's still drinking – not much, but definitely some. She has been ordered to behave, and is trying, but it won't last. I've been there so many times before. Unlike you, she has spent a fortune on what she's wearing tomorrow, and right now is probably in The Sanctuary being pampered. I think that she's making a big effort not to screw up again with Graeme ……"

"I doubt if they'll have much to do with each other really; he'll be busy fussing over his new business partner and she won't be seated anywhere near them, believe me."

Eleanor meant it, food was meant to be enjoyed; she'd worked hard on her seating plan so that Fiona was nowhere near Graeme. Mark nodded with approval.

"Good, though I don't really believe that there'll be a repetition, she's a lot calmer these days. You know, I do feel sorry for her – but that's all. It isn't a good enough reason to carry on and though I dread the inevitable scene….. I've got to get a life, and honestly – I'd like that life to be shared with you." Mark hadn't intended to be so direct, but seeing Eleanor's face right now he was glad he had.

"God – that makes me feel a bit nervous – and happy too. I want the same, but there's a long way to go, and Graeme will make it as hard for me as he can. It doesn't matter that I gave him everything I had, he can never get enough – money, power, women. It's a sick situation but it's over, after this weekend. That's as long as I can handle this farce."

Eleanor was suddenly full of it; she hated the knowledge that she had gone along with such arrogance and deceit.

"Oh come on Eleanor, let's just enjoy being together right now. Let's face it, we've both been had. We can't change what's gone before, but we can make the future happen if we want," was Mark's answer, not wanting her to lose the happiness. She nodded at him,

"You're right, what's done is done, but God it annoys me nonetheless. As you say, 'let's look forward', well, I am trying…." she gave a little shrug.

"I know you are, and don't stop whatever you do – eh?" Mark's hand had reached for hers again, she loved the feel of his strong fingers playing with hers. They sat for the last few minutes of their time together, touching and looking.

"I have to go, Mark."

"Me too," he answered, as they reluctantly came back to reality.

"I've got people to see, and you've got people to cook for. How's your American guest settling in?" He asked as he settled the bill.

"Och, he's easy. Jack likes home cooking, old houses and reminiscences. I've always got on well with him, he's actually good company. No, he's no problem; it's Christine who's a bit down though." Eleanor gathered up her bag.

'Bit down' didn't come close to describing it; Graeme had already told his sister to 'pull yourself together, for Christ's sake.' In contrast, Eleanor had spent hours listening to her.

"I've only met her a couple of times, I think," said Mark, as they moved towards the door.

"She's totally different isn't she? I mean, compared to her brother…"

"They have nothing in common except their mother, and that isn't enough," said Eleanor, having heard plenty the night before.

Christine had talked; it had come out of her at such a

CHAPTER 32

rate, a spewing out of what had hurt and damaged her, and it had had nothing to do with the amount of alcohol taken. She had hollow legs that one, could drink for hours or not at all; she decided which. Either way she was sharp. Eleanor had been surprised at how much her sister-in-law knew. Graeme would've been shocked, but for Eleanor, it gave her hope.

"Anyway, I'd better get back and start working. Christine can help me with the preparations and we'll get a chance to talk some more. She is nice, you're right, but not happy at all. With Graeme and Jack out tonight with the Belfast boy – he's due in this evening – we can have the place to ourselves and maybe I can cheer her up a bit," said Eleanor, looking round for a taxi. He held her close and kissed her gently.

"See you tomorrow then, and just keep the future in your head," he said, before opening the door for her.

"I will Mark, and don't be late. This hostess regards late guests with hostility!"

With that she left, much happier. Mark turned to walk back to his office; he was unaware of Thomas following him, already talking on his mobile to Drake.

CHAPTER 33

Friday, Belfast

"Yes I know, I know, yes, I've got it, yes. Look, there's nothing more that I can check. I can't tell you any more than I've already told you. Okay, yes, I'll 'phone you tonight when I've seen them both. Right then Kevin, leave it with me. Yes, I will..." Sam Hudson ended the call as his wife came into the room. She could feel his annoyance from the doorway.

"What is it, Stella? I'm busy right now," he snapped, before she could open her mouth.

He was at his wits end with the hassle of this deal. Kevin, his brother-in-law, wouldn't leave him alone, couldn't let him get on with it. Endless pointless bloody phone calls when all he wanted to do was concentrate on his part. Everyone was the same, the anticipation of this delivery meant that they were all running round like headless chickens.

"I only came to tell you that I've packed your case for you and that your tea's ready..." Stella got it out in a rush, he made her nervous when he was like this; she never knew how he would react. Could be a smack on the mouth for disturbing him, or he could be nice – what it depended on she could never work out.

Despite all her efforts these past few weeks to stay out of his way, to keep him happy, she'd often felt his fist as his frustration grew. She'd be glad when whatever he was up to was over.

"Good. Did you do them shirts the way I showed you?" Sam asked, coming towards her. She flinched as he got closer and it pleased him, she'd been so easy to train.

"Yes Sam, and I've put your good shoes in a wee bag, like you said." Her eagerness to please wound him up, made him

Chapter 33

worse. She irritated him, this pathetic door-mat looking for praise.

"I don't want any tea, after all; I'm heading off early to the airport. There'll be a car coming for me in a wee while – did you put the case in the hall?" he asked as she stood back to let him pass. Her disappointment was plain to see, she'd made him his favourite food as he'd asked. That pleased him, and kept her in her place. He watched her scuttle upstairs to fetch his case.

"Right, look after yourself," was his parting advice as the door closed behind him with a bang. Stella sat at the bottom of the stairs, letting out the breath that she hadn't realised she was holding in. She rang her son as soon as the sound of the car faded. Living locally he was there in minutes, able to visit his mother only when Sam was absent.

"Ma...Christ almighty, what's the bastard done to you this time?!" The young man was livid at the sight of his mother, her face mottled with old and new bruising, grip marks on her wrists, an eye still puffy. Holding her in his arms, he could feel the trembling in the thin body.

They had all suffered throughout the marriage, Sam meting out his justice as he saw fit – but it was Stella who'd borne the brunt. Taking beatings to protect her kids, shielding her son from Sam's irrational jealousy as he grew up – she'd paid, again and again. He and his sister had their own lives now, but his mother stayed on.

"This has got to stop Ma, you have to get out – he'll kill you one day – he will..."

Stella couldn't answer him, could only shake her head and look down. How could she possibly leave? Who would be willing to help her knowing who her old man was? And the thing that frightened her most of all – Sam's threat:

Friday, Belfast

'Tell anyone, and you'll regret it. Try to leave… and I'll have you, and yours, fuckin' shot.' Stella believed him.

Sam, meanwhile, had been delivered to the airport; passing through all the security checks he headed straight for the bar, his mood improving slightly. Turning his 'phone off after Kevin's last call had helped – that and getting away from the bloody house. Nursing his drink, he went through the list in his head.

It wasn't the business itself that wound him up so much as all the palaver surrounding it, he decided. It wasn't his scene at all; off his own patch, with a bunch of snobby gits, eating posh food and talking about fuck all.

'Christ, give me a hard meeting in East Belfast any day over that lot,' he thought, 'at least there I'd know what the score was.'

The fact that it was all in Graeme Ward's control was the other major worry; the man had better get it right.

'Or he's fuckin' dead,' and with that thought, Sam went to join the queue to board the plane.

Watching him go up the steps and disappear inside the aircraft, the man in the terminal waited until it had taxied down the runway before making the call;

"Hullo, it's me. Due in an hour."

"Okay."

He hung up immediately and walked briskly away, paying no attention to the woman waiting for the 'phone. She dialled the number quickly, and spoke briefly;

"Yis, I seen him. Yis, for sure. I'll find the car nar."

CHAPTER 34

Friday evening

Jack Barnes took his time getting ready. Showering after his sleep that afternoon he was calmer, looking forward to the evening out. He and Graeme had talked that morning, able to discuss the details without fear of being listened in on. His friend was stressed out, true, but it hadn't affected his business acumen. As they had paced the garden in Putney they had gone over their plan and had come up with only one concern, and that was currently beyond their control.

"Let it be, Graeme, we'll have the confirmation by the time the match is over," was Jack's advice and belief, and Graeme made an effort to go along with him.

"Yes, I know, it's all in the lap of the gods right now, I just hope to God your man doesn't blow it. When I think of how it's going to be, afterwards……"

"That's it, don't look down – I'm not. Just keep the picture of your new life in your head, not another worry for as long as you live..." Jack put his arm round his friend's shoulder. Christine, watching them from her bedroom window, had been surprised by their closeness.

Hearing them come in she went downstairs to meet up with them in the kitchen. With Jack around, she found it easier to be with Graeme, the emotional dilution caused by another presence restraining them from picking at each other's sore points.

"Hi, I was going to make some more coffee, any takers?" she asked, as they wiped their feet.

"I won't thanks, Christine, I'm planning to get some sleep in after lunch," Jack replied, giving her a smile, pulling out a chair at the table.

"You, Graeme?"

"A small one would be good thanks. Any word on those tables and chairs yet?" he asked as she handed him the mug.

"Don't worry, it's all done, I took delivery while you guys were down the garden. No, don't panic brother, even I can count!" she retorted seeing the look on his face.

"It's all there, it's been checked and signed for. I didn't really think you two would want to be disturbed, so I just got on with it." Christine couldn't believe how stressed out her brother was, for Christ's sake it wasn't exactly rocket science.

Jack had swiftly started talking; talking to ease them away from each other, pulling them into a story. Generally he loved coming to stay in this big family house, so comfortable and welcoming, but this time the whole atmosphere was different, there was nothing but heavy tension everywhere. By the time his tale ended they had calmed enough, their good manners rounding off the job for him. Christine finished her coffee and excused herself, pausing just long enough in the hall to overhear her brother's comment to Jack.

"You've not said a word about the domestic bliss you've walked into." It was a flat comment, the bitterness underneath. Graeme was looking for male support.

"I don't think you'd want to hear my thoughts on that one," was the quiet response.

She decided against listening further, moving quietly up the stairs. Jack was aware of her, waiting until she was out of earshot before he spoke further.

"Just you make bloody sure that nothing, and I mean nothing, you do in the next twenty four hours upsets what we've planned. You've totally hacked Eleanor off, that's painfully obvious, but she'll do it – provided you don't cock

CHAPTER 34

up. Got it?"

Accepting Graeme's nod, he went on,

"Keep her happy and it's one less worry for us. As for you and your sister, well – talk about kicking someone when they're down! You were a mean bastard to her last night, and this morning's not much better. Get a bloody grip on that too."

Graeme had paid attention to Jack, going so far as to take them all out for lunch in Putney by way of a peace offering. Christine had made the effort and it had been a good result in Jack's eyes.

Stepping out of the shower and drying himself, Jack reckoned that he'd handled Graeme pretty well. He'd advised against Graeme's welcome plan for Sam tonight, pushing instead for Graeme to have a quiet dinner with him once Sam had been settled into his hotel.

"He's as uptight as we are, Graeme. Let him have the night to himself; judging by what you've told me about him, he'd probably enjoy room service and the adult channel far more than where I want to take you for dinner…"

He'd left it there, had slept well and now, looking smart in his dark suit, came downstairs, heading straight for the kitchen.

"Hello Jack," said Eleanor coming over to kiss his cheek. Graeme and Christine were busy bringing in boxes from the utility room.

"Are you the one responsible for taking up valuable fridge space?" she teased.

" Hi Eleanor, yes, but only temporarily – I'm going to get them out right now." As he spoke he took the champagne out of the fridge. He knew she adored it; Graeme did too but only served it to impress guests. Eleanor appreciated the thought.

"Lovely! Just what the cook needs... Graeme tells me that you two are going off soon?" she went on, as he began opening the bottle.

"Yes, we're off to collect Mr. Hudson from Heathrow and then we'll see him to his hotel. Did Graeme mention that I'm taking him out for dinner after that?" Jack asked, giving her a glass.

"Yes, I think that's a great idea – I'm going to be working late on this lot. Cheers everybody!" Eleanor made the toast, the others joining in.

The men had left within half an hour, their driver arriving on time. Jack reckoned that it was long enough for everyone to remain pleasant.

"Right, Christine. Now they've gone let's start with another glass of fizz and a new list," Eleanor said, glad to have the house to themselves. Sitting down at the table, she watched her sister-in-law approach with the bottle – Christine looked better, brighter.

"That's fine thanks – I take it Jack's responsible- not just for the fizz?" she asked, as Christine joined her.

"Yes. I'd say Graeme's had his ear bent. He was his usual horrible self and then suddenly we're all off for a friendly lunch. I just went along with it, didn't want to spoil Jack's peacekeeping efforts. My brother is one ignorant shit though !"

"I'll drink to that," said Eleanor swiftly.

"How the hell do you put up with that crap? And can I light up in here?" Christine had been so good about smoking outdoors, now she was dying to have one with her drink.

CHAPTER 34

"Go ahead, I'm making the rules tonight – there's an ashtray on the windowsill".

"As for putting up with stuff, I did it for the sake of the kids, to keep it stable for them. Just as I wanted to bring them up myself, not fobbing them off on a nanny. Olivia was always there for you lot, wasn't she? And her life was no picnic…."

"Och, Daddy was never as bad as Graeme; he just wasn't aware of what Mummy needed, never gave it too much thought, I suppose. But Graeme, he's got a side to him that I find quite cruel. What's that look for?" She asked, as Eleanor pulled a face.

"I was agreeing with you, but only up to a point. You can see your brother's nasty side – sometimes feel it – I live with it. But it wasn't like that in the beginning, he became it over the years. Your father, though, never changed his opinion – in his eyes I was wrong for his son, and that was it – all because of my father. Come on, Christine don't tell me you don't remember?"

"I remember it only too well, it was wrong and yet I went along with it. I've regretted it Eleanor, believe me. I didn't want to believe that Daddy was such a bigot, I suppose…"

"He was dreadful – but despite him Graeme and I started off well and the marriage did work."

"You mean you made it work.."

"Maybe – but I believed that it could last, that it was worth it."

"Do you still believe that?"

"Let's say that Graeme has changed so much that I find it hard to recognise him and leave it there – eh? As for me, I've got the big 'do' tomorrow – which I intend to get right

227

– then I might take a break for a few days…" she smiled at that; a real one.

Christine was surprised at how positive Eleanor sounded, considering everything.

"Funny, I feel like asking you whether you'll even be holidaying with Graeme?" She asked, fishing. Eleanor just smiled again, and ignoring the question, pulled the pad and pen towards her.

"I've got to get started here; look why don't you decide what you'd like to eat tonight, while I start sorting out where I'm going to begin. We can have anything you fancy," she said, pointing to the notice board with the takeaway menus.

Christine took the hint and left off, Eleanor would do it her own way. At least she felt a welcome from her if not from Graeme.

"Fine by me Eleanor, but if you do want to talk about him, I'll listen. You've heard my nightmares, I'd like to help you, if I could."

"Thanks Christine," said Eleanor, and she meant it.

"When I get to the point where I can talk, I might take you up on that. Now let's concentrate on feeding ourselves, that's your job, and then feeding the rest," she added.

Christine went to the 'phone to order. Eleanor's smile was inside her now, as she thought of Mark.

★★★

Heathrow was bunged, and Graeme was glad that he'd made the arrangement with Sam. Crawling off the M4 on to the slip road to the airport they could see complete congestion ahead.

Chapter 34

"Christ, it just gets worse here!" said Jack, "we're going to be seriously late." He looked at Graeme, who shook his head. He'd never had any intention of meeting Sam in the terminal.

"Relax, it's not a problem. I've sent a driver to pick him up and take him to the Holiday Inn, he can wait in the bar. I thought it was best."

"Oh, good one," commented Jack, wondering what else Graeme hadn't told him about, as they inched along. He turned on the radio to listen to the news, both of them alert to any item regarding shipping.

The hotel was busy, with coach loads of passengers cramming the foyer, baggage being unloaded everywhere. They excused their way through to the bar, Graeme spotting Sam over in a corner. The introduction was brief in the extreme, Jack's proferred handshake ignored by Sam, who gave him a nod.

"Right. Good to meet you."

"Yes, and you," replied Jack, dropping his hand. "Good flight?"

Graeme left the pair of them to it as he went to get their drinks, not staying to hear Sam's attempts at small talk – let Jack find out for himself.

They'd only stayed for another drink because of Sam's insistence that he would buy his round, thank you. No-one really wanted it, but he was already on his feet, leading with the chin.

"Don't panic Jack," Graeme said, eying Sam as he went to the bar; "he has no notion of how to talk to people, he really can't do it. But when it comes to business, he's hard to beat. Just have the drink and then we'll leave – otherwise we get into a loss of face game – believe me, he's touchy."

FRIDAY EVENING

Jack listened, watching Sam's approach; 'I hope he's right,' he thought.

Graeme and he had made idle chat, Sam listening but saying little. Needless to say he'd bought them huge drinks – Jack could feel them hitting the champagne.

"Right – let's go… shall we?" Graeme announced as soon as he could. They all needed to talk business.

Quiet during the drive to the Tower hotel, they'd let Sam get on with checking in, joining him in the lift. Graeme had decided to impress, and it succeeded; as Sam opened the door to the suite he was dumbstruck, as Graeme had hoped.

It did look good, all the trimmings and a view of the river. Jack thought it okay, but Sam thought it was the ultimate. Graeme gave him a couple of minutes to check it all out and then called for order.

"Come on, we've got a little bit of business to do, and then we can all relax. Water anyone?" He asked, pulling out a chair at the table.

They joined him and they talked, quietly and purposefully, each one seeing and feeling the strengths of the other. Jack felt reassured, as Sam's sharp mind impressed him. Graeme was super efficient, glad to be actually dealing with something. Sam trusted neither, but would be able to say that so far things had gone moderately well.

"I'd say that that'll do it for today. Next step will be the big one, so let's leave it there and wait for the call, eh?" Graeme announced within the hour. He looked at his watch and seemed pleased. The other two were in agreement and were just standing up when the doorbell rang. They were startled, but Graeme was already heading towards it.

"I'll get it – this is my treat Sam," he said, as he opened

230

CHAPTER 34

the door. He stood back to let her walk in, enjoying the look on his face as he caught sight of the prostitute.

"This is Sonia, she's here for as long as you want. Say 'hello' Sonia.." Graeme prompted. She did, moving on into the room towards Sam.

***

In Islington it was tranquillity itself. Mark, returning to an empty home, had relaxed and had just finished eating when Fiona arrived. She looked great, if brittle, handling her shopping with caution in case she damaged her nails. Sober and chatty, it was a refreshing change for Mark. They'd been able to stand and talk a little, neither of them wanting to sit down in case it formalised it in some way.

"I met up with Daddy for lunch, and then he took me shopping." Fiona waved at the expensive bags, knowing that Mark would be relieved. He was a real bore about money, always going on about it.

"That's good, where did you lunch?"

"The Savoy of course, it's the only place he ever takes me to, but yes, it was good. Then we ended up in Knightsbridge," she said, "and he thought I deserved a treat or two. Anyway, what about you, what did you get up to today?" The question was so non-committal, Fiona was proud of herself as she watched him. Mark topped up his wine as Fiona poured herself a tonic water.

"Quite boring really, meetings about meetings, and a working lunch. Nothing exciting," came his calm reply. She didn't believe a word of it, but smiled sympathetically anyway.

"Damn!" she said moments later, "that was the last one –

I meant to get more on the way home and forgot."

"What's that, tonic water? There's plenty in the cupboard surely...." Mark went over to check.

"No, I've been drinking a lot of the stuff and forgot we were running out, it's just a bloody nuisance. I fancied another long one." Fiona placed her glass on the surface and waited. It didn't take long.

"If you really want more, I'd be glad to pop out and get some, it'll only take a few minutes." Mark's offer was genuine and Fiona was delighted. She'd poured all the tonics, bar one, down the sink that morning.

"No, don't worry, you've had a drab day, I can have some mineral water," she said sweetly, relying on his memory.

"It's alright, I'll go. I know you hate that stuff. Won't be a minute."

"Oh, thanks Mark, that's kind," she said to his back as he left, picking up the mobile he'd left behind.

CHAPTER 35

Saturday, Midday

Dun had been up since dawn; everything was ready in the flat. She knew she'd missed nothing, she'd paced it out so many times, checked her tools, her stash. Her last job was to pick up her small bag, lock up, and leave.

"Be right down," she yelled from the walkway to the car below. Locking the door she hurried down the stairs. Nico was on time, and she quickly climbed into the front seat of his dark saloon.

"Good one. We've got to pick up my friend, just the other side of the Walworth Road. And there's an extra wad in it for you tonight, I need a small favour." Dun passed over the envelope, Nico had a look inside.

"What's the favour?" he asked, reckoning the amount – Dun had pitched it generously right.

"I want you to hang around in Putney, not come back for us later. I'm fucking uptight about something holding you up, or maybe the whole show ending early…and here's your mobile." Dun passed over the recently 'recycled' mobile; she had one the same.

Nico was happy to take the money. It wasn't a hard job, two women and a third punter later. He could cope with that, especially at his premium rate; he drove out of the estate and on to the main road. Dun waited for his reply as he edged his way on to the Elephant and Castle roundabout.

"Okay, right, I'll park up nearby; you call me, and I'll come. Now, which street for your friend?" He asked, slowing down.

"Second left, halfway down on the right. Here."

Later the trendy neighbours would carefully describe how lovely old Mrs. Ward went off with two men in a dark car, late morning.

233

SATURDAY, MIDDAY

Olivia joined them, getting into the back seat, she was uncertain why Dun had decided to sit in the front. It upset her for some reason. She couldn't tell what was churning inside her friend's head: the anticipation of revenge, the sheer buzz of going with the flow, not fighting it. That given a few minutes, Dun would start her plan.

Greetings exchanged as the car moved quietly off, Olivia leaned back, tense and dry mouthed. She was watched by Dun in the mirror.

"Can you pull over?" Dun asked Nico. He was prepared, she'd told him what she wanted on this part of the job.

"Sure, one minute."

As soon as the car stopped Dun got out and went to the boot. The box wasn't big, and it clinked as she lifted it. She had wanted to do this herself; it was her way of easing her friend's day. Climbing into the back, she put the box between them.

"Time for a quiet drink and smoke. Couldn't quite do the fizzy stuff, so this'll have to do." Olivia took the ready mixed gin and tonic bottle from her, and they toasted each other. It was weak, but helped the dryness.

"To us."

Dun didn't light up the spliff until the car was moving again; it would keep Olivia smooth and happy. She loved her friend, would always protect her. Nico was keeping an eye on them in the mirror – this was one strange job. Dun's 'friend' could be a posh version of his grandmother; only it was inconceivable that she'd have a smoke….

"It's all sorted, I've covered the lot; all you have to do is chill out, trust me." Dun's voice was low and confident; Olivia nodded.

"I do, Dun, you're about the only one I do trust. It just

234

Chapter 35

seems an enormous step..."

"Which I'll take for both of us; here finish this off, we're in Wandsworth already," she said firmly, and passed the spliff over. The traffic was heavy but moving, they'd be at West Hill in minutes. Nico was checking out the passing side streets, parking would be a nightmare.

"That's it, up there on the right."

Nico eyed the large house; it was immaculately maintained, shouted 'money' at you. Pulling over, he let them out, Dun letting Olivia start walking before she spoke:

"See you later, Nico. Make sure that you come down West Hill to get us. See the side gate there, that's where I'll be."

He nodded, and she left, hurrying after her friend.

"They're here!" Christine called out to Eleanor, who was busy in the kitchen, as Olivia rang the bell.

"Can you get it please?"

She stayed where she was, letting Christine welcome her mother and the 'help'. Putting the kettle on for coffee, she was ready for a break.

"Hello Eleanor," said Olivia, as they came in to join her, Dun at the rear.

"Olivia, how are you? Come on in a have a seat, I'm about to stop for a bit and see where I'm at." She moved towards her mother-in-law, her welcome genuine. Olivia felt the warmth. She and Dun sat down while Christine got out the mugs.

"The house looks wonderful, have my flowers arrived yet?"

"Yes, and thanks. I haven't done anything with them though! I thought that maybe you'd be able to help me out with the dreaded flower arranging?" Eleanor was being honest; she had buckets in the utility room full of them.

It was all so normal really; the men off to the rugby, the

235

SATURDAY, MIDDAY

women preparing for their return. Dun sat and watched as they all skated on their polite surfaces; game playing, with the real match buried underneath.

"Shall I show you where to put your things?" Eleanor asked Dun; she'd cleared the laundry (next to the utility room), giving her somewhere to retreat to. Just a chair and some soft drinks, but Dun was pleased by the thought. She couldn't be with a load of people all day – they'd only wind her up. Even better was the direct access to the yard, where she'd be able to smoke, and eventually leave by.

"Thanks," was all Eleanor got, and she left Dun in the room.

"Let's just leave it there Christine… drop it now…." was what she overheard as she came in to join the others. The tone was such that she knew not to ask any questions. The pair of them were obviously glad she was back.

"Right. Dun's just putting her things away. Now, first we'll sort out a quick lunch…" she said ignoring the tension between the women.

"Christine, could you give me a hand?" Eleanor asked, but it wasn't really a question. There was absolutely no way that she was going to allow some bloody Ward feud upset any of her arrangements. She was running it her way, and they would follow. She decided that they'd have wine with their sandwiches after all. If it made the pair of them sleepy, she didn't care. Cooking for forty was a challenge, let them argue the toss later.

Eleanor got the Frascati out of the fridge, as Christine got the corkscrew and glasses.

★★★

Drake's Saturday had started early. The reports on the ship's progress had been increasing, the likely drop zone close to

Chapter 35

Malin Head, Co. Donegal. He knew where it was, bang on the top of Ireland, with a choice of two countries to hide in. The border between North and South, left or right.

"Hope to God that it's on our side, not theirs. I don't want to have to get into any niceties with the Gardai, Thomas. It's better if we can keep it within the family, so to speak. No diplomatic crap and distant relations to bother with." He aired his thoughts as he ate a huge breakfast. Thomas agreed with him, having privately covered both angles – just in case. He needed a chance to get out to make a discreet call – and knew every working pay phone within a mile radius of Jermyn Street.

"Indeed sir. We should hear where it's definitely going to be by 1400 hours; that's the current estimate. As that's pretty certain, I thought I'd go out early and get what's needed; it's not a lot, but this could be a long day and I'd like to have it all sorted." Thomas' voice was its usual calm sound. Drake didn't even bother looking up from his newspaper.

"Yes, that's fine, you go ahead," he said, then paused, looking over his half moon glasses.

"Where's our little troupe right now?"

Thomas loved his turn of phrase, sarky bastard.

"All of them are heading off to Twickenham, they're meeting in the car park we think. Ward has organised a fleet of cars for everyone, all very smooth. They'll be there for the duration, especially as Ireland hasn't a hope of winning."

"Oh dear... how disappointing for them – never mind eh?" He said with a small smile, returning to his paper. Thomas left him quietly, he had time now to get the first call in.

★★★

Saturday, Midday

Mark had sent Eleanor flowers, ordering them before Fiona had surfaced. He didn't need to send a message with them, she knew they were coming. Distracted by the thought of her, wanting to hear her voice but knowing he couldn't phone – the day seemed long.

For Fiona it would barely be long enough. She had her own agenda, and on it was the determination to outdo every other woman at the party. Her preparation was meticulous and lengthy, every inch of her body would be scrutinised, cleansed, toned and fed. She had chosen what to wear so carefully too.

'Just the thing to spark up my Mick friends, with their provincial little wives,' was her thought, looking at the 'dress'. She'd so enjoyed buying something so outrageously tarty.

'That'll give them something to talk about,' she said, draping a large pashmina over the chair. She had no intention of letting Mark in on her little act, let him see her when they got there.

'He might even fancy what's on offer,' was her wishful thinking, but the reality was her hurt pride – she couldn't help it.

***

At Twickenham the group was subdued as Ireland took a hammering. They drank and watched, urging their team to try harder. Jack Barnes was beside himself, nearly forgot the business as he roared,

"C'mon Ireland, c'mon....oh God. look at him..." as the referee disallowed the try.

Sam was unmoved by the whole thing – rugby wasn't for

Chapter 35

him. Standing at the back of the box, he let the others get the best view. Still hung over but with a feeling of total sexual satisfaction courtesy of Graeme's treat the night before. It had been everything he could have wanted, bloody heaven.

"Alright Sam – need anything?" Graeme asked, signalling to the waitress to bring over more champagne.

"Not for me thanks, I'm fine with this." He had a lager, had been nursing it since he arrived.

"Och, c'mon, have one of these, help me drown my sorrows." Graeme pressed the glass on him. Sam took it reluctantly.

"Any news?"

"Not yet, we'll have heard by the end of the match, Jack reckons." Graeme spoke quietly; he was keyed up, trying not to show it.

"Your lot are ready to move?" he asked, aware that he'd gone through it before.

"Aye, just give us the word and we'll be there," Sam said; "no sweat."

"Cheers."

Sam watched him as he moved off to speak to other guests. He put the glass down and went off to the bog. His drinking wouldn't start until later, until there was something to celebrate.

CHAPTER 36

The Party starts

Eleanor lay in the bath, tired and happy. Up to her neck in foam, she couldn't think of anything she hadn't done. The house looked superb, 'en fete', the food was done bar, the serving and Olivia and Christine were guarding it all whilst she stole some time for herself.

A little time to think pleasant thoughts, and they were all about Mark. She'd smiled when his flowers arrived; discreet and apt, they had been dwarfed by Graeme's hideous 'floral arrangements' – he never learned. She'd been tempted to ring Mark, but hadn't, had made herself concentrate completely on the day's effort. It had flown by, and she'd been glad of the help in the end; Dun had been a silent presence who efficiently cleared up after her, retreating to the laundry when not required.

With two hours to go, she expected Jack and Graeme within the hour. Ireland had been demolished at Twickenham, she'd heard it on the radio, so no doubt there would be some drowning of sorrows. She could imagine the attempted singing later – Jack couldn't hold a note at the best of times. As for the rest of the guests, there was nothing she could do other than make the best of it and pray that Graeme's mix would work in the flesh – she had no control over it,

'So there's no point in getting wound up, just give them the best the house can offer, that's your part of the deal,' she told herself, 'Graeme'll be working hard tonight though….his choice, not mine.'

Climbing out, she went into the bedroom, ignoring the 'phone ringing.

'God, my hair's a mess.'

CHAPTER 36

It was Christine who came to the door a minute later.

"That was Graeme on the 'phone. He and Jack are on their way, and they're bringing the guy just over from Belfast, Hudson, with them. He reckons they'll be here in about half an hour. Okay?"

"Yes, that's fine, thanks Christine. I'll be down in a bit," Eleanor called out. Thirty minutes – she'd be pushed to be ready.

It was forty minutes later when she appeared, just in time to hear a car pulling up in the drive.

Opening the front door she waited as the three men extricated themselves from the car.

"Welcome home, was it as bad as it sounded?"

"Oh God, Eleanor, it was a massacre," Jack answered, reaching the doorstep.

"You look great, really great," he went on, and it was no lie. She was one classy lady, simply classy. Sam's reaction was similar, except he couldn't speak, and his hands were sweaty already; he was dreading the social side of this deal.

Graeme made the pretend peck on the side of his wife's face. His own was flushed, but he wasn't drunk, they were all keyed up with the business in hand. Jack had had the news, the shipment was being got ashore, now....

"Everything alright dear?" he asked. "You look nice..." he added, then turning, said;

"Eleanor, meet Sam Hudson – Sam..... meet the wife."

Jack tried not to wince at Graeme's manner, but Graeme was oblivious; he wanted Sam to relax a bit.

"Very pleased to meetcha," was Sam's mumble, as Eleanor moved into the hall.

"Come in Sam, make yourself at home," she said, opening the drawing room door.

241

The Party starts

Eleanor didn't like what she saw at all, and the handshake had been so damp and soft. She was taller than he, could see his scalp but not his eyes as they shook hands. Sam could feel her reaction, and the correction that followed.

Graeme went into bustle mode: coats, drinks, lots of fuss. It broke them up, and the arrival of Christine and Olivia diluted it further.

Jack made a beeline for Christine, he needed distracting and she was the perfect antidote. Her velvet trousers and silk top were a sexy combination, and she could be fun he knew.

"I feel the men won't have made the same effort as the women have tonight – love the pants..."he said, giving her a glass of champagne.

"Cheers Jack. They're trousers, not pants. Pants are knickers," she grinned at him. They clinked glasses and laughed.

"Point taken – anyway whatever they are, they look great," he smiled back at her.

Olivia found herself with Sam, Graeme introducing them. Unlike Eleanor, Sam couldn't tell what the old lady thought of him. She was quite a good looking old biddy, but seemed a bit vague.

Olivia studied him, a bit stoned, but very tuned in to what was happening in the room.

"So, you're my son's new business partner Sam, is that right..?" she asked him quietly, taking in the appalling clothes, wanting to hear him speak before making up her mind entirely.

"Yiss, that's right, me and your son's doin' a wee bit of bizniss – aren't we, Graeme?"

Sam answered her with an effort, looking at her son.

"Yes, it's our first venture, and that was Sam's first trip to

CHAPTER 36

Twickenham too," Graeme said smoothly, changing the subject. Olivia however, refused to run with the ball.

"How nice, and what a shame Ireland didn't win. Anyway, tell me more about this venture," she asked. Sam let Graeme deal with it, he'd done his bit.

Olivia listened to Graeme's words, hearing the lack of truth in the smooth comment, but before she could respond, Jack had joined them.

"Chewing over the unfair referee again are we?" he asked, aware of the tension.

"Not quite Jack; you'll have to excuse me, I promised Eleanor to keep an eye on things in the kitchen," she announced, catching sight of Eleanor disappearing out of the room. Two could play the lying game, she thought. She left them to it, Sam was repulsive and her son's smug deceit disgusted her.

"Good God, isn't he dreadful!" was her comment as soon as she reached Eleanor, who was pretending to check the dining room.

"I know! what a little creep, yuk... I only came in here for a breather, I know that I'm going to be roped in next to make polite conversation with him," said Eleanor, with a little smile.

"Do you know what it's all about, this business deal?" she asked Olivia.

"No. I do know what it isn't, however. Graeme couldn't tell the truth if you paid him," the tone was bitter.

"Oh I know Olivia, I've decided just to try and make the best of it tonight, do the same- drink his champagne like water and just talk to the people you like. Look who I've put you with," Eleanor showed her her table and the place cards.

"Only the old safe faces; you'll be well looked after."

The Party Starts

They both heard the car doors slamming; people were arriving.

"I'll just check that everything's alright in the kitchen," said Olivia moving out to the hall.

"Right."

Eleanor checked herself in the mirror, getting ready to open the door. She was excited and nervous; joined by Graeme they both stood on the doorstep. The taxis moved off, and half of their guests came up the drive.

"Hello, how are you?" came from all sides, as the women air kissed each other and the men shook hands.

"Aren't you looking great, Eleanor," boomed Dan Thompson, giving her his gentlest, prop forward hug – even so, she winced.

"Och thanks Dan, it's been too long since you've been here. How are you?" Eleanor's voice was gentle; she had a soft spot for the huge guy, he thought she was the business. Nonetheless she didn't take in his reply, disappointed that Mark wasn't here yet. She'd no idea how Graeme had organised the taxis for everyone, had hoped that Mark would be among the first to arrive. They moved in dribs and drabs, Graeme chivvying them into the drawing room, champagne at the ready.

Sam and Jack watched as they entered the room, Jack moving towards them to meet and greet; easily, confidently. Sam stayed where he was, watching how it was done, knowing that he wasn't even going to try.

By the time the next lot arrived the noise was unbelievable, voices had risen in competition, greetings had become far less formal as the bottles popped. Eleanor's smile was fixed, Mark and his wife hadn't shown yet.

"We'll give them another half an hour and then we must

CHAPTER 36

eat, Graeme," she told him as he opened more bottles – he agreed. The Batesons were the least of his worries.

Dun was out in the yard having a smoke when Olivia found her.

"Is he here yet?" she asked, passing the spliff over.

"Yes, and I've met him as well. He's a real charmer isn't he? Something about the man makes my skin creep – he's acting the part and his cold eyes tell you so, yet Graeme is treating him like he's someone really special."

"Go with what you feel, trust your instinct; Graeme's only brown nosing him to get the deal done. Now tell me, are they all getting the drink down them?" Dun's question wasn't an idle one, she needed the drink to flow.

"Well he's drinking champagne, and probably wishing it was a lager – but he's certainly had more than he thinks. He's like a fish out of water in there, to be honest." Olivia replied, passing the smoke back.

"How long before they'll need me?" asked Dun. Her timing was crucial, yet was completely under the Ward's control.

"Currently the last lot has arrived, all except one couple. Graeme's driver will have his ear bent if it's his fault, I can tell you. Eleanor won't let a meal spoil for the sake of politeness, so I'd say they'll be sitting down within the hour, probably less. I'd better go back in and make polite noises."

They finished up and went back inside; Eleanor was in the kitchen looking for her mother-in law.

"There you are, I've got the Hendersons asking for you, can you come and have a word? Everything alright Dun, do you need anything?"

Dun shook her head and Olivia went off. Eleanor hesitated by the telephone, then joined her. Where the hell was Mark? From worry to annoyance in one easy jump.

Chapter 37

Late arrivals

"Go and tell him I'll be down in five minute." had been Fiona's answer to Mark's call.

"You said that fifteen minutes ago!"

"Yes, and I'm coming as fast as I can; he's a bloody taxi-driver Mark, he gets paid to wait."

"Oh that's all right then, never mind the fact that we're late. Come on Fiona, we have to leave. I'll wait for you in the car, you lock up." Mark was worried, he should've been there by now; Fiona wasn't worried at all, she intended to do it her way.

"Fine, you do that, I won't be long, promise," she called out, checking herself again in the mirror. Minutes later she climbed into the car, totally ignoring the driver.

It was a quiet journey, the driver doing his best to make up for lost time, and Mark doing his best to breathe.

"Shut the window please Mark, there's a draught," was her only comment.

He didn't argue the point; putting up with her overwhelmingly cloying perfume was a minor hassle.

'Bloody expensive air-freshener,' he thought, pressing the button.

"Sorry dear, didn't realise," was his response, as they hurried along. They were embarrassingly late.

It suited some people however; as Eleanor kept things ticking over, she couldn't help noticing how there was a steady procession to and from Graeme's study. Jack had already been twice, and now Sam had been. En route to the kitchen, she watched as Graeme went in.

"Are you going to be long?" she asked opening the study door. Graeme was on his mobile, listening intently.

'I'll be out in a second,' he signalled to her, turning his

Chapter 37

back on her.

He'd finished off quickly, not pleased with what he'd heard.

When the doorbell rang he was nearest, with Eleanor coming out of the kitchen to join him.

"You made it, come in, come in. Fiona, Mark, welcome. Here, let me take that for you..." said Graeme, taking her pashmina.

As Fiona slipped it off she gauged the reactions. Graeme was delighted, Mark was appalled, and prissy Eleanor was disapproving. Just as she'd expected.

"Thanks Graeme, and forgive us for being so late, my fault entirely..." she oozed charm at him, letting him have a good look as she air kissed him.

"And Eleanor, of course, so sorry. I'm sure you've been thinking we'd got lost!"

Eleanor made the right noises as the women leaned towards each other, neither intending to actually touch the other. When Mark kissed her cheek it helped, a bit.

"Right, let's get you two something to drink and introduce you to some people,eh... Fiona — what would you like?" Graeme took her by the arm. He was affability personified; he liked her tarty look.

Eleanor and Mark followed, carefully not touching, neither saying anything.

"Would you look at the state of that!" was what Sam heard from the woman in front of him. He'd been shamelessly eavesdropping on her conversation with her two friends; their husbands talking rugby close by.

"God almighty, talk about mutton dressed as lamb!" said another.

Fiona had wanted the attention, and as Graeme ushered

her into the room, she got it, full on.

"Call that a dress, I'd have more self-respect than to be seen out that like. How embarrassing for her husband."

Their tuts of disapproval made Sam move so he could see what was making the women cluck so much.

'Yes,' he thought, eying the little slim blonde; great legs in a short red dress, low at the front and even lower at the back, 'that's very nice.' Compared to the matrons around him, she was sexy. Most of the men, had they been free to speak, would have agreed with him.

"Hello, yes I think we have met, wasn't it the Gala…?" Fiona asked, feeling the ripple in the room, it made her smile.

On top form, she concentrated on the men, reminding them of who she was, and what she was. The other women's feathers were definitely ruffled, flirtatious behaviour was not the norm, not at all. In a funny way her entrance united the guests. They at least had one thing in common – disapproval.

Mark was relieved to see her sipping the dry ginger that she'd asked for. He hadn't heard her change the order and couldn't tell the difference between that and the brandy and champagne that Graeme had been happy to slip her. Not much difference in colour, but a wonderful difference in effect; it made her glow.

CHAPTER 38

The Seaside

"Look, you can see the lights on it," the man said, pointing out the vessel anchored well off shore. It was about the only safe and sure comment he could make about boats, ships, whatever; his colleague wasn't much better.

"Where's our lot then?"

"They're coming in from the other side, they left Ballintoy hours ago – look out for one of the fishing boats."

The men stood on the foreshore, they'd been following the progress of the ship as it moved slowly across the top of Ireland. Neither of them knew a damn thing about boats and navigation, it wasn't necessary. They had a map and a car and had been driving and stopping for most of the day, reporting its progress.

"What I don't understand is why we have to follow the fucking thing. I mean why the hell didn't they just tell us where the drop would be?" he asked with a whine.

"How many bloody times do I have to tell you – you thick plank. This one's different, this is the one that nobody, and they mean nobody, is going to know about in advance. I tell you, they're fuckin' paranoid about this one. So shut it – tell them that it's stopped, and that I don't know whether it's in the Republic, or the UK. At the moment it could be either."

That was exactly how the captain had planned it. Take a map of Ireland and follow the international borderline between Northern Ireland and the Republic of Ireland. Where it heads north from the city of Doire, Derry, Londonderry – whatever ever the name, the geography remains the same. Right now, with judicious reading of his charts, the captain straddled the boundary, in Lough Foyle. He made his call to London, and soon after the men on Magilligan Strand watched the ship move off towards Inishowen Head.

Chapter 38

"It's not this side at all, fuck me, it's over the border.." was the man's shout as he grabbed the mobile.

"We're bloody decoys!"

He made his call and listened carefully.

"C'mon, that's us done here. We've to get back to Belfast. Tossers!" he spat, stalking off to their car.

The boats that went out to unload the cargo were fast, the men businesslike, and Kinnagoe Bay was ideal. It would all be shifted and hidden in hours, transported over the border and buried in Co. Antrim. Graeme had spent serious money buying the passage; everybody had to have his cut and the further up the ladder you went the pricier it got. He would only relax when it got to Co. Antrim, then his part was over.

"Yes. When?.... Yes, good," was all he said on the 'phone when it was confirmed that they had crossed the border.

He gave Jack and Sam a slight smile and a shrug when he came back into the drawing room. Jack was in high spirits, but Sam was still on edge – it would all be over in a couple of hours. He drank more champagne, wishing it was a lager.

★★★

The party of six from England had been at the Bushmill's Inn for nearly a week. All keen on the golf and fishing they were thoroughly enjoying their bachelor's outing. They were keen walkers too, and had taken the advice of the hotel on where to explore. Close to the famous Bushmill's whiskey distillery, on the magnificent Antrim Plateau, they had had a great time. Peat fires and excellent food, with air that seemed to knock them out, they were easy guests. They'd offered good money too, and the barman had had a word with his cousin about a bit of night fishing. Twice they'd been out now, and never caught a thing. Tonight they were hoping to get lucky – and there was a new guest at the

CHAPTER 38

hotel who'd joined them – 'just for the fishing like.'

Thomas' call from London today had warned them of the man's arrival, it meant the job was on, the waiting over. A different regiment from the rest of them, he too had old scores to settle from his tours in Northern Ireland. Tonight they'd fish with a difference, clear the debt from twenty years ago – with no worries about the Geneva Convention either.

"Good to meet you Jock, what'll you have?" asked the ex-soldier, while his mates propped up the bar, noisily swapping golf stories about their hard round at Royal Portrush.

"Mine's a pint, pal – and we can sit over there," the Scot replied, pointing towards the fire.

Drinks in hand they'd talked briefly, watching the smoke of the turf fire, looking like two relaxed tourists, joining their group in time for dinner.

In the base in South London it was quiet; those who weren't out on 'obbo' were subdued, there was none of the usual buzz. Thomas came in with another coffee for Drake.

"Any word?" he asked as he put it on the desk.

Drake shook his head – the waiting went on.

CHAPTER 39

Dinner is served

Eleanor gave Graeme the sign and he began to move people through to the dining room. The champagne had flowed and the mood was happy as they went in.

"Oh my goodness, isn't that just gorgeous," came the first of many exclamations. Eleanor had excelled herself; the muted blue silk-lined walls of the dining room were the ideal backdrop. Lit only by candles, the tables were perfect; crisp Irish linen cloths and napkins, with the Waterford glass out in force. Helping them find their places, she was already more relaxed, this was the best bit for her.

She hadn't been able to resist it, and now as her guests read the little menu on their tables, could hear the comments.

"Haven't a clue – here you have a go…"

"Are you sure that it is? Let Maura have look, she was always good at languages.."

Christine had egged her on the night before, and she had done them well; beautifully hand written, Jack having already enthused over them.

"Genuine souvenir for me Eleanor!"

Bradan Deataithe Dhun na nGall, agus Oisri o Tigh Mhorain an Chora.

Brollach Sicin in Uachtar Gaelach Baileys.

Almost everybody in the room was Irish, one way or the other, and not one of them had a clue what it meant. Her English side smiled, and her husband thought that she was responding to his smile of pleasure; Mark though could read her mind, and she couldn't resist glancing over at him. Fiona had nothing better to do than to watch her husband as the man on her left bored her. She saw his eyes change.

CHAPTER 39

Graeme tapped his glass and made his short speech, his mobile vibrating against his leg.

Mark was glad that he'd been given the translation, his table thought he was wonderful.

"The oysters are from Moran's of the weir – you've heard of them haven't you? " he asked, passing the wheaten bread.

"Oh yes, but no, shellfish isn't for me thanks – and what did you say the other was?"

"Timbale of Donegal smoked salmon."

"That's more my style, I find those other things far too slimy for me."

Mark ate his with relish as the woman continued her tale. Fiona was picking over her food, but at least was making an effort. He tried to catch her eye, but she was still sulking over where they'd been seated. Without doubt she'd been tucked out of harm's way, her back to the action – not quite her style.

"Excuse me please, I'll be back in a moment.." she murmured to her neighbour, heading off to the loo, again.

As Eleanor crossed the hall towards the kitchen she watched Fiona heading upstairs. At the half landing the woman's glance down was icy. She hurried on through to the kitchen, where Dun was busy.

"Only one isn't eating, he hasn't managed anything other than the wheaten bread..." she commented to the woman. Dun took the tray from her, she'd have known what Sam Hudson liked – nothing rich or fancy.

"Och, there's always one," she said, as the door closed – Eleanor had already gone back in. Dun could hear the swell of noise as the door to the dining room opened.

Upstairs, Fiona heard it too and hesitated. She had found the handbag, tucked down by the side of the bed. Black and practical, it was Eleanor all over. Hearing no footsteps, she

253

unzipped it quickly. The mobile was in the third pocket.

When Graeme came back with more bottles the room was relaxed enough to elicit a bit of a cheer, led by the prop forward. They'd all eaten superbly, were mellow and resting after the superb food and glorious wines. As the Irish cheeses and vintage port appeared, the men began preparing their cigars. Eleanor's *pièce de résistance* for pudding would be her last task.

She knew she had happy guests as she eyed the room; replete and relaxed, conversations were breaking out between some unlikely people as many of the women headed for the loo.

Mark was watching as Graeme poured and then leaned over to speak to Sam Hudson. Brief and rapid, the little man's demeanour altered on hearing it – not by much, but visible to a watcher.

It was done, the deal was done, he was sure of it. He waited to see how the American would react. As Jack raised his glass with a smile Mark touched his mobile in his pocket, he needed to get out to make a call.

Fiona heard noise, lots of it, coming towards the master bedroom. She pressed the button quickly.

"Excuse me, I have to take this, " said Mark embarrassedly; he loathed mobile phone intrusions. Only Drake would ring him, he knew that. Leaving the room he went into the drawing room.

"What – Eleanor..? Hi! This is bizarre. Darling, where are you….?"

Fiona listened to her husband's voice, warm and deep. Snapping the phone shut, she stuffed it and the bag into their laundry box and flushed the loo.

'Eleanor Ward – he couldn't, she wouldn't….' she said to

Chapter 39

the face in the mirror. She could hear the women getting impatient outside as she got her reserves out of her bag. She downed it and threw the empty into the laundry box. With a quick check she was out the door, their conversation stopping dead as she appeared.

"Really sorry – you know how it is.." she said brightly, not giving a shit what they'd been saying about her. She was beside herself inside, disbelieving and yet knowing it was true....she couldn't remember the last time Mark had used that warm tone of voice with her. But bloody hell, Eleanor!

Leaving the bedroom she headed downstairs, not quite catching the parting comment from the women.

"A right wee madam, that one…"

★★★

They looked so pretty, the ice-bowls; she'd spent ages decorating round the edge of the ice, and now with their dishes of coffee ice cream on top she was delighted with the result.

"Christine, would you take the jugs of sauce in for me please? – I'll take the last of these in." Eleanor picked up the bowl.

"God! How much whiskey did you put in the sauce!?" Christine smelt the Irish coffee sauce.

"Lost count…don't think it'll matter too much though, do you?"

They were both laughing as they came out of the kitchen, but it stopped the second they met Fiona in the hall.

"Who's rattled her cage then?" Christine demanded as the woman stalked past; "talk about rude!.."

Eleanor said nothing, she wanted to have a word with Mark.

Dun sat in the kitchen eating the leftovers, stolidly lining her stomach.

The noise level went up again as the dinner ended and the relaxed table swapping began. Jokes were told and the fug in the room increased, Graeme going so far as to offer his Havanas around. He was one happy guy, moving round the room, making the women laugh at his almost risqué jokes, at ease with the men.

Sam made the most of the change around, slipping out of the room and heading for the kitchen, in serious need of air. He knew he shouldn't have had the port, it was a toast too far.

'But Christ! What a result!' he thought, as he fumbled with the door handle.

Fiona had moved table and was now able to watch, pretending to listen to the prop forward's long tale, her beady eye raking the room. There was bloody Eleanor, but where was Mark?

"Fiona! There you are, how are you – tell me, are you having a good time?" Graeme demanded, his sweaty hand stroking her bare back as he joined them. He was 'well on', as they say, high and loud, free with everything – everyone his friend. He'd even smiled when Jack attempted to get off with his sister. Nothing really mattered anymore, he'd done it – he'd bloody done it!

Olivia watched his progress, so too did Eleanor – both women glad that this would be the end of it.

"Eleanor, wonderful meal. Really great," was what Fiona guessed he was saying as her husband approached the

Chapter 39

hostess. She waited for him to ask the question, watching Eleanor's face.

As the woman shook her head and looked puzzled, Fiona raised her glass. That was what they saw when they couldn't help looking her way.

Dun was enjoying her after dinner smoke when the back door opened. She was in the shadows and watched as the man came out, taking deep breaths and moving unsteadily. She recognised him immediately.

'Talk about the luck of the Irish,' was her thought as he threw up in the yard. She remained still, hearing the sound of the zip on his trousers. "Aah God, that's better, aah... " he said as he pissed down the fence, leaning his head on his forearm. It was as though the fresh air had finally cut the legs from under him.

"Who's there?" was his slurred question as Dun came towards him as he finished.

CHAPTER 40

Exits

Graeme poured her the large brandy; Mark could see her taking the glass from him with a sly smile.

"Oh God," he said to Eleanor. "I know that look..." as he started moving towards his wife. Unable to speak, watching as Fiona got to her feet, chair falling backwards – she'd no idea what to do.

It was Jack who took over in the end; Jack who came between them, stopping Fiona from striking out. No-one, however, had been able to stop her foul-mouthed outburst that had cut through the stunned silence.

"Hey Graeme, instead of pawing me why not shag me, fuck me – he won't..." she announced loudly, pointing towards Mark.

"No, he's too busy screwing little Miss Perfect over there to have time for his wife! Didn't you know ?? Oh, well just ask them.. Go on Eleanor, tell your husband all about it..." she screeched across the room.

The guests were embarrassed, some edging away from it, slipping out into the hall – others were enthralled.

Eleanor went white, and Graeme tried to get sober, fast. He was dumbstruck at first, then fucking angry. She was his wife dammit, mother of his kids, how dare she play around..

"I knew she was up to something..." Christine said to Jack, but he wasn't listening.

"Quick, you get between those two," he snapped at the prop forward, as Graeme made a lunge for Mark. Tables went over with a crash, making some of the women shriek and push for the door. It took two of them to restrain him, the prop forward pinning his arms down, Jack helping push him into a corner.

Chapter 40

"Graeme – enough. Leave it – it's not worth it…" Jack's words weren't getting through, the man was seething.

"You – sit down and shut up." Mark said to Fiona, shoving her into a chair.

"And Christine, get the cars round for these people, quickly." As he finished saying it, Fiona lunged.

The ice-bowl hit the wall, quickly followed by another. Shards of glasses and melting ice went everywhere, clearing the room of the rest of the guests. Christine's call went out with the sound of breaking glass and Fiona's foul-mouthing in the background; Olivia, appalled, went to tell Dun.

Mark's cuts were superficial but they bled, Fiona was glad to see. As for the drenched Eleanor, she'd have to wait; the hall was chaotic as everyone milled around, wanting to be gone.

Dun made the call.

Chapter 41

Yes Minister

"Yes, tell the Minister I shall be there, and yes, I am aware of how busy he is." Drake's voice was clipped and ultra polite. The call had been brief and peremptory and not unexpected, but that didn't help his mood. He hung up, pausing for a moment to think before acting.

"Thomas, in here, now!" It came out the way he really felt – furious.

"Sir?" was the cautious answer.

"Meeting with the bloody Minister within the hour. Meanwhile I want to hear nothing from you other than 'yes' and 'sir'. Got it?"

"Yes sir."

Drake had heard the news hours ago, had blown his top at the cock-up, was still beside himself.

"I'll be ready to leave for his office in forty five minutes," he snapped, on his way to shower and change. Being hauled in to explain the mess was not what he had had in mind for his Sunday.

"Bugger!" he exclaimed as he stripped. Thomas went off to fetch the car early, he'd rather not be near the boss when he was like this.

'But he's one smart bastard all the same.' "Yes, sir.." was his mutter as he stepped out into Jermyn Street.

In the shower Drake went over it again and again, sifting the pieces of information. He needed to be able to put some spin on it, make it seem better than it was. The facts were pretty damning and he'd spent most of the night working on them. It had all been going so well..

He'd moved quickly when he'd heard, knowing that the media would be hot on the trail. The early morning news

Chapter 41

bulletin had been as he had wished, no point in having clout if you don't know when to use it. It would buy him a little time, but not for long.

'Two officers suspended, effective immediately,' had sent out his angry message to the team. That one was the lovely Louise had made it worse, but he was ruthless.

"You want me to believe that you and your colleague, on an important obbo, were unable to keep track of one pathetic little man. That a large number of people were able to leave and you couldn't do anything about it. Do you think I'm stupid? Tell me exactly how this was able to happen."

He had not interrupted the silence that followed his question; always good at waiting, knowing that most people couldn't handle more than two minutes without saying something.

Oh she tried, Louise really tried: big eyes, big sniffs, she was truly penitent. Drake wasn't interested, he pushed until he got the pathetic truth out of her.

"He'd only been about fifteen minutes, had gone to get some food. I'd assumed that we had bags of time, that nothing'd happen till later. Then suddenly it was chaos sir, cars pulling up and people piling in – I wasn't able to see clearly and couldn't approach without him."

Drake knew she was lying about the length of time, but the rest was the truth. He'd eventually got hold of Mark Bateson and had listened in disbelief to his tale of woe. As things stood they'd be hard pressed to convince anyone that they weren't involved in some way.

"Sit down Drake," said the Minister coldly, as his secretary left the room.

They didn't like one another; the Minister disapproving of Drake's privileged background, and Drake contemptuous of the man's fake working class act – (deprivation and struggle, my arse.) Right now though Drake had to be able to win him over.

"Thank you Minister, and I appreciate you agreeing to see me."

"Hardly able to avoid it. What the hell's going on – we're fielding questions and delaying – but I've got to see the Prime Minister later and he's not happy either. So explain."

When Thomas drove him home an hour later Drake was in better form, he felt that his version would be honed and reduced, but best of all believed.

"Turn the radio on Thomas, it's time for the news."

They both listened to the moderate tone of the announcer, as Thomas drove sedately along Whitehall.

'Security forces in Northern Ireland have confirmed the seizure of a large shipment of arms in Co. Antrim, following an anonymous tip-off. They are currently investigating the discovery of two bodies at the scene, both young men. Their deaths are being treated as suspicious, and may have links to terrorist organisations. The possibility of a feud between rival factions is not being ruled out. Now the sport….'

"Thank you Thomas, that's fine. I've just been told by the Minister that the Security forces are in fact screaming that a covert operation has been carried out without their knowledge. That the two men were garrotted, with bloody fishing lines, and that it stinks. I was able in all honesty to tell him I didn't know what the hell they were on about. Apart from one watcher, who left Northern Ireland on the flight after Hudson, I didn't have any operatives over there. That we were totally reliant on the normal channels." His eyes were in Thomas' mirror – the man's understanding in the look.

Chapter 41

"Indeed sir. Any word on Hudson?" came the calm answer. Thomas' trust had been well placed in his boss.

"No, and that is the most serious cock-up so far as I'm concerned. We've got Ward and Barnes, but not the little runt. I'm due an update soon, they're pulling the car company to bits – we should soon know which one he was in. The hotel's been done, he hasn't been there since he left for the rugby yesterday. There are voices being raised regarding his disappearance."

Thomas didn't comment, he had no idea what was going on there; now if he'd been dealing with Hudson…

CHAPTER 42

Reunion

He was propped up on a chair in the yard, smelling of sick and grateful for the can of coke that took the foul taste out of his mouth. Dun had told him to stay put while she got a bucket of water. In his fuddled state it seemed like a good idea; he took a good slug of the drink.

"Get in there and make a brief good-bye, c'mon Olivia, we have to go… now…" she urged her friend. It didn't seem to be going in, the woman sat on at the kitchen table.

"Olivia, just stick your head round the door, come on!"

Pulling herself upright Olivia went to the door; when it opened it was like bedlam in the hall. The cars were arriving and everyone wanted to be in the first ones. She tapped the nearest person to her,

"Tell Eleanor that I've gone on home would you – I'm too tired for any more of this."

"Of course Mrs. Ward, – are you all right?" The man was concerned at the old lady's drained face. He didn't get an answer; Dun took her arm and closed the door.

"Out into the yard, while I get my bag," her voice was different; excited, but under some control still. Olivia moved as quickly as she could, stepping into the yard, she saw the man slumped on the chair.

"Get the gate open, that's it – close it after me."

'God bless the tradesman's entrance' was Dun's thought as she lifted Sam up, gripping him firmly and moving off down towards the road. From a distance it looked like a friend helping a very drunk mate into a dark saloon. But then they were all dark saloons, with doors open and pissed people hurriedly climbing in.

As the cars moved off Nico's was indistinguishable from

Chapter 42

the rest as they headed down West Hill.

"Christ!" was the only comment from him, the smell of sick still lingering on Hudson.

"Don't worry, he won't puke in your car." Dun told him from the back seat,

"He's out for the count," she added, "mixed his drinks.."

Nico nodded, not caring that much. His flight out of Heathrow the following morning was much more important.

Olivia was silent in the front, not seeing the journey; surprised when they were back in the Elephant and Castle, driving into the estate. She was one step removed from it all.

"Olivia, I want you to stay in the car until I come back for you. Okay?"

The question brought her round, Dun's voice firm and kind; hand touching her shoulder.

"Yes, I'll sit here."

Nico and Olivia sat in silence as Dun angled the man out of the car. Draping Hudson's arm round her neck she half hoisted him, starting up the stairs like a pair of drunks. The stairwell was disgusting, but the occupants were busy elsewhere. Dun took it steady, talking to him as though he was alert.

"Nearly home now, c'mon there, just one more, and another one… that's it," she encouraged as they reached the landing – her door yards away. She could feel the rush building inside her, couldn't help smiling.

Unlocking the reinforced door she got him inside, quickly taking him into the kitchen, dumping him onto a chair. She paused to admire her work, with his head now resting on the table he looked so peaceful, harmless even.

"You sleep a wee while now, till I get her in…" she said,

patting him on the back.

She felt so strong, so up. She'd only given him the tiniest amount in his Coke and she had him, just like that. Carefully locking the door, she went down to fetch Olivia. They had to be together, she felt better with her close by.

"Here, that's half – check it. Okay? the rest comes in a few hours. I'll call you as soon as I'm ready."

Nico took the envelope from her. He didn't need to check that it was all there, without him the last stage couldn't happen.

"Fine, I'll wait to hear," he said, and driving off left them by the stairs, the dealers' BMWs doing a brisk trade on the other side of the yard. He watched in the mirror as Dun took Olivia's arm, heading up.

"More balls than many men, and stronger too!" was his mutter. He had hours to kill, he needed good coffee.

★★★

If you'd looked at her across a room, you'd have admired the old lady. Elegant and with character; straight backed and with a style. Close up you'd see the age of her, the deep lines and the blue veined hands, but you'd still be moved, especially by her eyes. They said it all; once they must have been so striking, now they were so full of her life's toll that you felt for her. It was her eyes that worked on Dun, made her try so hard.

"Here, you take this and go into the bedroom. Stay there until I come for you, alright?" Dun moved Olivia out of the kitchen and into the small room. Her friend moved tiredly and was glad to put her feet up, have her drink and rest. She didn't want to think about the evening. Dun gently

CHAPTER 42

propped her up with the thin foam pillows, putting the large whiskey on the Formica topped table beside the bed.

"Thanks, I won't come out. I don't feel anything, just numb." Olivia looked gaunt in the dim light, Dun putting a shawl round her shoulders.

"Leave it all to me. If you can, sleep a bit; that is…. if you can ignore the racket."

The block was throbbing with drum and bass, people were indoors but their noise was everywhere. It would go on most of the night, above and below them.

"Is it always like this?"

"Pretty much nowadays. I'll come in and get you as soon as I can, okay?" On getting Olivia's nod Dun left, and closed the door firmly. Crossing the hall she re-entered the kitchen and turned on her own music, loudly. Bob Marley didn't waken the man at the table.

Olivia drank the whiskey quickly, wanting to feel even less. Leaving the light on she burrowed down, the different sounds and rhythms competing with each other. The warmth got to her; despite everything she fell asleep. It was the best thing for her that night.

Chapter 43

The facts of life

"It really doesn't matter that you can't answer me, I just know you're hearing me, that I can tell you anything, Sam, and you'll have to listen," she said to the slump in front of her.

This was her turf, her time, and inhaling her spliff deeply... she savoured the moment, the reggae keeping her company.

"You're such a big man, aren't you? A big, important man, eh?" She prodded him across the table, pinching and twisting his ear hard. It stirred him, the effort of raising his head making him groan out loud, his eyes flickering open.

"With no business with the likes of me, oh no, moved on to better things. No problems – no worries for Sam Hudson – a cushy life for some – not me though – never me."

Sam was hearing her, his eyes had responded to his name.

"You don't fucking recognise me do you? You haven't a notion who I am – yet I know you so well. All about you, every detail, over all these years." Her mouth was dry with the buzz of the power over him. She'd tell him, and he'd listen – it was on her list, and Dun never deviated . She slapped him hard across the face; her monologue would stoke her up for the job ahead, the stored pieces of bitterness talked of for the first time.

"It's me Sam... Tess – from the farm. From the time when you were banished, those early days. Remember ?" If Sam did, he showed nothing.

"I had your child, you know. But you, you had to kill it, didn't you? That time in Belfast, I was knocked up when you dumped me. The only time in my life when I thought I could have something of my own to love. You and your 'sex aid specials' – you left me ripped inside, I couldn't keep

Chapter 43

it, could never have another either. Fucking nightmare it was – you took it away, took it all away from me..." her low voice was so angry, her foot beginning to tap its agitated rhythm. Sam didn't move, Dun stood up and began pacing.

"And you killed her as well. Her – Olivia – my balance. Left her in the half dead world of the parent who wasn't allowed to see her dead son. He was too much of a mess they said, she wouldn't recognise him they said, it could traumatise her they said! You'd a hand in that somewhere along the line, I know it.... didn't you ?" She stopped and bent down to peer into his face. His slight movement was all she needed for the off.

"What you need is a drink, boy. Here, let me help."

She force-fed him the whiskey having added the rest of the liquid ecstasy. Pinching his nose so that he would have to swallow it, she ignored the gagging. It was a great feeling this, sharp and strong – and building all the time.

Her list sprang back into her mind as she watched him slide; meticulously planning and ticking off, she was like a little machine.

"You're never going to waken from this one Sam. I'm the very last person who will ever speak to you. I'm going to decide your future for you, just like you used to do. No-one is ever going to find you. There won't be a body, there won't be a trace left of you. This is the best thing I've ever done in my life."

She waited until he was comatose then took him through to the bathroom. Just like riding a bike, you never forgot how to butcher.

It was no more awkward than hanging up a pig in the end, a bit more floppy perhaps. The line took the weight as she spread his legs, his head dangling down into the bath.

The hooks she'd got from the DIY store were ideal for his ankles. She was suited and booted, had masked the bathroom with yards of plastic sheeting creating an inner lining; not perfect but close to. She wore nothing under her suit, it would be hot, if not hard, work. There wasn't that much of him to be honest.

'Scrawny bastard,' she muttered, as she cut his throat. Compared to a big hog at 250 lbs, he wouldn't take long. She was supremely efficient, good at her job, and happy as well. As she left him to drain she checked that her drain cover was in place. Nothing like being paranoid for getting it right. Skinning up, she was so on top of her lists, it was like clockwork, and so soothing. She could hear the trickle of the water and blood.

The offal containers were ready; five litres of blood wouldn't take that long, and she had the whole night. The party fiasco had given her extra time, and cover she couldn't have dreamt of.

'Nico's extra was the best wad I've ever spent covering my back,' was her thought; his nearness had been crucial as the shit hit the fan.

'And the next best is Flash – bless him.' Her deadline was his departure for the river, she'd make it, she had the muscle and the mincer; worse still she'd enjoy the challenge.

She went to check on her friend, smiling at the sight of Olivia asleep on her bed. It put her in mind of a child's song, she'd no idea where she'd heard it, but she'd never forgotten the line about the sleep that was 'free from all care' – it just fitted right now. Olivia had done well, it had been a fast switch for her, but she hadn't wavered.

Dun went back to work, boning knife and hacksaw, bucket and hammer.

Chapter 43

Nico was only minutes away, arriving by the staircase soon after her call. "Nice one. I need you to help me load up," she said, as he turned the engine off. The first signs of light were in the sky. Both were in a hurry to get to Flash's, needing the extra time.

"They'll fit if you drop the back seat…"

Nico did as she suggested, then helped store the containers. He couldn't help noticing how fresh and clean the woman was. Olivia slept on while the block rocked.

CHAPTER 44

Aftermath

Whatever Fiona might have done by way of damage, it was nothing compared to what Drake's team had done. They had been thorough all right, and when Eleanor and Christine were brought back in a police car after questioning, they were stunned at the sight.

"Oh God – look at it!" had been Christine's wail. It had been comprehensively turned over; drawers with their contents sticking out, everything moved. Drake's fury had spurred them on. The computer had gone of course, and everything of Jack's. They walked round the house, feeling violated.

"Look.." said Eleanor, on the landing, pointing upwards.

"They've even been in the loft !"

The cover hadn't been replaced properly, she would notice a detail like that.

"Eleanor, c'mon, leave it – let's go and get ourselves a drink." Christine pulled her away. They were both wiped out by what had happened, walking downstairs they avoided the dining room, retreating to the warmth of the kitchen. Christine poured a brandy for Eleanor.

"Here, take this, while I ring Olivia."

"What are you going to tell her?" asked Eleanor.

"The truth, what's the point of trying to hide anything from her? She'll have to be told sometime about bloody Graeme, why not now?" Christine was blunt; they'd all have to live with what he'd done. Even now they hadn't been told any of the detail, but what they had heard so far was bad enough.

Eleanor sat sipping as Christine dialled.

"Just her answerphone," she said, leaving a brief message.

Chapter 44

She came to join Eleanor.

"What am I going to tell the kids, Christine?"

"Nothing yet; you heard the police, they may need us again. The best thing right now is for you to finish that and try to get some sleep. I'll stay up for a bit, just in case."

When she had gone, Christine got started on the clearing up. It wouldn't be to Eleanor's standard, but at least it was something. Her mind wouldn't switch off; how could her brother be working with terrorists?

Eleanor lay awake on the bed, with similar thoughts. She listened to Mark's messages on her mobile, not able to return his calls. She felt so cold and afraid of what could be said.

'Like I'm considered a bloody security risk and he can't see me again…'

***

In Southwark, Dun paid out another wad while Nico waited in the car. He knew what was going on in there, in the lockup, it had been used before. Pay enough, and anything can be put through the industrial mincing machine. Dun's preparations made it a quick run, and Flash was able to get away on time with his rancid meat load. He knew the tides, needed to be much further down the river. Two grand though for an extra load was good money, he reckoned.

Dun was high with it, over the top; she'd got back into the car, talking to herself. Nico could feel the charge of the energy in her.

"Nearly done, nearly done."

He drove her back to the flat; silent but very aware of her, even wary.

"I'll be as quick as I can," she'd said, and she meant it. Two trips in all; loading the bags into the boot she'd passed him the last of his pay.

"I don't want Olivia to get upset, so check it now, will you?" and she went back up the stairs, full of energy. The change in her voice was marked, she was gentle sounding.

She went over the flat for the last time, she'd never return; this bit of her life was ending, the best bit.

Check and check again, even she couldn't find anything she'd missed. She went to get Olivia, helping her up.

"Come on, let me take you home. You can go home at last Olivia, in peace."

Her friend looked at her, silently asking; Dun nodded.

"Everything is sorted, it's all over. Let's go."

She double locked the flat as always, then carefully helped Olivia on the stairs.

Nico began the drive to Olivia's.

"Just go round by the recycling for me Nico. That's great." Dun asked, getting out to empty the bags.

She'd washed all Sam's clothes, didn't care that they were sodden, it would give the bleach rinse time to work. They dropped down inside the recycling bin, his bleached shoes following with a thud. She pocketed the bags; she was so calm now, in the eye of the storm, knew that she was right.

"That's it, home now."

Nico dropped them off at the top of the street as Dun had asked, she wanted Olivia and her to have the short walk in the early morning together. As he drove away to Peckham, he knew he'd make the flight to Cyprus.

CHAPTER 45

Sunday

Drake waited impatiently as the last of the team filed in, letting the silence grow before he spoke.

"Right. You can see we're two down, let's hope that there won't be any more. What have we got, apart from this monumental cock-up?" was his only greeting.

It was Darcy who answered him; primed by the others, he was seen as the least likely to wind the old man up.

"Sir. Currently we have Ward, with his fancy lawyer, being interviewed again, he's saying little. Barnes, we feel, will be a little more forthcoming, given time. He's a sad dreamer, it's Ward who ran the show." He moved along the display board, pointing out the links, Drake let him continue.

"We've interviewed half of the guests so far. No-one appears to know anything about Hudson. They may have spent the day with him, but it would seem that the guy didn't talk, except to Ward and that wasn't much. We should have the rest done by late evening, but I don't expect to get much from that angle."

"The cars..?"

"That's a bit different. The company is completely legit., can account for all the vehicles, and has given us the list of drivers. We're nearly done on that front, and are pretty sure that it wasn't one of theirs. That leaves the only other vehicle known to have come to the house at that time, a taxi from South London for Ward's mother. We're working on that one at the moment, sir."

"Ward's home? Has it been done?"

"Thoroughly sir, and his office. We've pulled out all the stops…"

"Pity the same level of efficiency wasn't applied last night

– we wouldn't be in this shit now, would we?" Drake retorted.

"Obviously there's a watch on airports and ports, but so far, nothing, sir."

"Bloody marvellous. Hand picked team and this is the best you can do ?!"

Standing at the back, Thomas could feel the team's reaction, their annoyance. Drake could too, and knew when to back off.

"Right, that's the bollocking; and now this is the information that I've gleaned, courtesy of having my ear bent by the Minister," he continued.

"Hudson's vanishing act has sparked off an unholy row and we're currently being blamed. So far we've got the ship, the non-English speaking crew, and a conveniently stocious captain. We've got the arms, and two men murdered; plus the anger of our security forces over there, who think we mounted a covert action and forgot to tell them. We've got two of the players and have managed to lose the third on our own patch.

We also have a Minister who has the ear of the Prime Minister, and whose granny is Irish, all the way. Right now, we don't have quite enough friends, do we? …. So, find the car, find the bloody driver – that's your priority. As for me, I'm heading off to Paddington Green, check out how the brave boyos are doing. That's all," and he left them to it.

"Right, you heard him, hit all the cab companies.." Darcy encouraged them – all of them well aware of the numerous unlicensed cab businesses tucked away in Southwark.

"And lunch is on the Guv. – look…" he said, showing them the folded notes that Drake had slipped him.

"Nice one," was the consensus as they got stuck in.

CHAPTER 45

★★★

At Camberwell Police station that day, the burnt out car on the Croft Estate warranted little more than a mention at the briefing. The incoming shift was asked to keep an eye out for the two youths seen fleeing the scene as the car had erupted. It was a regular occurrence on that estate, an estate so tough these days that officers go in in threes.

The descriptions were of little use; medium build and height, with baseball caps, trackie bottoms and hooded tops. It could fit hundreds on the estate, and they weren't likely to get much more help from the residents; minding your own business was a real life skill.

★★★

Dun and Olivia hadn't bothered opening the curtains when they went into her house. They'd headed straight for the kitchen, pulling up the chairs to sit by the Aga, Dun helping her friend get comfortable.

"There, you rest, I'll get us something warming." Dun said.

She knew that they wouldn't be interrupted, the now trendy street allowed itself a lie-in on a Sunday, few surfacing much before ten. She'd unplugged the phone when they'd arrived; now it was just the two of them, the way she liked it. She warmed the milk and added a lot of brandy, and sugar; it would do the trick.

"Och Dun, I'm too old for all this; can't understand where it all went wrong, can't see it ever getting any better, can you?" Olivia's voice was flat and sad. She took the mug from Dun, drinking deeply.

"Was it worth it though?" Her friend moved closer to

her, wanting to smell her.

"The kids, yes, the rest.... not really; a non-life, that about sums it up."

"I feel such a bloody failure, Dun. How can I say that the kids were the best part? Look at the results! One dead, one hand in glove with terrorists, and the last one unable to hold her life together. God knows how it'll all end, but I don't want to be around to find out this time. Give me my chance now Dun, help me go, not to ever come back, please..." her voice was urgent, her hand reaching out for her friend.

Dun soothed her, not saying what she thought, it was too late for that. Maybe, after all, it was time for the daughter to have to face reality without the cushion of the parent. Tough, but then, compared to many she'd never had to really struggle. Olivia came first in Dun's mind, her wishes were more important than any child's – no matter the age.

"Finish that up, and I'll make you another one, eh?" she said, reaching out for the mug.

This time she added much more, masking it with the sugar and the brandy.

As Olivia drank, Dun talked to her, so softly; giving the last scraps of love she had left inside her. Warm and safe, stroked and held, Olivia felt like a child again, Dun her protector; soon the loudest sound was from the kitchen clock.

Leaving the house later, Dun went out through the yard and down the narrow alley; moving quickly, wanting the distance between them. You'd have almost thought she'd been crying, but when the police picked her up later there was no trace of any softness left in her.

★★★

CHAPTER 45

"Unprovoked and vicious attack on a busker at the Elephant and Castle, sarge. He's been admitted to St. Thomas' hospital, serious facial injuries. Couple of witnesses say that the woman just went berserk; took four of us to contain her," the young constable announced to the custody sergeant at Carter Street Police station on the Walworth Road. Dun stood in front of his desk, passive and calm, judging the timing of her comment. She had to be able to pull it off, to hide any trace of her mental state. Being sectioned now was definitely not part of her plan.

The sergeant looked down at the little middle-aged woman. She didn't look like a dosser, didn't look off her head; ugly cow maybe, but that wasn't a crime. As he took her details she was performing brilliantly, seemingly letting her indignation get the better of her.

"He snatched my bag in East Street market, yesterday, left me without a penny for the weekend. Little toe-rag, gets away with it every time. You lot do nothing about it – it isn't even worth my while reporting it. So I when saw him poncing about with his guitar, I couldn't help it, I hit him with my bag of shopping. Didn't mean to do any damage, just wanted to give him a dose of his own medicine," she blurted out for their benefit, well aware that many of the residents in her block had had similar experiences, had given up hope of anyone helping them, of protecting them.

The bloodied carrier bag with its tins of Tesco's Value baked beans, corned beef and grey budget loaf had been bagged up; swung with force, it would have done serious damage to any face.

She was charged with actual bodily harm and enjoyed their cups of tea whilst waiting to be interviewed. She knew their procedure so well, felt safe in custody, out of harm's way in a sense.

'Tomorrow morning I'll be up in court and then, hopefully, on to Holloway Prison,' was her thought after her interview was over. It would be the perfect solution to her final problem. She slept deeply, unaware of the noise around her; it had been a manic time.

CHAPTER 46

Growing up

Christine picked up the keys to Eleanor's Mercedes, while Eleanor looked for the spare set of keys to Olivia's house.

"Don't worry, if I get lost I'll pull over and check the A to Z," both of them well aware that map reading wasn't one of her skills. It didn't matter really, she'd find her way eventually, and she needed to be moving. Eleanor's lethargy was so heavy, impenetrable; she couldn't get it through to her sister-in-law that she was worried about Olivia. She been trying to reach her for hours now, and had an unease inside her that wouldn't go away. She couldn't touch her brother's car, it was taped for the police, but wanted to be mobile, and alone.

"Take the bloody Merc., it's in the garage and I never drive it - ever," had been Eleanor's sharp answer to her query. He'd bought it for her one Christmas; red, vulgar, and ostentatious – everything she hated.

"Sure? I'm not the best of drivers…" Christine didn't fancy the responsibility; in her old car at home it didn't matter that her parking was atrocious.

"Listen. Like this place, I couldn't care less if I never saw it again – believe me Christine, I mean it," came her stark answer.

"You go and check on Olivia, and I'll stay here – just keep your mobile on. Go on, I'll be fine. Anyway, I think we both need a bit of space – I find it hard to believe all that's going on…" Eleanor paused, shrugging.

"I know. One step at a time. You think about yourself while I'm gone, decide where you'd like to stay for a start. We're not staying here." Christine took the keys from her, and unusually, gave her a hug. Stiff at first, Eleanor responded.

"Go on, it's all right," she said, pulling away – much more and she'd break down.

Christine left her, cautiously driving away, but stopping a few minutes later to make a call on her mobile.

"Mark? This is Christine Ward… "

If Mark was surprised to hear from her he didn't show it, he listened to her message and thanked her for the call; afterwards, he immediately rang Drake.

When Christine finally pulled up outside Olivia's house she was completely frazzled by the drive. She tended to avoid right hand turns, and had consequently taken a huge detour, getting lost regularly. Watching her trying to park amused the two men from Drake's team parked several doors away.

"Oh, look at her – who let her drive a classy motor like that!"

"She can walk to the kerb from there.."

Christine gave up on her third attempt and left it as it was, moving quickly towards the house. As she got out the keys the men were already beside her.

"Police. Can you tell us who you are please?" asked a polite voice. Even with warrant cards on show it still made her jump.

"This is my mother's house, Olivia Ward. I'm her daughter, Christine."

They all went in together, calling out their presence, switching on lights. Christine reached the kitchen first, wanting to believe that Olivia would waken, had just nodded off in the chair. She knew when she touched her that it wasn't so.

"Oh God no, Ma. No!" Her wail went up as she knelt in front of the chair, feeling for her hands. Drake's man felt for

CHAPTER 46

a pulse in Olivia's neck and thought there was a faint one, but very weak.

"Quickly, get an ambulance!" he snapped at his colleague Darcy, who immediately put the call out – police priority would help.

"Talk to her, try and talk to her," he encouraged Christine, who was stroking her mother's arms.

"She told me she was going to do this, that no-one was going to stop her. I didn't want to believe that she would, didn't want to hear what she really wanted." Her voice was quiet, the tears rolling down her face.

When the ambulance came Christine carried a bag full of drugs that she'd found in the deep kitchen drawer. Every kind of antidepressant, sleeping pill you could think of, kept over the years, enough to kill a horse, as they say. It would be hard to tell what she'd taken without tests.

Sitting with her in the ambulance Christine knew in her heart that it'd be too late; she'd been warned and hadn't heeded it. Olivia was going 'home', and wouldn't allow herself to be brought back. Not long after their arrival at the hospital, when they came to tell her that her mother had died and that they had done their best, she felt a complete calm.

Remembering to thank them politely, she followed the nurse to see her. Left alone with Olivia for a few minutes, it was enough for her. Standing, looking at the peaceful face of her mother, it was so like a deep sleep that she had to touch the head – just once more.

She even tried to tell her mother that it was alright, that she understood, but she couldn't. She left the room like a robot; she had to tell Eleanor.

"Can I get you a cup of tea, coffee?" Darcy asked her,

standing up as she came out of the room. She was surprised to see him, but supposed that thanks to her brother this was how it would be, police checks.

"Coffee, please. I need to get outside and have a cigarette," she said, walking on down towards the exit.

When he found her minutes later she was already lighting up another one.

"Here," he said, handing her the coffee, "and I'm really sorry about your mother. "

"Thanks. It hasn't really sunk in yet. Part of me is trying to work out what I'm supposed to do next, you know? It's down to me now to decide what happens. I have to talk to Eleanor, but what else?"

"Nothing else needs to be done tonight. I'll drive you home when you're ready – sorry, back to your mother's house," he corrected himself.

"Yes, actually, that's where I'd like to go. I'd rather not leave the area, you know, want to feel near to her." Christine said, nodding.

"Is your colleague still there?" she asked, expecting the answer.

"Yes, he's just had to check out a few things with regard to your brother." Darcy told her honestly.

"Ah yes… Graeme. I'm never going to speak to him again. Do you think it'd be possible for you to have him informed about her?" She was asking seriously and Darcy understood. Part of him agreed with her, Ward's behaviour would impact on everyone, and none of it would be good. He didn't blame her for not wanting to have anything to do with him. She was regarded by his lot as clean, as was Ward's wife; their interviews had been so straightforward, their lack of real knowledge about Ward's businesses obvious.

Chapter 46

"I'll make sure that he's informed. Ready?" Darcy asked gently.

They travelled back to the house in silence, the short journey made even quicker by the lack of traffic. Darcy wanted to say something to her, to ease her in, but couldn't. Going back to the house after a death was always a hard one, and coupled with the rest, she would need to be bloody strong.

They went straight into the sitting room, Darcy's colleague quickly getting to his feet as they came in.

"It's cold in here, I should light the fire," was all she said, busying herself with paper and kindling. Darcy shook his head and the other man gave a sympathetic shrug.

Fire started, Christine turned to look at them, standing up and going to the drinks' tray.

"I'm going to have a drink, would you join me. Please?"

Darcy accepted on their behalf and they drank the whiskey in silence as the fire took; Christine sat in her mother's chair, trying to not feel so small.

"Can I stay here?" she asked, not sure how the police worked.

Darcy had already sorted it all with Drake, this would be kept quiet, under their jurisdiction for the time being. No local plods to be involved, and no reason for the daughter not to stay at the house. Suicide was not uncommon in cases like these, and a thorough check had been done whilst they were at the hospital. Darcy had been impressed at how sympathetic Drake had been.

'Poor bloody families who now have to live with the consequences of their relative's actions. He'll be doing a bloody degree in Sociology in prison, while they live with the reality – you're tainted, suspect. Ward's mother has threatened this for years, be co-operative with the daughter, she's an innocent in all this.'

Darcy leaned forward to reassure her,

"Yes, you can," he said, "I've checked it out and that's okay – we'll come back in the morning if we have to. But we'll ring first, so don't worry. Are you sure you wouldn't like someone to come and stay over with you tonight?" He meant it, she looked so lost.

"No, I'll be fine," she said, getting up, "thanks for your help, and…"

"Probably see you tomorrow." Darcy put down his glass; they took their leave of her quickly. Christine locked up after them, hearing the silence come over the house.

She sat thinking for a long time before making the call, deciding in the end not to tell Eleanor – she wanted, needed, the time for herself.

'Let it all wait,' she thought as she rang, trying to make her voice sound brighter.

"Hello, Eleanor – it's me. Yes, I made it, in the end. Are you okay?…I know – it's grim."

She listened to the flow at the other end, not taking it in, interrupting her;

"Look, I've decided it'd be a good idea to stay here tonight – no, not great – och you know… yes, I'll give you a ring in the morning… bye." Cutting the connection, she curled up in the chair; awkward and uncertain how to be in her mother's house without her, and yet swamped by her presence.

CHAPTER 47

Paddington Green Police Station

"In you go – mind your head," the man said as he angled Graeme into the unmarked police car.

He couldn't grasp what was happening, couldn't see Jack or Sam and was desperately trying to sober up. As the car moved off he saw some guests still on the pavement, huddled in groups, staring at him; he looked away.

It was a silent journey, light traffic making it a quick run, and Graeme had been the first to arrive at London's most secure police station; hustled out of the car in the yard at the back, well out of sight. Tucked alongside the flyover, with its often televised frontage, it didn't seem much different from any other to him. Being taken inside soon changed his mind; the double security system on the door had been the start. Caught in the airlock, doors locked behind and not yet opened in front, he'd fidgeted, hating being hemmed in on all sides. The men bringing him in exchanged knowing glances – it never failed to get to people – like a cut off point from your world into theirs. A reminder that control was out of your hands.

Drake's latest instructions had been followed to the letter, with clearance from the top. Graeme was assisting police with their enquiries; other than confirming his details he'd decided to say nothing further until his lawyer arrived.

'Let him – don't try to do a thing with him. I want him sober, able to let it all sink in, before we really start on him. Once he starts thinking properly he'll realise what a heap of shit he's in – only he won't know how big it is. Just make sure that nothing is missed – food, drinks, breaks – leave no room for any legal wriggling because we didn't stick to the rules. Utter politeness to be shown.'

When Richard Matlock bustled in later to see his client, he too received the same courtesy. Not kept waiting, quickly issued with a security pass, he was taken to the room and shown in. A dishevelled and flushed Graeme got up to greet him, his handshake sweaty.

"Glad to see you…" he said as the door closed on them, and they began their confidential confab.

In the adjoining room the door was locked, off limits to everyone except Drake and his team. They'd bugged three interviewing rooms in all – done in the weeks of waiting under the guise of maintenance. The tiny audio cameras were the best the Service had, top of the range and proving their worth already.

Jack Barnes hadn't a clue where he was being taken to, but he was clear how he would play it when he got there. Carefully treated by the men bringing him in, he was soon able to make his phone-call and was waiting for an official from the American Embassy to appear – until then he would say nothing.

Outwardly he was presenting as controlled and calm. Inside it was different – more sober than Graeme, he knew already that the heap of shit they were in was huge. He'd heard it in the tone of the Embassy official when he'd got through. Cold and efficient, like he knew already where and why Jack Barnes was being held and didn't like it.

'There may be some delay before someone is available to come to the station. Hopefully it won't be too long,' was the only comfort that Jack had received – that and a cup of tea.

He had a long wait in the end; his embassy checking everything twice with Drake's lot before bothering to get to him. Now, though, it seemed someone had finally shown up, he thought – as the door opened and a man came in.

Chapter 47

'Jesus…' was Jack's reaction 'they've sent the office junior..' as he watched the fresh faced young guy in a Burberry come over to him. His heart sank as they shook hands and sat down, he needed someone with experience and knowledge, not a greenhorn like this. He began to talk.

★★★

Drake arrived in the room, pleased at the sight of so much quiet activity. Standing behind them he watched the screens; unable to hear the voices, he read the body language instead. Ward was holding his head as his lawyer paced and talked. Barnes was doing all the talking, gesturing as his man made notes.

Touching the sleeve of his senior man, Drake jerked his head, and moved towards the door. They slipped out into the corridor and headed off to an empty office.

"Looks promising in there — now give me a rundown of what we've got so far." He listened intently to his man's summary, delighted by what he was hearing; cutting in with comments that helped fill in more of the gaps.

"The Americans are more than keen to have Barnes back. All those names that he's asking the Embassy guy to contact on his behalf — I bet every last one of them will have run for cover, conveniently forgetting they ever knew him. However — those who were involved in the U.S. are having their doors kicked in right now by the FBI. I'd be delighted to send him home — he'll certainly serve a longer sentence there…."

"What about Hudson, sir — any word ?"

"No — not yet," said Drake, frowning. "We're working on the last few cab companies in Southwark — I'm expecting

289

to hear some results soon. Ward and Barnes are assuming we've got him, and we'll keep it that way. Barnes isn't a major player – in my view he's been dragged in by his pal on the old sentimental ticket. No – we focus on Mr. Ward –he's the one who can give us what we want – when we find out which button to press. I'll be sitting in on his next interview – it's due to start within the hour."

The man nodded in agreement, and wasn't surprised to hear that Drake intended to be present.

"His lawyer'll be giving him earache right now, sir – which should help..."

"Oh yes – and even that clever bastard will be pushed to find a way out for his client. Right – time to get back, I think...." Drake stood up, smoothed his suit, and left the room – so sure of his next move.

Richard Matlock had done more than bend his client's ear. Hung over, and feeling increasingly panicky, his client was reeling with what he'd been told. Concise, clear, legal advice – it was what he paid for, and he was certainly getting his money's worth this time.

'Bloody bleak' was the best of the lawyer's predictions, as he finished outlining where they stood.

Graeme broke out in a real sweat, and was wiping his face as the man entered the room with Drake – the next interview began.

When it was over, Drake's team divided into two camps of opinion regarding his move. No one could doubt that it had worked, Graeme Ward was now going to co-operate fully, his brief said so, but still...

Drake was uncaring, he'd been given a trump card and had used it perfectly. Ward had become exhausted towards the end, but still wouldn't give enough. Time was running

CHAPTER 47

out, and any vestige of compassion Drake might have had for the man – about to be told of his mother's death – went with it.

"So sorry," he'd drawled, "I was asked to give you this earlier – completely slipped my mind..." passing the note they'd got from the senior registrar at the hospital. He watched coldly as Ward's face registered the news and crumpled. The lawyer read it quickly and looked to Drake to confirm its bald statement of Olivia's death.

"Yes, I'm afraid so," he'd said, adding, "a sad loss – like they say – you never miss your mother till she's gone."

At that, Graeme Ward had broken down and wept like a child, as his lawyer asked for time to confer.

"Of course – take as long as you like," was Drake's polite parting shot.

CHAPTER 48

Broadmoor Psychiatric Hospital

The allocation meeting for the psychiatric social workers had been businesslike for once, finishing on time and all cases dealt with. Neil Guppy had taken on only one new case. He was already overloaded but had agreed to do an initial assessment at least. It made him look keen. His senior had beamed when he'd agreed, the rest of the team nodding their agreement as she spoke:

"That's great Neil, I appreciate that you're really under pressure at the moment, but her assessment must be started within the next couple of days. It should be fairly straightforward, Holloway has sent their background info, such as it is, and there may be other earlier stuff to track down. See me early in the week if you're having any problems. Good, that's all everybody, and thanks."

He took the slim file handed to him; scanning it for the details he read;

Tess Dunlop, born 1.2.1945. aka 'Dun', with a south London address. Single, no family, currently calm and co-operative. There was little there to alarm him; compared to some of the really big names in his caseload, names that the British public reviled for what they had done, she was small fry.

These scanty notes, with the accompanying legal forms, suggested a paranoid schizophrenic who hadn't taken her medication and had blown. He'd closed the file before reading the medical notes, in a hurry to get to the statutory review on another patient. There was never enough time to fit it all in, never enough support even in a practical sense. Down to one admin clerk for the entire team, the chaos was alarming.

'I'll fit her in tomorrow; start a background check in the

CHAPTER 48

morning, get some more stuff on her before I see her,' was his thought as he hurried through the building. It would mean he'd have to finish the other report this evening; more bloody overtime – unpaid of course.

Neil Guppy, born in 1960, single, no family, currently close to breaking point and not able to be co-operative much longer.

'That just about sums me up, and the rest of the bloody team. This job is impossible, we can barely cover our statutory duties because we can't recruit social workers, yet we can spend thousands on more sodding managers, and their focus groups!' His moan was a familiar one, and one that the big bosses always ignored.

Like many of his colleagues he was demoralised, overloaded, and under constant pressure to take more on, without sufficient support. Neil had been a keen social worker once; he had ideals, principles, a wanting to do something worthwhile in society. Now he felt as though he rushed everywhere, achieving little, doing basic tasks that should have been done by others.

'And who suffers? The patient, cos then I don't have enough time to do the proper casework...' he puffed, nearing the meeting room. 'All can I hope for is that one of my cases doesn't blow up in my face – that's job satisfaction in my book.'

He paused outside the door and tried to smooth down his hair and beard; they were a stuffy lot. Making an apologetic entrance and moving quickly to join them at the table, he started digging through his briefcase for the relevant file.

"Right, ladies and gentlemen, I believe we're able to start now. Mr. Guppy, may we have your report please." The chairperson's voice was crisp and efficient, but his annoyance at Guppy's answer was instantaneous.

"I beg your pardon?"

"I said that I appear to have brought the wrong file. I'll have to go back to my office – I'm really sorry everyone."

Neil could feel their collective annoyance with him and left the room, mortified. The file was on his desk, many locked doors away, the report inside a rushed job.

'But it's better than nothing….what a bloody mess…' he muttered, getting his pass ready. This would throw out his entire day, another hour to be found somehow, and absolutely everybody would be pissed off with him. He was glad he'd gone to the off licence, he'd need his prop later.

It was gone nine that night when he stopped at the Chinese to get his takeaway, Crowthorne village so quiet and normal, with bedlam round the corner. Drained and down, he drove home to Bracknell on automatic pilot.

However, Tess Dunlop's day in Broadmoor had turned out much better.

'She's a transfer in from Holloway. Attempted murder of a screw, various suicide attempts. Hasn't said much, been docile really. Due for her first assessment in the morning – Neil Guppy's her PSW.'

Dun was aware of being looked at through the window, couldn't hear clearly what they were saying, just the rumble of their voices. She didn't care, she was where she wanted to be – she'd bloody well pulled it off after all.

Broadmoor Psychiatric Hospital; where if you were smart you could make your time an absolute doddle. She'd been there a week – well more like five days really – she'd been so liberally dosed for the journey from north London to the Berkshire village. It was the most locked up place she'd ever

CHAPTER 48

experienced, but like all the others it had its parallel regime which she'd already started to key into.

Same old rules, baccy and 'phone cards, sex and drugs. She understood them and was pacing herself; some of the faces she recognised from the TV news when they had been sentenced, they were seriously sick and fucking dangerous. Not like her, no, that wasn't how it was with her, she was different. They hadn't a bat in hell's chance of ever getting out, they knew it.

For Dun, this was a long respite, she needed it; right now she was busy working out her next step. They'd told her she'd be seeing a psychiatric social worker within a day. She was good on social workers, could read them like a book. For her they came in three categories; the posh do-gooders, the Jesus' sandal brigade, and the ones who'd been round the block a few times and were less malleable. They were the awkward ones; she was hoping she'd be lucky, get a duff one. She closed her eyes and dozed; warm and comfortable, with the good food coming soon.

★★★

The next morning saw Neil starting with energy and resolve, coming in an hour early to catch up, but sighing as he caught sight of his desk. Always untidy, the piles had grown, with their urgent messages underlined – many going back days. The hour he gave to it didn't seem to make much difference, but he cleared a hole big enough to start on the Tess Dunlop case.

First stop for him was the Social Services Department in Southwark, London, who had confirmed that she had been known to the department, and that the admin clerk would ring him back. Somewhere in the filing cabinets were the official forms requesting information, he'd do those later, but with a reply taking over a month these days, he couldn't wait. What he wanted now was a quick summary from a Duty Social Worker on the woman. He'd hardly sat down with his new cup of coffee when the 'phone rang.

"Neil Guppy."

"This is the London Borough of Southwark, Social Services Department. You rang about a former client of ours, Tess Dunlop?" the voice asked.

"Yes, and thanks for getting back to me so quickly. Have you got a file on her?" Neil was delighted by the unusually speedy response. It was short lived, as the voice went on;

"I am not at liberty to discuss it with you. I have passed your request to our Duty Social worker who will ring you when she's free. As you know we are a very busy department and I can't guarantee when that will be."

Neil thanked her anyway, and got on with it. He knew by looking at his own desk that his request would get little priority in Southwark. It was urgent only to him, the woman was banged up already, wasn't a risk to anyone. His colleagues in London would weigh that up against a child at risk case, and his would have to lose. They hadn't the staff or resources either to do an efficient job – covering all the areas of their work was not remotely feasible. He went through what the prison had sent, this time checking the medical forms.

'Christ, she's had a pre-frontal lobotomy. Done a long time ago, but nonetheless...'

For him it was a barbaric treatment, he had enough trouble coping with ECT, never mind drilling into the skull. It meant that there would be plenty of info on her though.

Chapter 48

'You don't get one of those done for nothing,' he said quietly, putting the file to one side. He had two meetings before he was due to see her.

She'd recognised his type, knew exactly what he would be like as soon as he had arrived into the room. Late and apologetic; clutching his bulging briefcase, with long hair in a ponytail and straggly beard, she had him tagged. Eying his socks and sandals, she smirked. He took it for a smile of acknowledgement, and wished that he had more on her background. Introducing himself gently to her, he began.

"Don't call me Tess, just call me Dun," was her first interruption. She watched him begin again, and thought that her luck was probably in with this one.

'He's a right little eager beaver, but he hasn't a notion about me. Thinks he's going to be my fucking pal – my only one in the world – that's handy.'

Know what the professionals want and feed them a little bit at a time, so they feel that they are making progress. She had been working it out as she lay on her bed. Planning always paid off for Dun, it was an obsession with her, and this place gave her the peace to work on her latest story. Compared to Holloway, with its overcrowding and incessant racket, Broadmoor was a haven, despite the locks.

It had been so hard for her to keep the lid on, to keep some control over the voices and the white anger. When they'd taken her to Holloway prison she'd been able to finally let go, and give rein to her paranoiac schizophrenia. It wasn't something she could remember clearly, or that's what she let on. She could recall vividly the screw's face as she throttled her, how it had taken three others to drag her off. It'd been a real buzz, and had got her into Broadmoor.

'You can always count on them not checking up

properly, one way or the other,' was her thought as she settled down to run the interview. 'Always.'

Neil tried hard, bless him. Outwardly quite co-operative, Dun manoeuvred him on to the path she'd decided on. She reckoned she could buy herself time by making him start at the very beginning with her. Take him back to her childhood, give him the first strand that would lead to her subsequent dramatic disclosure of child sexual abuse. That would tie him up for a while, would whet his appetite.

He went with it, he didn't have much choice. She was sullenly silent when he tried to steer her round to what he wanted to know; avoiding any eye contact and tapping her foot rapidly. When she did speak it was rapid, full of references to places he'd never heard of, going back years, full of anger and pain.

Ending their session, half an hour over its time, Neil felt swamped by the amount of information, but told himself that he'd write up his notes that very day. He said it every time and never did, relying on his memory and his scribbled notes, too pushed for time. He knew that he was months behind with his record-keeping, that any barrister would have a field day should he ever end up in court over a case. But knowing that wasn't enough, he couldn't catch up, no one could. As he left to return to his office he began to rationalise the session in his head.

'She's one powerful woman, and she ran the whole show, Guppy – you let her,' was his thought; honest if uncomfortable. He had a team meeting to go to and was in no hurry, they'd still be wading through the minutes of the last one.

'Take the time to sort your head.' His thought was interrupted on meeting his senior in the corridor,

Chapter 48

hurrying along.

"Just finished my first session with that Holloway transfer. On the whole I think it went quite well; there was some resistance, but I think we could be looking at very early abuse here. I'm going to let her feel her way through this, you know? Let her give it to me, at her pace." He knew how to pitch it for his senior, allay her worries.

If he sounded confident enough he could buy a little time, get a few summaries done on his cases so that he wouldn't have to cancel another supervision session with her. It was the only place that the holes in his work could be spotted. He'd been making excuses to avoid his supervision sessions; afraid that she would immediately spot that he wasn't coping, that his caseload wasn't managed at all – it was beyond him.

"Oh good, I wasn't entirely sure that you'd have time to fit her in. Shouldn't have worried though, you're such a safe pair of hands Neil, a valuable member of the team. Are you coming to the meeting?" Her face, with its warm smile, studied him, seeing what she wanted to see; another surrogate son for her to mother.

"I'll try my best, might be a little late though," he said giving her his most earnest look; he had hoped to grab a quick fag and coffee first.

"That's fine, I'll make your apologies. See you shortly," and she was gone, hurrying on to the small conference room. Neil went to the office and sat down at his desk.

'Coffee first, I think,' as he looked round for his mug: already swiped by a colleague, it wasn't that that made him swear out loud. It was the yellow sticky on his `phone, with its urgent message:

'Tel. D.O., LBS, re T.D. NFA'd in '77 after no contact.

Poss. file hs.bn. m/fiched. Pl. ring b4 3.'

"Shit! I might have guessed I'd miss it!" he exploded, as he grabbed the phone and started dialling; he might just catch the Duty Officer in Southwark.

"Trying to connect you, please hold...still trying to connect you..." the tinny Vivaldi rang in his ears. As he held on – and on, Tess Dunlop was arriving back in her room, well pleased with how it had gone. Better still she knew that there would be some 'blow' coming in later that night, and she was in a position to barter for a quarter – maybe more.

'Never ask where it comes from – just be glad that it gets there,' was the maxim.

'Too right' she thought, 'time to chill out and unwind after all that pain, eh? Work out what the next step should be – it's the "shrink" tomorrow.' Lying back, she closed her eyes.

Later, the log would read: 'although Tess had been very subdued following her session, she managed to eat well and had seemed to cope with recreation – even if she only stood on the sidelines.'

Tess would confirm that, but would have added that it had been a profitable exchange – she'd scored well.

As for Neil, his long wait for the Duty Officer didn't help him. She was brisk and in a hurry, unwilling to spend more than a couple of minutes on the case.

"No, there's nothing held here on her, she's had no contact with the department for over twenty years. If there is anything it'll be on micro-fiche, and that's held centrally in Peckham, I think. Yeah, try them – our switchboard'll have the number. Sorry, that's all I can do – we're really busy at present," she finished. He could hear her other line going, her asking the caller to hold on; he didn't keep her.

Chapter 48

"Thanks anyway, just one more thing, is there any mention of her having had a child?"

"No. All I've got is the absolute minimum, and nothing about any children. Alright?"

"Yeah, and thanks again. Bye." He'd hardly started the words when the line went dead.

'And it'll take ages to get hold of her file, buried in some bloody central microfiche storage system. Shit.'

CHAPTER 49

The Savoy

The person ringing the doorbell wasn't giving up and Eleanor couldn't ignore it any longer.

"Mark," she said flatly, opening the door a little. "You should've 'phoned first, I'm not fit company…" making no move to invite him in.

He stood in the porch, patiently waiting for the pause. She looked so wretched, her pale face drained, eyes puffed – he was desperate to comfort her.

"Eleanor – I've been ringing you all day and you haven't replied once. So, this was the only way – and I'm not going away without seeing you. I'll just stand here and wait." He was determined, and Eleanor hadn't really got the energy to argue. She let him into the hall where they stood eyeing each other.

"I don't want to talk Mark, I haven't got anything to say…" she tried to control her voice and couldn't. She wept as he wrapped his arms around her, holding her tightly.

"Come on, let it out," he said, "don't push me away, Eleanor, we've got to sort this out together, it's for the best."

Eleanor let the hug go on, it was strong and comforting, so good to be held.

"I'm afraid Mark, afraid to be alone, or with you. Afraid of the scandal and how it's going to ruin so many lives – I can't believe how bad it is. How am I going to do it all? All! That's a joke, I don't know how to bloody start!" Her voice had risen, she'd pulled back from him to shout. Dishevelled and tear streaked, she was a mixture of despair and rage; conned and conned again, she'd always come back for more, ever optimistic. Mark took hold of her again, talking quietly to her, moving her into the kitchen where it was warmer.

Chapter 49

"You're not facing this on your own, that's the most important thing to remember, right? I've been desperate to talk to you, wanting to be able to give you some of the better bits of information, rather than undiluted doom.." he said, stroking her face.

"What information?" She sniffed at him, finding the box of tissues.

"Like Fiona has been checked into The Priory, and I've moved out of Islington. Like, you've been avoiding me and it isn't necessary." He was pushing it, pleased as Eleanor rose to the challenge;

"Oh, it's alright for a servant of the Crown to have a relationship with the wife of an arms smuggling, terrorist sympathiser is it?"

Mark responded quickly.

"You're not the guilty one here – Graeme, Jack Barnes, Sam Hudson – they're the guilty ones. You weren't involved, that's patently obvious – I mean if you were, I don't think you'd be here, more like Paddington Green Police station, eh?"

"What about guilt by association?" she asked miserably.

"That's different, and you know it. I know what you're trying to say and you're so wrong. I've spoken to the police, I have a contact, and believe me they regard you and his sister as not relevant. I've also discussed it with my boss and that's why I'm here."

"You've discussed me with your boss !?"

"Eleanor, you know some of my work has been sensitive at times, and that no matter who I'm with, they get checked out –you passed. Dwell on that, not the negative bit."

"What did you tell him about me?" she asked, incredulous that she'd been discussed.

"It's not like that," he replied, recognising female insecurity and going for the bland reassurances.

"There are a few things that we'll have to deal with, but in general terms, it was fine."

"You actually sound like a civil servant Mark!" Eleanor interrupted, but he shushed her.

"Listen to me. You're not responsible for what Graeme has done, but I don't doubt that you'll pay for his actions. Currently this is being kept out of the press, they are co-operating, but as soon as the embargo is lifted, you'll be under siege. We only have a little time and I want us to make the best of it. No, don't look shocked – for once, let's put ourselves first, not our former spouses. So, Eleanor Clarke, you're going to pack a bag and come away with me. All the way into town, right now – you're not staying here." He was hopeful, but could see her trying to think of reasons why she shouldn't go.

"Well…"

"I've gone mad and taken a suite at the Savoy!" he added.

It was quite true; totally extravagant and out of character, he'd booked it earlier. Drake had been approving when Mark had told him where they'd be if he needed them.

'You seem pretty sure that she'll take up your invitation?' had been his other comment, and Mark had been sure, if given a chance to talk to her.

"You're joking – the Savoy?" Eleanor was warming to the idea. She knew Christine wouldn't be back till sometime tomorrow, and …

"Yes, why not – you did the Ritz, I seem to remember…" She did, and that clinched it, already running her fingers through her hair, wondering about how long she had to get ready.

Chapter 49

"Not too long, please," Mark smiled as she agreed.

It was the idea of being able to run away, to get out of the mess, give up responsibility that made her hurry. Mark was impressed by the swift turn around, the shutting up of the house took minutes and they were out of it.

"Tell me that you think this is a brilliant idea," he said to her in the taxi, his arm around her. He felt happier than he had in weeks.

"I'm still deciding, but so far, yes..."

It was; from the moment she arrived at the Savoy she basked in it. Letting them look after her, not having to worry about a thing. Currently the hardest decision was what to wear for dinner.

"Decide as you soak in the bath, with some more champagne to help you think." Mark suggested. He had his own ideas about what to wear for dinner, room service seemed a wonderful idea. In his head he thanked Christine for the call, hoping she and Mrs. Ward were having a quiet time together...

***

Drake returned home in better form but it didn't last long. There was no trace of bloody Hudson, and the Minister was pushing even harder.

"Christ, Thomas, would that our minister expended the same amount of time and worry on finding the good guys – this little runt Hudson is getting the kind of treatment I'd expect for a damn dignitary, not a bloody terrorist.." Drake was fed up with the pressure,

"Next I'll be told that he had an invitation to a Buck House garden party!"

Thomas' views were similar, if more extreme; his answer however, was tact itself.

"I know sir. It does seem a little strange. What have we got on him at present?"

Drake had got up from his desk and was pacing, counting off on his fingers, as he answered.

"That's the thing; we have traces of vomit and urine in Putney, we have the hotel room with his belongings. The taxi for Mrs. Ward hasn't been found and now she's dead."

"That's harsh..." said Thomas, "bit of a double whammy for the wife and daughter.."

"It is Thomas, and I think it's the first tragic reaction to Ward's antics. She was a sad and unhappy woman, his mother; another one of the forgotten victims of Northern Ireland and its bloody 'Troubles.' But that's how it goes; families and the fall out from the last thirty years. She deserved better, she never knew who'd murdered her son, he wasn't important, not like Hudson." Drake's voice showed his contempt; it didn't often appear, and Thomas understood its import.

"Right now however, I have a problem with the hunt for Hudson. According to the Minister we should be concerned and anxious about his welfare but I'm not sure why. Come on Thomas, you've read the display boards; the more we found out about the man, the more we were repelled. What has this man not done? The further we dig, the worse it gets. Torture, intimidation – probably murder – why should we be we so desperate to ensure he's safe and well?"

"It's P.C. sir. Only reason, must be."

"Precisely. Our Minister would rather we danced to the P.C. 'keep the boys happy' tune, than the 'bang up the murdering criminal bastards' one that I want. So, what now?"

"A bit of your 'lateral thinking' I suppose sir."

"Yes, and that's my only bloody option. I'm trying not to see Hudson's vanishing act as one less piece of scum to worry about, but it's hard. We go on with the hunt of course, but I am pushing the Minister to see that the overall result was a success, and that the media will be quick to see that too. He rather liked the idea of good press coverage.." Drake half smiled as he remembered the Minister's fleshy face as it registered his suggestion. – T.V. lights at the end of the tunnel..

"One break through," he went on, "he's taken on the N. Ireland murders – accepts that we weren't involved, and I assured him that that was the case. He'll formally put that to them, and advised them to look within the Province for the killers. So at least that's one off my list." Drake said it carefully, his back to Thomas, not wanting to see his face.

"Anyway, that's where we're at – at the moment.. Now, it must be time for an aperitif Thomas, surely?"

"At once, sir."

CHAPTER 50

Belfast

"Dear God, what's that? Who's there?"

At four in the morning, alone in her house, Stella Hudson was terrified by the banging on her front door. Pulling on her grotty dressing gown, she felt her way downstairs in the dark, too afraid to turn on the lights in case someone tried to shoot her.

The chain snapped the second the door opened, a boot kicking it out of its screws.

"Get on in there," she was told, as they bundled her into the front room. She knew their faces, knew them from the social club, especially the woman.

"We're going to have a wee talk, so we are," the woman said, pushing Stella hard, making her fall backwards into the armchair. She looked at them and felt sick inside; she'd heard of the people who were taken away in the night, their kids left to hunt for the body.

Their wee talk was coldly efficient – the PACE rules didn't apply. Stella couldn't give them what they wanted and had taken a serious beating as a result. They left her bruised and battered – traumatised – but with a gem of information: Sam was missing and it didn't look good.

"And I hope the wee fucker's dead and all," she murmured, trying to put the cigarette to her swollen lips, her bruised hands shaking.

As her 'interviewers' drove away, the talk in the car was sporadic.

"Christ! How thick is thick? She doesn't even know who her man really is….." said one.

"I know – but I tell you what, I fuckin' know who's responsible – and it's not the fuckin' Brits, neither…" said

Chapter 50

another.

The debriefing afterwards with their commanding officer, Kevin, was definitive; it didn't take much to spread the rumour – and that was all it was, just a bloody rumour. Within hours the security forces in Belfast were aware of a major feud. 'Tit for tat' had taken on a new lease of life.

"Some bloody ceasefire this!" shouted the squaddie as the next shout came in at the barracks.

"Youse lot have got our man. Give.." was the demand at the end of the gun, just a few streets away.

★★★

In London, Thomas was heading off from Jermyn Street to find a pay 'phone. He'd cooked Drake a wonderful meal and had left him nursing a generous brandy. Punching in the numbers quickly, his old mate answered on the second ring.

"Jock?.. It's me," he said, the instant he heard the voice.

"Good result all round," he went on, "check out the news tomorrow. Oh, and give my best to the wife."

"Great. Will do – and thanks mate – it needed settling."

He hung up and walked on, ignoring the tourists. Settling the score had taken years and patience, but it had always been when, never if. The remnants of his platoon had kept their promise to their butchered mates – pay back time, one day.

'And the best part is that they'll blame each other over there, Drake's seen to that.'

Thomas felt justice had been done.

CHAPTER 51

Wind up

"What's going on here?" Darcy asked the woman with the folder, standing looking up at the balcony.

"Squatters or crack house, probably both," she answered, only on seeing his warrant card.

She was the unfortunate new housing welfare officer for the estate, checking up today on a report regarding No. 10, Brook House, tenant: Tess Dunlop.

"What brings you here?" she asked him, keeping an eye on the front door of Dun's flat.

"One Tess Dunlop, aka, Dun. Any chance of getting in there?" Darcy was anxious, he'd been going over all the evidence and this was the last link, he was sure of it.

"Give it a little time, and you can. I've decided that it's most likely crack, and have asked the police to attend – they should be here any minute." Her voice was crisp, she'd found that alleging drugs was a sure-fire way of gaining instant access. New to the area, but wise to the games that went on, she'd also got her eye on a potential dealer on the third floor as well.

They waited together in the filthy yard, watched on all sides – and left severely alone.

When the cars and van came it was over in minutes; Darcy getting in to the flat as soon as possible afterwards.

"Oh shit!" he exclaimed as he walked through. It was trashed, other people's crap everywhere; drugs and the paraphernalia, half eaten takeaways, cans and bottles. Dun's sterile little place, scrubbed with bleach everywhere, was now unrecognisable.

"Just in time, I'd say – give them another few days and believe me, it'd be really bad," was housing welfare's view.

CHAPTER 51

Darcy sat in his car when he'd finished in the flat, uncertain how to break the news to Drake.

He would put forensics in, but the druggies had had a field day – they'd be lucky to find much. The tenants in Dun's block had been united in their unhelpfulness, the neighbouring blocks were all apparently occupied by the blind. It was stone-walling on a grand scale, and he decided to just come clean with his boss, not try to impress. He was surprised though when Drake himself answered the 'phone.

"Darcy, sir," he blurted in answer to the curt query.

Drake was a good listener, and Darcy was honest and at his most earnest. When Drake ended the call, he sat for a long time, digesting the detail. Giving Darcy free rein had been valuable, and he agreed with the young man's summing up.

'And that takes me back to my original dilemma,' Drake thought to himself . 'Do I actually give a shit about Hudson? Sitting here alone, I'd say honestly that I don't. We've stopped a lot of grief happening to ordinary people, and we lost a nasty piece of work on the way. Good luck to whoever was responsible is what I'd like to say, and not waste any more time trying to find out for certain. Instead, I ought to make the call…'

It was a brief one, and his resignation was swiftly accepted. He'd sit and write the formal blurb later, and the Minister would express his regret and dismay at the loss of such a fine officer.

'And we'll both know that it's all bollocks. He's looking out for his future, no-body else's.' He poured himself another drink, then made the next call. He'd tell Thomas later.

"Rupert! Drake here. Sorry I couldn't get back to you

sooner. I'd be delighted to be considered for the post – who else is up for it?"

"You're top of the list, despite your little set-back." Rupert's lazy drawl was famous in the Foreign Office, his influence vast. They'd been to school together, firm friends from the start, they'd kept up the friendship.

"Thanks Rupert – I'll fill you in on that one over dinner. What's the score on the new job then?"

"Ah, Drake. We'll have to leave that until we meet. One could summarise it I suppose…it's the same old story, but with different headgear – tea towels this time eh!" he chuckled.

"Let me come back to you in a day or so, and we'll get together. I fancy Claridges, if that's all right with you…"

"Done. I'll ring you at the end of the week, and thanks again." Drake rang off and pondered which Middle Eastern country would end up as temporary 'home' to him and Thomas.

★★★

In Broadmoor, Dun was settling in well; staff were ensuring that she took her medication, and she was making sure that she could score the rest. Time had shrunk to hospital routine, the outside world of little relevance. She was warm and well fed, smashed most days, and only had to perform for her social worker once a week.

'And even that's not happening at the moment. Poor guy, off sick with stress – again,' she told herself with a little smile. She was happier now, much calmer – she didn't 'do' stress any more, didn't need to – everyone else around her absorbed it for her.

CHAPTER 51

'Fucking social worker doesn't know what's hit him, and I've hardly started.'

She was having fun, couldn't seem to recall much of her recent past, but was contentedly spinning the detail of her earliest years – and it was slow work.

Neil Guppy, with his 'safe pair of hands' was at home in his shared house in Bracknell, burning papers in the tiny back garden. He couldn't face what was coming, he'd been off sick now for three weeks, and he knew the call would come soon. Depressed and ashamed he took what he thought was the best option; burn some of his files, and deny everything, claim they'd been lost.

His senior would've had to have checked up on his work as cases blew up in his absence. She'd have instantly seen the lack of recording, everything months behind – the total chaos. Cupping his hands, he lit another match, watching his lack of work burn.

It was Neil Guppy's senior who had to tell Dun that her flat had been completely vandalised. Dun didn't smile until she was alone,

"Brilliant," she said.

★★★

Christine couldn't face going into the kitchen at first. She stayed on in the sitting room, opening up her mother's bureau. After she found it, and pouring herself a large one, she made herself read the envelope's contents. The old photos had fallen out first, stark reminders of the happy childhood times. Tom's passport and school reports, and finally, a short letter, for her. It was something she would keep forever, those few bald lines of explanation. Maybe she'd get to understand it, given time. She burned the photos, though, unable to bear the memory of those dead, and then the sight of the living brother.

'She'd prepared for this, fastidiously...' was her observation as she looked further.

In the battered bureau every pigeonhole had been cleared. Once famous for its bulging overflow, most of its contents had now gone; only a small clutch of papers remaining.

She read all that had been left for her, not caring that she was now financially secure, just sad that there would be so few to contact, to mourn Olivia's passing. Leafing through her mother's address book, it was grim to see so many crossed out, dead. Like so many before her, when she finally went to bed, her head was full of the 'if only I'd...' – the insoluble regret. She closed over her mother's bedroom door, and went to try and sleep in the spare room.

★★★

When Eleanor woke she couldn't believe how late it was; she'd felt Mark getting up earlier and had thought she'd lie on for just a minute or two.

"You should've called me," she said, coming out to find him reading the paper. Wrapped in the big bathrobe, she leaned over to kiss him, still warm and sleepy from their bed, smelling of them both. Mark got up to hold her, as the feeling in the pit of his stomach increased.

"Why? You were happily dreaming – well you looked pretty happy to me..." he replied with a smile. He'd been up since seven, feeling great, knowing that she was with him – at last.

Chapter 51

"You know I am, Mark, and it's an amazing feeling..." Eleanor smiled, after last night she felt so alive and wanted, knew what it was like to be loved.

They were disturbed by the knock, both wanting to laugh at its timing.

"Room service."

"Now Eleanor Clarke, breakfast in bed or breakfast and bed?" asked Mark, as the waiter left.

"I think I'll start with breakfast."

★★★